Dating the It Guy

Krysten Lindsay Hager

Clean Reads
www.cleanreads.com

To Justin who always believed
and in loving memory of my Aunt Joan Frances

Chapter 1

MY MOTHER ALWAYS told me I was a day late and a dollar short. So true. For one, I had this amazing intuition where I could sense things before they happened…except I never realized what it was trying to tell me until after it was over. Like last Monday, when I was at my friend Kylie's house helping her color her hair to be dark like mine, and I made this joke about her mom's lawn gnomes getting attacked by a cougar. I don't know why I said it, but she said that no self-respecting cougar would touch those ugly things. That night it was on the news an escaped cougar was seen in a Detroit suburban neighborhood carrying a small elf. Now I walked around saying, "Hot soccer players are wandering around upstairs," but so far, nothing.

I've tried to blow stuff off in front of my friends because I didn't want them to think I was weird, but it was hard to deny I didn't have some sort of psychic insight when last week I sensed my grandma was sick. Later that day we got a call she had a stroke.

That's why I never ignored my instincts and why, on the first day of summer school, I had this feeling my life was going to change. I wish I'd also had the instinct to wear a cuter outfit, but like I said, it only takes me so far. Besides, I figured nothing exciting was going to happen in summer school. After all, I was only taking a four-week class because my internship at the local newspaper had been cancelled after they said you had to be sixteen with a driver's license to intern there. You'd have thought they would have put it in the requirements or something, but the editor told me it was a new policy they forgot to post on the website. But I had felt something was going to go wrong with the internship from the get-go. That's why I didn't waste my money buying new clothes for work.

So now I was stuck in a classroom while some other jerk got my internship, all because my mother thought I needed something "productive" to do this summer. Like watching *While My Children Wept* wasn't productive. By the way, I didn't know if it was my intuition or the writers' crappy writing skills, but I always knew what was going to happen on the show—even without reading the Internet show spoilers.

The class I was taking was supposed to be a gender and media class. I heard we were going to be watching videos and talking about current events, so I figured it wouldn't be too bad—maybe even fun. When I got to class, our teacher, Mrs. Rae, handed out the syllabus. I couldn't help but notice we were only watching two videos. Plus, we had a ton of written assignments. Would the fun ever stop? Mrs. Rae said we'd be doing a lot of group work over the next few weeks. Group work—two words that struck fear into my heart. I glanced over at Kylie.

"Emme, don't get mad, but I promised I'd work with Zach if we had any group projects," she said.

I nodded. After all, he was her boyfriend, but I didn't know anyone else in the room.

"Okay, does everybody have a partner?" Mrs. Rae asked. "Because this is who you'll be working with for the rest of the semester."

I felt stupid raising my hand—especially as Mrs. Rae scanned the room for another friendless loser. I thought she'd let me work with Zach and Kylie since everybody else was paired up.

"Well, there's another student who's not here yet," she said. "So just get started on the assignment until they arrive."

Everyone started working while I watched the door for the new student to arrive. I hoped it wasn't the weird girl from gym class who always gave me funny looks like I just ran over her dog or something. As the door opened, I held my breath, and in walked Brendon Agretti, the senator's son and possibly the hottest guy in Michigan, okay, the entire western hemisphere. Last fall, Kylie's mom accidentally hit the curb in front of the school while watching him jog. He reminded me of this underwear model, Michael Kahlo, who was on a poster that was stuck to the door of my friend Margaux's locker. The picture had been glued in the locker a zillion years ago, but to be honest, nobody had tried to remove it. I had spent many nights staring at Brendon's social media pages and reading all the gushing comments girls left him.

"Brendon, you'll be working with Emme," Mrs. Rae said, pointing to me.

Part of me wanted him to be my partner, and the other half of me wanted to run in the other direction. He walked over and tossed his notebook and keys onto the desk. He had on a navy blue V-neck shirt with the sleeves pushed up and seemed like he should be in one of those preppy clothing ads. Meanwhile, I had chosen today to put my dark brown hair in a ponytail and wear my jean overalls. Zach called it my "Engineer Fred" outfit, and I appeared closer to five years old than fifteen.

Brendon sat down next to me.

"Hey, I'm Brendon," he said. It was cute he thought I wouldn't know who he was. So humble, so...oh crap, I was supposed to say something.

"I'm Emme."

"Cool, so what's the assignment?" he asked.

I handed him the worksheet about comparing the way men and women are written about in magazines. "It's due tomorrow, so Mrs. Rae said she would let us spend class time researching in the library," I said, wondering if my voice always sounded so squeaky.

"Should we head to the library then?" he asked. I nodded, and as soon as we got to the library, Brendon headed over to the magazine section and grabbed a bunch of them. All the couches were taken, so he asked if I wanted to go somewhere else. We tried the cafeteria, but the cheerleaders were using it to make posters for a car wash.

"There's this place outside we could sit," I said and led him to this garden area behind the track. It was a memorial garden for a girl who had died in an accident years ago. I always wondered who the girl was because it seemed so sad all that was left of her was a plaque with her name on it.

"I never even knew this was here," he said, sitting down.

"I come here a lot to write." I wished I could have said I shot my swimsuit calendar here.

"Oh yeah? What do you write?" he asked.

"I mostly write short stories."

"Cool. Have you been published in the school's lit magazine?" he asked.

I shook my head, but I didn't admit I hadn't submitted anything because I was scared of the editor, Lauren Hartnet, who was also his ex-girlfriend. Lauren was also in the media class with us, and she was one of those perfect, overachieving types who managed to be involved in everything, get good grades, and still have bouncy hair. She was basically the anti-me. Not like I was a slug or anything, but my idea of a good time was shopping and watching TV, and my hair was more windblown than bouncy.

"I used to be on the board for it, so I'd be happy to read some of your work sometime if you were thinking about submitting anything," he said.

I nodded, but like I'd let *him* of all people on the planet look at my writing. After all, I never let anyone read my stuff. In fact, I was panicking over the fact I had signed up for creative writing in the fall, and I would have to read my work out loud. I decided to change the subject and pulled out one of the magazines.

"This magazine listed the makeup they used on the model, but I mean, look at this male model. He's definitely wearing makeup, and nothing is listed for him," I said.

Brendon nodded as he flipped through the pages. "Yeah, a lot of these guys have eyeliner on. How did I never notice that before? And no guy has skin *this* perfect."

I almost said, "You do," but managed to keep my swooning to myself.

As we worked, I noticed he didn't take any notes, and I didn't have to use my intuition to figure out I would end up doing the whole project myself. Why did cute guys always think they were too good to do their own work? Brendon leaned forward to look at my notes, and part of his dark hair flopped in his face. He smoothed it back, leaving a trail of cologne. I was tempted to ask him what brand it was so I could buy some to spray around my room.

"Oh crap, I completely forgot I have to pick my friend up from tennis practice," he said, looking at his watch. "Sorry about this. I'll see you in class tomorrow."

Great, I bored him, and he had to make an excuse to run off. I knew I'd get stuck doing the whole assignment. I made a mental note to wear something nicer tomorrow. The other girls in our class had worn cute summer clothes, but I knew the school cranked up the air conditioning in the summer, and I didn't want to freeze. I was starting to wonder if the school rented out part of the cafeteria to a morgue in the summer or something. It was weird how cold the place was when it was eighty-five degrees outside.

—

THE NEXT DAY I wore the jeans that made my butt look good and strappy red sandals instead of my usual sneakers. I walked in feeling pretty confident.

"Hey, Emme, you're pretty dressed up for class," Zach said as Kylie punched his arm.

"It's just jeans and sandals," I said, as my face got red. Brendon came in and waved me over, so I got up to move.

"Too good for us now, huh?" Zach said, and I rolled my eyes at him.

I sat down next to Brendon as Mrs. Rae passed out our next assignment.

"Each group will pick a sitcom and examine the gender roles of the main characters," she said.

"What show do you want to use?" Brendon asked.

"I don't know. Maybe a comedy like *The Templetons*," I said. "It's pretty funny, and the mom and dad characters would give us a lot to work with."

"I love that show, and I've got some DVDs of it. Do you want to watch it together?"

"You could come over to my house if you want," I said. I could not believe those words had just come out of my mouth.

"Is that cool? I could bring over a pizza or something," he said. I tried to steady my shaking hand as I wrote down my address on the inside cover of his notebook. We decided to meet at six, which gave me approximately three hours to clean the house. He asked what I liked on my pizza, and I told him I didn't eat meat, but I could pick off pepperoni if he wanted it. I tried to give him money for the pizza, but he wouldn't take it. Well, the least he could do was buy me dinner since I did all of our assignment last night.

Mrs. Rae told us to hand in our homework before we left, and I pulled my sheet out.

"Oh, I did it, too," Brendon said. "I guess we can hand in both of them."

I had assumed the assignment had been dumped in my lap since he had run off yesterday. He took our papers up, and Kylie asked if I wanted to go with her and Zach to meet our friend, Margaux, after class and get smoothies. Zach drove us over to The Big Chilly. Margaux was sitting in a booth, playing on her phone. She had cute red shorts and matching high-heeled sandals on with a white tank top. As usual, she appeared like a cover model with her light-brown hair blown out to perfection. Kylie, Zach, and I ordered our smoothies and went to sit with her.

"So Brendon is coming over to work on a project," I said.

"That should be interesting," Kylie said.

Margaux moved to the edge of her seat. "Wait, Brendon Agretti? Mr. Hotness is coming over to your house? Whose idea was that?"

I said I invited him over.

Zach rolled his eyes. "Why do girls go nuts over that guy? Seriously? What does he have that I don't?"

"Well, I don't actually know him, but I'm guessing class and hotness," Margaux said.

Zach's mouth dropped open, and Kylie nudged her.

"Just kidding," Margaux said unconvincingly. "But he probably has a croquet set with his name engraved on each ball and mallet."

"So he has a few bucks and looks like an actor?" Zach said, poking at the floor with the toe of his sneaker. "He's probably all stuck on himself."

"He's smart, and he seems like he'd read, do you know what I mean?" I asked.

"Oh yeah, he's a reader," Kylie said, nodding. "Is he nice?"

I nodded, but didn't mention I thought he blew me off yesterday. He probably went to pick up some super-model/honor student potential girlfriend who was also a gourmet cook and protested against toxic waste in her spare time.

"Has he taken you for a ride in the royal car?" Zach asked.

"I don't know what he drives," I said.

"I'm sure it breaks down less than the thing you drive," Margaux said, rolling her eyes.

"Big Blue-y is a classic," Zach said. "You don't appreciate its timeless quality. Besides, unlike the three of you, at least *I'm* old enough to drive."

"I'm just happy to see you getting interested in someone again, Emme," Kylie said. "I know you haven't wanted to date anyone since you and John broke up."

"Well, who could blame her? Dude had been talking to his ex-girlfriend behind her back the *whole* time they were dating," Margaux said, her brown eyes widening. "You're *so* much better off without him."

I bit my lip. Kylie was right—I hadn't even wanted to date another guy since John because I was afraid of getting hurt again.

After we finished our smoothies, Zach dropped me off at home, and I began picking up the magazines littering the family room. I was in the middle of vacuuming when my dad called to say he and my mom were taking my grandfather out for dinner.

"What's that noise?" he asked. "The disposal on the fritz again?"

"No, I'm vacuuming. A guy from school is coming over to work on a project," I said. "Is it okay? I mean, I thought you guys would be here."

"It's fine. I'm just surprised you knew where the vacuum was," he said. "Is it some famous celebrity? Just curious who would cause you to tidy up."

"Ha ha. I just wanted the house to look nice. He seems…clean."

"Well, I like him already if he's got you cleaning. See ya later, kid."

I tried to make the bathroom look decent, but spilled cleaner on my jeans when I tried to refill the spray bottle. With ten minutes until he arrived, I ran upstairs to change. I put on another pair of jeans, but they were too tight to sit in. The doorbell rang just as I had taken my jeans off. Great, he was here, and I wasn't wearing pants. Fabulous. I grabbed the closest pants to me, which unfortunately happened to be my baggy time-of-the-month jeans. There was no time to change, so I raced downstairs to let Brendon in.

"Hey, I got half pepperoni and half mushrooms and olives," he said when I opened the door.

We walked into the kitchen. "Do you want juice or bottled water?" I asked as he stared at the bottle of guava juice I was holding. He seemed a little grossed out at the fruit floating on the bottom.

"Um, it's all natural juice, which is why it looks a little…"

"Chunky?" he said. "Water would be great."

I poured two glasses of bottled water and grabbed some plates and silverware from the cupboard. We went into the family room, and Brendon showed me the DVDs he had brought over.

"I figured we could watch a couple episodes and then decide which one we want to use," he said.

We started to eat, and suddenly it was like I had never worked a knife and fork before. Why was I so awkward? He picked up his slice and took a bite without having mozzarella strings hanging from his mouth or getting grease on his chin. He even ate cutely and was considerate about the pizza toppings. Oh wow, he even put a coaster under his glass. Where did he find a coaster in my house? I leaned forward and realized that the green box that had sat on the coffee table for years was a coaster holder.

Normally I ate at least three slices of pizza, but today I only had two, which I ate with a knife and fork. He had four pieces and some of the breadsticks that came with the pizza. I gave him the magnetic notepad off the fridge to take notes on the show and about died when I realized that it said, "Shop Your Buns Off." As I started writing down what the dad character had said to the kid, the screen went black for a second. I saw Brendon staring at me in the reflection. Was he staring at me in a good way, or did I have pizza sauce on my face?

We watched the episode twice and then answered the homework questions.

"So how'd you end up taking this class?" he asked.

"My summer internship at the newspaper fell through, and my parents wanted me to do something productive."

"I did an internship at the state capital last summer. It was the most boring thing ever, and I lost respect for almost all the people I had to work with. Some of those people are seriously phony, and I don't even think they realize how much of themselves is fake—it's like they start to morph into this human sound bite—does that make sense?" he asked.

"Totally."

He seemed more, I don't know, human or something. I used to watch him at his locker with his rich friends and wonder what it would be like to be in his world. What did he and his friends do for fun? Where did they hang out on weekends? They certainly didn't go anywhere my friends and I spent time.

When he left, he gave me his cell number and e-mail and told me to call him if I had problems with my half of the paper. Normally, I always gave anybody I worked with my phone number right away, but I had been afraid to give him my number in case he thought, "How pathetic. Why don't you just throw yourself at me?"

I knew I wouldn't call him, but it was nice that he gave me his number, and I wondered what I could get for it if I auctioned it off online. When I went to put the number in my phone, I accidentally knocked my affirmation journal out of the bookshelf. It opened right to the page where it said, "Visualize something twenty times, and you can make it happen." Now, I had read that line a trillion times, but I never did it. Sure, I had pictured myself with a new purse or those cool boots that Sierra on *As My Children Wept* always wore, but I had never done that with a guy. Still, what could it hurt? It wasn't like I was altering the universe. I was just picturing Brendon and me walking through the halls at school...while holding hands. He didn't have a girlfriend or anything so it was completely harmless, right?

THE NEXT DAY, I woke with this weird feeling my laptop was going to act up. In fact, when I checked my e-mail in the morning, I was kind of surprised it switched on at all. I figured I was just being paranoid about not getting my rough draft done, or maybe it was because the planet Mercury was in retrograde, but I tried to ignore my feelings. We had the day off from class, so I didn't start working on my paper until later in the evening. I had just started typing when my screen froze. Feeling panicked, I hit Control-Alt-Delete and restarted the laptop, but the screen went blue and started flickering. What was it doing, and why was there a little gray box on my computer telling me I had sixty seconds until it shut down? Fifty-nine...fifty-eight...fifty-seven... This was just like the episode of *As My Children Wept* where Samson had to stop the bomb hidden in Sierra and Aristotle's wedding cake. Did it mean the laptop was going to blow? On the show, the cake blew up, and everybody thought Aristotle was dead...well, until he showed up at Sierra's next wedding, and was Sierra's new husband mad...probably just as mad as Mrs. Rae would be when I didn't turn in my assignment.

"Mo-om! My laptop's possessed. Fix it!"

"Why don't you just ask me to get out my fairy princess wand and throw pixie dust on it," she shot back. "I'd have better luck with that."

Sarcasm was not cute when you were having a crisis. I tried calling Zach, but his mom said he was working late. I was desperate, so I asked his mom if she knew anything about computers.

"There's a guy at Mary's Little RAMs who works on mine. I could give you his number, but they closed at five tonight."

I hung up defeated. I didn't know anybody who knew a thing about computers. Oh crap. I *did* know somebody who knew about computers. Brendon. He had mentioned he took a computer class last semester, but could I call him? Usually I'd have no problem calling a guy for something, but this wasn't a normal guy. He was what Margaux would call a "Hottie McHotHot." Okay, what was wrong with me? He was just a regular person like everybody else. He put his pants on one leg at a time and went to the toilet like everybody else...but I bet his bathroom was super clean and everything in it matched. I pictured the whole room done in some manly, rich-person color like "hunter green" or "maroon." And there would be lots of dark mahogany —

"Emme? Do you want to use my laptop to work on

your paper?" Mom yelled up the stairs.

"It won't help," I replied. "I saved it on the hard drive because I'm an idiot."

Stupid Mercury retrograde. I should have known better than to expect a computer to work right. I should have backed up my work or e-mailed it to myself, but no, I was too worried about ordering new lip gloss from lickity-lips.com. Now I had no paper, no gloss, and probably after I called Brendon begging him for help, no pride. I called and left a message on Brendon's phone. He was probably out with some amazing prelaw, premed student who donated blood to anemic puppies and did puppet shows for the elderly while knitting booties for—

My phone rang, and Brendon's name popped up on the screen.

"Hello?"

"Hi, Emme, it's Brendon. What's up?"

I explained about my computer, and he started giving me suggestions, which would have been helpful if I had known what he was talking about. It was like he was speaking in Aramaic. He offered to come over, and the second I hung up the phone I went to fix my hair. Normally I didn't do much with my hair. It was long and always seemed messy no matter what I did with it. Kylie always said it was tousled like something out of a magazine, and yeah, sometimes I agreed with her and even loved my hair...and other times I feel like strangers on the street were going to walk up and hand me a hairbrush. My hair had been in a ponytail all night, so I couldn't wear it down because it had a ponytail holder crease. I wound it into a loose bun and put on my ruby lip stain. I was digging through my hamper for my cutest top when the doorbell rang. I threw it on and ran down the stairs.

"Hey, thanks for coming over," I said as I answered the door. I told him my laptop was upstairs, and I felt weird, like I was trying to lure him into my bedroom or something. He followed me, and I realized I should have made sure my dirty underpants weren't half hanging out of my hamper when I shut it. Of course it wasn't a cute pair, but the big momma pants. Why didn't I just wear Little Bo Peep pantaloons?

"See, it does this weird countdown thing when I turn it on," I said. He sat at my desk and started messing with my laptop while I sat on the bed. I wondered if he washed his hands or used some hand sanitizer because I had this strict "clean hands" policy about my keyboard. I mean, I heard on the news those keyboards were playgrounds for bacteria.

"It's probably because Mercury is in retrograde," I said. He stared at me as if I had said, "I was sacrificing a goat in here before you came in, please excuse the stains on my ceremonial robe." I tried to explain. "It's the planet that rules communication—never mind. Do you think you can fix it?"

"Not sure yet," he said. "I think I can retrieve your paper though. Do you have someplace else to finish it if I can't get this computer to work?"

I started to answer when he said he had brought his laptop over for me to use while he worked on my computer. So I could either go downstairs and type on my mother's boring laptop and leave Mr. Hotness alone in my bedroom, or I could stay here and work on it while we were in my room. Together. Alone. In my room. I loved the planet Mercury.

Chapter 2

WHILE I TRIED not to drool, Brendon put the computer in "safe mode" and was able to save my paper to a drive. He started up his laptop for me, and I leaned over him while he explained how to use it. The side of his ear and neck were hot. I never knew anyone could have such amazing ears. People take things like ears for granted when it comes to the cuteness factor.

"Did you get all that?" he asked. I had no idea what he was referring to, but I nodded. Why couldn't I keep my head around this guy? It wasn't like I had grown up in a convent or something and this was the first guy I had ever seen. I never had trouble talking to guys before, so why was I thrown by him? Well, other than the fact he was amazingly hot and nice. Nice. I didn't even believe in the myth of the "nice guy," but Brendon seemed to be one. I had noticed last year that even when his friends would make fun of people in the hallways at school, he never did. And who else would have come over to try and fix my computer and bring along his laptop in case I needed it? Okay, I needed to focus. After all, my grandmother always warned me about falling into the whole "knight on a white horse" thing. She said women did not need rescuing and I could take care of myself, and with the exception of this laptop thing, I could. So why did I act stupid around him?

"I think it's a virus."

"Huh?" I glanced up.

"I think you have a virus," he said. "You should probably take it in and have it checked out. Wish I could fix it, but what can I say? I'm not that smart."

A guy who admitted he couldn't fix something? Grandma didn't warn me about that happening. In fact, she wouldn't believe such a thing existed.

"Well, thanks for trying and getting my paper off there. I can use my mom's computer if you want your laptop back. I hope I didn't infect you…" *Ugh*, why couldn't I just be normal for two seconds? "I mean, I put this drive in your computer—"

"I have tons of virus blockers and stuff on there. It should be fine. Are you sure you don't need it anymore?" he said. "How's your paper coming?"

I shrugged. "It's coming. Thanks again for coming over. I thought I was going to have to throw holy water on it to—" *Shut up, shut up, shut up, you little weirdo.* "I mean, thanks for coming over. See ya tomorrow."

As soon as he left, Mom came into the room to ask if my computer was fixed.

"No, but my friend was able to get my paper for me. I guess I have a virus."

"So your *friend* was able to get it for you," she said, smirking. "How interesting you called a guy to help you."

"What? Oh, because only guys know about computers. That is so sexist, mother."

"I *meant* because you got ready like you were going to the prom," she said. "I can't remember the last time I saw you wearing makeup just to do your homework."

I rolled my eyes and told her I had to get going on my

homework. She made smooching noises as she got her laptop for me. It would be nice to have a mother who didn't have the social skills of a six-year-old. Before I got back to work, I decided to light some candles. It was Tuesday, so I lit my pink cotton candy scented soy candle to draw love. Grandma was the one who had told me how different candle colors meant different things and which days you should light which candle. My mom wasn't into that sort of thing, although she did light blue candles for safe travels before we'd go on trips. I wondered if the pink candle thing actually worked. It had never done anything for me before, but what if this time was different? Chances were nothing would ever happen with Brendon and me, but what if he was my soul mate? Stranger things had happened. Like the time I had a dream years ago about a player throwing up during basketball finals. I mentioned it to my dad, who had seen me predict stuff before, so he bet a ton on the game with some of his friends. Well, I was right about the guy having the flu, but he still played, and his team won. And my dad was not happy. Grandma told him that's what he got for trying to "abuse my gift for profit." However, my "gift" wasn't helping me figure out how to talk to Brendon. Okay, forget talk, I wanted him to fall for me the way the singer Nick Bettis fell for my favorite actress, Grai—wait, they didn't exactly work out. Or did they get back together? Once my subscription to *Starlight Magazine* expired, it was like I wasn't up on anything anymore.

I sat back on my bed. I couldn't think of one other person who would have dropped everything to come over to help someone they barely knew. It had to mean something, right? I had a weird feeling he and I were supposed to be more than just partners in class. Well, even if the candle thing didn't work, it still made my room smell good.

I tried to picture what it would be like to date Brendon and imagined him taking me to a restaurant on the water. One of those places that put up Christmas lights year round so everything's all romantic and sparkly. It would be private and dark, so I wouldn't have to worry about getting sauce on my chin or trying to use my knife and fork. I was convinced back in the day I had missed the lesson on how to properly use silverware. Maybe I was sick that day like I was the day when everybody learned how to tell time, which meant for the rest of my life, I had to pretend I couldn't see my watch clearly whenever someone asked what time it was. I was sure Brendon could tell time easily with his expensive Riley Turner watch. The price of his watch could single-handedly save the rain forest. Okay, maybe not, but it *was* expensive. As I sat there, I wondered if he believed in love at first sight and the whole soul mate/kindred spirit thing. Then I wondered if he had any feelings for me at all. I couldn't sleep, so I went to talk to my mom. She was in her room, reading, and I noticed she had a bunch of green candles lit on the coffee table.

"For Grandma?" I asked.

"Yeah, she was always lighting green candles when people got sick," she said. "Maybe now it'll work for her."

I wasn't sure whether or not to point out the light-green candle in the middle was actually suited more for getting pregnant than getting well, but I thought I'd let it go. Maybe the exact shade of green wasn't as important as Grandma had led me to believe. Or maybe I'd have a new brother or sister soon—eww. I couldn't even let my mind go there.

"I've been lighting them, too," I said.

"I know, your father's been complaining you're going to burn the house down. He's afraid you'll forget how many you lit."

I had never forgotten to blow out a candle—fine, okay, once. I had lit an aromatherapy stress candle, my friend Margaux called, and I was on the phone for over an hour. When I came back, the candle had burned so low that I didn't see the flame, and I didn't remember it was lit until I switched off the lights to go to bed. If it wasn't for the tiny glow, I would have fallen asleep without blowing it out, but even if I didn't blow it out, it was in a container, so I'm sure it wouldn't have caught my dresser on fire. Besides, it wasn't like we didn't have insurance.

"If nothing else, the green should help us with prosperity," she said.

"I thought purple was for prosperity."

"You should know, I guess. You always paid way more attention to what Grandma was saying about the superstitious stuff than I did."

"Do you think she's going to be all right?" I asked.

"She's a fighter, but *you* need to get to bed. You don't want dark circles under your eyes for when you see Brendon—" She started laughing. "Sorry, that sounded like something an old-fashioned sitcom mother would say. Get your butt to bed, kiddo."

"You know, it wouldn't kill you to be a little more sitcom mom-ish," I said. Mom said she'd work on teasing her hair up and wearing an apron to make breakfast in the morning.

Chapter 3

I got to class late and didn't get to talk to Brendon until it was over. He asked if I wanted to go over to the student lounge and get something to drink.

"Did you finish your rough draft?" he asked as we sat down.

I started to say that I was pretty much done with it when my mom called on my cell phone to say she was going to visit my grandma this afternoon, so I should get a ride home with Zach and Kylie. Unfortunately, Zach and Kylie had already left, so I was going to have to take the bus.

"Everything okay?" Brendon asked.

"My mom can't pick me up because she's going to St. Mary's to see my grandma. My grandma had a stroke recently."

"I can take you home," he said, and we walked out to his car. "My grandfather had a stroke a few years ago."

I nodded, but didn't know what to say because I had seen that on the news when it happened.

"Every Labor Day we go up to my grandparents' house and hang out, and it's hard to see him this way," he said. "He was a senator, like my dad, and now my grandma cuts up his food like he's a little kid or some- thing. Some days she even has to feed him — it sucks."

"My grandma had to move to the rehab center be- cause she can't walk too well now. It's so depressing to go there," I said. Margaux's eyes glazed over if I talked about visiting my grandmother, but Brendon seemed to be pay- ing attention.

"My granddad's still able to live at home with my grandmother, but my family checks in on them. It's a big house, but he can only get around the first floor in his wheelchair," Brendon said as he traced the steering wheel with his finger. "It sucks because he used to be pretty ac- tive. They even have a tennis court in the backyard."

I couldn't imagine having a tennis court in my back- yard. Last year we had a rabid gopher and animal control had to come out, but that was the extent of any interesting stuff going on in my backyard.

"Hey, do you play tennis?" he asked.

"Yeah. I'm not good though."

"I reserved a court time for tomorrow night, and my friend backed out. I hate to waste it. Any chance you'd want to play at the country club with me?"

"I don't belong," I said, blushing.

"I can get you a guest pass. You in?"

"Sure, why not?"

THE NEXT MORNING, as I got ready for class, I realized I had no idea what you wore to play tennis at an *actual* ten- nis court. My friends and I played on a cement slab in the park, and we wore shorts and T-shirts, unless we were too lazy to shave our legs, then it was sweatpants.

During class, Mrs. Rae called on several people to read their rough drafts out loud. I saw this girl Rory slide down in her seat when Mrs. Rae called on her partner, Kirk. It was pretty obvious Rory had written most of it since Kirk read it like he had never seen the paper before. The air conditioning wasn't working, so we had all the windows open, and there were three fans running. With all the noise, I could barely hear anyone who was reading, so I started daydreaming about a story I was working on about three sisters. Being an only child made me obsessed with writing stories with siblings.

"Emme, do you have any suggestions for Kirk?" Mrs. Rae asked, breaking me out of my trance.

I shook my head, and she asked me to read my rough draft next. Crap, I hadn't blinked once since I went off to la-la land, and my tinted green contacts were off-center so I couldn't see my paper, much less read it. I tried blinking hard to get my contacts to move, but it felt like I had tiny pieces of sandpaper inserted into each eye. Blinking hard, I opened my mouth to begin, when the bell rang. Whew.

Brendon waited for me outside the classroom. He had shown up looking cuter in shorts and a T-shirt than most guys look in a tux. Meanwhile, I was in yoga pants and a long-sleeved T-shirt, which hid the fact I had zero muscle tone. I started to walk out to his car when he pointed out I had forgotten my racket in the classroom.

"Oh right, hold on."

I came back out, and he asked where my sports bottle was. I didn't own any sort of bottle with the word "sports" on it, so I said I'd grab a bottle of water from the vending machine on the way out. Now I had to hope its un-uniform appearance wouldn't sicken him. I had put a rose quartz crystal in my pocket, hoping to "draw love" to me, but I should have checked to see if there was a don't-make-a-fool-of-yourself-on-the-tennis-court crystal.

Brendon unzipped an expensive-looking racket bag and slid my old, naked racket in next to his pro racket. Next to the bag sat six containers of tennis balls. How long did he think we were going to play? Kylie and I would play until one of us neared breaking a sweat, and then we'd quit and go for ice cream to cool off. I had never played longer than twenty minutes and never used more than one can of tennis balls in my life.

"Um, you do know I don't play like, competitively, right? My friends and I try to see how long we can hit the ball without missing a shot," I said.

"One way to play. How many shots until one of you misses?" he asked.

"Four, possibly five."

"See? I knew you'd make it hard to return."

Actually, that was when we were *trying* to hit to each other. I began feeling self-conscious about my serve. I knew it wasn't great, but I couldn't change it now because I had been doing it like this since I was eight. Normally, I informed people about my "tennis rules" before I played with them. My rules were little things like the fact that I wouldn't run after balls too far out of my reach, and how I refused to share a court with little kids who were better players or any jerk who found it funny when he had to hit my balls back to me because my swing was off. I decided not to share those rules with Brendon, though.

We pulled into the parking lot, and the butterflies hit full force. What was I thinking going to a place where *actual* tennis players hit? What if people made fun of me? What if I passed out, and the only person who knew CPR was some nasty, oiled-up jock? We signed in and walked to the indoor courts. I was happy to see that each court was partitioned so no one could watch us. Brendon opened a can of tennis balls and a familiar rubber scent filled the air.

"Seriously, I just want to play for fun. No competitive stuff, okay?" I said.

"But that's half the fun. C'mon, you serve," he said, throwing me a ball. I hadn't played in a while, but it started to come back to me.

"Hey, Miss I-Just-Want-To-Play-For-Fun, I need to get something to drink," he said, panting after about ten minutes of play.

His shirt was damp around the neck from sweat. I kept wiping my face so he wouldn't see how greasy I was getting. I took a drink of water, and it dribbled down my chin. Lovely—I was sure all the girls at the country club drooled openly. Brendon walked over to my side of the court and asked if he could have some of my water because he had finished his sports drink. I never share drinks since I saw a story on the news about how meningitis was spread through stuff like that, but I handed him the bottle. I was surprised he'd want to drink after me, but maybe he was a step away from dehydrating, and it was between sharing my spit or death.

"Wanna quit?" he asked. I nodded and went to change.

There was only one other girl in the locker room as I washed up and pulled my hair up. I went out to meet Brendon, and he asked if I wanted to get some frozen yogurt. I started to answer when the girl in the locker room came out behind me.

"Hey, stranger. Haven't seen you around lately," she said, putting her hand on Brendon's arm.

"Hey, Cassie," he said.

"What have you been up to?" she asked.

I've seen dogs chase the mail carrier with more dignity. Brendon shrugged and said he had been busy. He introduced me, and her eyes darted over to me just long enough to size me up. I hated girls who acted like having another female in the room was competition.

"Well, give me a call sometime," she said, walking away.

What was her problem? She didn't know whether or not we were dating. It was like it didn't matter if I was his girlfriend or not because I wasn't "good enough." We headed over to the yogurt place, and he asked if I wanted to get together tomorrow. Did he mean he wanted to work on our project some more or he couldn't go a day without seeing me because I was so irresistible? Naturally, my intuition was no help when I needed it the most.

"We could grab lunch, too. So, are we on for tomorrow?" he asked.

Don't look too eager. Don't look too eager.

"Yeah, okay."

HE PICKED ME up the next day, and we went to a deli. We both ordered subs, except he had a turkey and ham sub on white bread, and I had a veggie sub on whole grain. My sub kept falling apart, and I had bits of sprouts everywhere. I must have wiped my mouth fifty times, while he stayed neat. Did they put glue in his sub?

He told me about a student council project he was working on, while I wiped shredded lettuce off my pants. He was always working on committees, and he told me his dad said it was important to build up your resume. His dad would cry if he saw my resume because I had to put selling cookies and babysitting on it to plump it up.

"We're also sponsoring a student artist this month," he said.

"Oh, the watercolor guy? I saw his stuff in the cafeteria. He's pretty good," I said. *Ask me out. Ask me out. Ask me out now.*

"I don't know anything about art, but there's an art fair in Royal Oak next weekend. Do you want to check it out after we work on our project?" he asked.

He wasn't into art, so I knew he wasn't dying to go, but did it mean he liked me? I said it sounded like fun, and he asked if I wanted to stop at the used bookstore on the corner.

"Someday I'd like to be able to collect first editions," he said as we walked through the bookstore. "I want to have a huge library and to have actually read the books in there, you know? Not like when you see some celebrity's library, and you know they haven't opened any of them. Or like my dad's office where most of the books were from the previous senator, and I doubt even that person read them. I hate when things are just for show, you know?"

I nodded. We browsed for a while, and I found a biography, which was only three dollars, and a book on numerology. He found two mysteries and a big book on Scotland.

"I like to collect books on different countries," he said as I flipped through it. "I have Italy, Jordan, Germany, France, Lebanon, and Ireland so far."

"Do you travel a lot?" I asked.

"Not out of the country. I did go to Italy when I was five, but I don't remember it. Hey, have you ever been to the big store in Detroit—it's near the old baseball stadium? It's like a big factory full of books. It's not too far, if you're interested."

I like to read, but I would have spent the whole afternoon at an actual factory if it meant spending more time with him. As we walked through the bookstore, I saw they had a young adult section. Out of the corner of my eye I spotted the series I had been obsessed with and my mom sold at a garage sale after she wrongly assumed I was "done with the Allington Heights books, seeing as you read them all." *Hello*, I reread all my books, and those Allington Heights books got me through my breakup with John. I escaped into their world and forgot about my own crappy one for a little while.

"Check out these classics," Brendon said. "Look at the covers. Aren't they amazing? Are you into Dickens?"

My only knowledge of Dickens were the cartoons made of his *A Christmas Carol* story, but I decided it counted, so I nodded.

"I'm super into him right now. It's like I go on these kicks where I'm into one writer and want to know every-thing about their work and then, boom—I'm over it and onto someone new," he said.

Did that apply to his dating life, too?

"Yeah, when I get into a writer, I want to know all about them—like how they work and what inspires them."

Brendon cocked his head to the side and stared at me. "Oh, wow. Well, yeah, as a writer I can see how you would."

He didn't say anything bad, but I got the feeling he thought it was different. It wasn't like he was judging me, but I could tell it wasn't what he expected me to say.

Afterwards, we stopped at a café, and he ordered something like a coffee slushy so I got one, too, even though I normally don't drink coffee. I was trying to think of an excuse to ask him when his birthday was so I could use the numerology book on him. I decided to bring the book out to see what he'd say about it. He picked it up and started flipping through it.

"You're into this stuff?" he asked.

"My grandma got me into it. She told me about this actress whose mother was into numerology and how the mother told her they shouldn't get on this plane because of the flight number and her age—just all these numbers seemed unlucky and then the plane ended up crashing," I said.

"Wow, pretty hardcore and creepy. Hey, it says you can find your destiny," he said. "How do you do it?"

"There are different ways to figure stuff out, but the easiest one is to add up your month, birth date, and the whole year to figure out your birth number," I said.

He pulled out a pen and started adding it up on his napkin. I saw his birth date and realized he was a Cancer— just like I suspected. Thankfully, he wasn't a Sagittarius like John. I was convinced all Sags couldn't settle down.

"Do I add the one and nine from the year, too?" he asked. I nodded. "Okay, I'm a three, so what does that mean?"

I flipped to the page on threes. I was more interested in knowing how threes and fives (my number) matched up, compatibility-wise, but I didn't want to freak him out with that.

"Okay, it says you're intelligent and used to getting your way. You have a great need to be loved and for emotional attachment," I said, leaving out the part where it said you could wind up jumping from relationship to relationship if you didn't find the right person. "It also says that you are energetic and you don't worry about the future."

"Well, that part's not true. I'm panicking over college applications and where I'm going to end up next year. What does yours say?" he asked.

Mine stressed how important freedom and ambition was, but I decided not to share that since he was a Cancer and stability and loyalty were important to them. There was a huge paragraph about number fives, but I just read him the good parts about my "sparkling personality," "generous nature," and "warm sense of humor." Next, we did the personal year ones where we added up the birth month and date with the current year. My birthday was in August, so mine was about to change, but Brendon had just had his birthday, and he was in his number two year.

"Let me read it," he said, pulling the book away from me. In a perfect world, it would say we were soul mates, and he'd fall madly in love with me.

"Emme, listen to this, 'This could be the year you find the right person. Love could be right around the corner, so take a chance. All your relationships will strengthen now, so go out and meet new people because the number two year is a partnership year,'" he said, as my heart shot up like it was on an elevator. "Hmmm…nothing about colleges, though."

Thank you, Mr. Romance. Didn't he see how fate was practically giving him a neon sign saying I was the one? Okay, maybe not neon, but pretty close. He asked what year I was in, and I explained I was in my number five year, but it would change in August.

"It says, 'A number five year often involves you meeting your soul mate. Sometimes these romances hit rough waters, but this will clear up by the time your sixth year rolls around. Five is a symbol of chance, so something could catch you off-guard, but it will be a turning point in your life,'" he said as he lowered the book. "So did you meet your soul mate this year?"

"Working on it," I said.

When he got up to get a bottle of water, I flipped to the section on compatibility and checked how threes and fives matched up.

"Number eight couples: You are both intrigued by each other's intellectual side—" Boring. "It's as if you've met your match and you feel as if someone 'gets you' for the first time." Here we go! "You'll see excitement in new things and feel like the universe is opening to you. It's like walking on air, and nothing seems out of reach. Everything is flowing for you—" Perfect. "—just don't sabotage it with negativity, jealousy, or low self-esteem." Crap. "Work problems out instead of running from them. Patience, compromise, and understanding your partner's core beliefs are important. People may question if it'll last, but if you hang in there, you can discover a close bond."

Well, the last part wasn't the sunshine and rainbows I had hoped for, but things *were* looking up. I wish I could tell if he was into me. If only I could get a straightforward sign or something. *Anything.* I mean, in *my* perfect world, he'd be holding my hand and writing me poetry, but he didn't seem like a poem-writing, touchy-feely kind of guy. However, minutes later, when we were leaving and walking out, Brendon saw his friend Sam. He went to cross the street and grabbed my hand—just like I had visualized a zillion times. My heart jumped. I mean, he only held it for a second, and it was just to lead me across the street, but it was still Brendon holding my hand.

"Sam, wait up!" he yelled. Sam jogged over to where we were. He was dressed in a pink golf shirt with light-colored shorts on and his overly gelled hair styled to perfection. He seemed more like a cover model than a regular guy.

"Sup," he said, nodding at Brendon.

"This is Emme," Brendon said. Sam nodded at me, and they started talking about tee times. Although I couldn't see Sam's eyes through his super-expensive sunglasses, I had the feeling he wasn't paying the slightest bit of attention to me. I could have been a stranger waiting for a bus next to him.

"Oh, my phone," Brendon said pulling it out. "Just a sec—"

Sam, obviously bored by the idea of waiting five seconds for Brendon to take a call, said he'd see him later and walked off without acknowledging me. Brendon put down the phone.

"Gotta go pick up something for my mom. I'll drop you off on the way."

I had been hoping to spend a little more time with him, but pretty soon I was back in front of my house, and he was driving off. Then I realized we hadn't even talked about the papers.

"Hi, Grandpa," I said as I walked into the family room where my grandfather was watching TV.

"Hi, sweetie. Do you know where Mom is?" he asked.

"She's in the kitchen," I said, thinking it was weird, since he could see into the kitchen.

"No, I mean *our* mom," he said.

"Who? You mean Grandma?" I asked. He didn't say anything. "Grandma Frances?"

"Yeah, where's Frances?" he asked. I stared at him, and then got up to find my mother.

"Mom, did they move Grandma to a new room or something?" I asked. She shook her head, and I told her Grandpa was asking where she was.

Mom sighed. "He was asking me earlier. I think he's just confused because there's so much going on. We're going to have him stay with us for a little while. I don't think he should be alone right now."

I went back to the family room, and Grandpa was looking up at me expectantly. I didn't say anything, and I hoped he wouldn't ask me about Grandma again, but he did.

"Remember, she's back at the assisted living place."

"Oh, that's right," he said.

I got out a deck of cards, and we played war until Dad called us for dinner. Grandpa didn't ask any more questions about Grandma, but I had a strong feeling he wasn't just "a little confused" and this was only going to get worse.

Chapter 4

BRENDON WASN'T IN class when I got there on Monday. Mrs. Rae put on a film about stereotypes, and most of the back row dozed off during it. Brendon came in late and sat by the door. Great, now I seemed desperate and pathetic sitting by myself like I was waiting for him, which I totally was. When the movie ended, Mrs. Rae passed out worksheets and told us to work with the person to our right. Normally, Brendon sat on my right, but today I had an empty chair. I saw this girl, Rory, sitting by herself and asked her to be my partner. We started filling out the questions when I heard somebody laughing. I glanced over and saw Lauren walk in late and then start laughing at something Brendon said. Why did his ex-girlfriend have to be in this class? I went back to Rory, who was peeling the price tag off her notebook.

"Did you finish your paper?" she asked. "My partner hasn't even watched the show yet. I knew I was going to get stuck doing the whole thing."

Her partner, Kirk Woodsen, with his bleached hair and a deep tan, talked loudly about the basketball playoffs. "He teaches tennis to five-year-olds, probably because they are on the same mental level. He told me he wants to get into modeling," she said, rolling her heavily lined eyes. "I should tell him my mom's an agent, and maybe then he'd do some of the work."

When class ended, I wondered if I should go over and say something to Brendon. I packed up my stuff slowly, hoping he'd come over to me. When I got up, I realized I was the only one left in the room. Meanwhile, Brendon was in the hall talking to Lauren.

"Hey, Emme," he said.

"Oh, hi," I said. "I didn't see ya there." Oh, how lame. I'm such a loser.

"I had a student board meeting this morning, which took forever. Did I miss anything important?"

I shook my head, and Lauren gave me the same condescending smile people give annoying children. And I *felt* like a kid next to her, with her high-heeled sandals and a short jeans skirt, while I was wearing a T-shirt with a cat on it and sneakers. What a femme fatale.

"Do you have a minute? Wanna grab something to drink?" he asked me.

I nodded.

"I'll see you later, Brendon," Lauren said, making a point to rub his arm as she left to meet her friend. Yeah, I always groped people when I said good-bye, too. Brendon and I went over to the Coffee Beanie Weanie across the street. He got an espresso and a cookie, and I ordered green tea. He offered me part of his chocolate chip walnut cookie and told me he was in charge of setting up tutors for the homework help lab. I offered to help, but he needed tutors in chemistry and advanced algebra. I barely made it out of algebra one and only because my math tutor went over all of my homework for me.

"I almost forgot. I got a bunch of teen magazines for our project," he said, unzipping his backpack. "I dropped this one in the store, and this woman looked at me like I was a pervert, but look at this singer's outfit. It looks like she was attacked by a mountain lion." He pointed to the ripped-up shirt and jeans the singer, Crystalline, wore.

"It says, 'You can look like Crystalline with Cosmic Powders makeup. She's wearing peony blush and shimmering violet lip cream,'" I said, making a mental note to check out the lip cream later on lickitylips.com.

"Look at this picture of Lorenzo Crawford," he said. "He's definitely wearing makeup, but you don't see the brand named."

I could have pointed out I was wearing the same shade of bronzer as Lorenzo, but I decided to keep it to myself. Brendon made a joke about how Lorenzo's last movie was all about him posing and being tan. I could smell his cologne as he leaned over. If it took the rest of my life, I would do everything I could to find out what cologne he used...without actually asking him and sounding like a stalker.

"You know Kirk—from our class?" he said. "He uses fake tan. I saw it in the locker room once."

I realized how close he was sitting to me, and I hoped my mint green tea was masking any bad breath issues.

"Rory thinks he wears contacts to make his eyes bluer," I said, not sharing I did the same thing to make my hazel eyes look like they were dark green.

He laughed, and we went back to the magazines. My head was reeling from sitting so close to him. I focused on finding examples for the project, but I caught him staring at me when I glanced up. He seemed embarrassed, and I figured he was probably staring at my messy hair.

"Since you're so busy with activities and stuff, I don't mind finding the articles for the next project," I said.

"No, it's okay. I found a couple last night, and there's a lot of stuff in this issue." He started to grab a magazine, but it slipped out of his hands. "Sorry," he said as he got up to get it.

He put the magazine between us, and when I moved forward to see it, he put his arm across the back of my chair. Now lots of guys did put their arms on chair backs, even Kirk did that with Rory, and he *definitely* wasn't interested in her, but I couldn't help but hope it meant something. I got this shivery feeling, and he asked if I was cold. I shook my head. I always got a feeling before something major was about to happen, and it has nothing to do with being cold, but I didn't know *why* I got the feeling. Grandma used to do the same thing and always said, "Somebody just walked across my grave." Somehow I didn't think Brendon would understand if I told him I needed to move my future burial plot to a less high-traffic area.

"Are we still on for the art fair?" he asked.

I had only been circling it with hearts on my calendar since he asked.

"Sure, I think I'm still free," I said.

We finished up our work, and he walked me out to meet Kylie.

"Okay, I'll pick you up at three tomorrow," he said, walking off.

"Can I ask a stupid question?" Kylie asked as soon as Brendon was out of earshot. "What's he like? Because he's so well-known, and I can't imagine what it'd be like to grow up with your whole life under a microscope. I mean, my mom remembers his first birthday party pictures being shown on the news. And he's hot, but he's not like I-know-I'm-a-hottie hot, but more like a confident, 'Yes, I *am* hot. Any questions?' I mean, he has to have noticed there aren't any guys who look like him walking around."

"I should tell him what you said."

"Don't you dare," Kylie said.

"I get what you mean—he's grown up with everybody knowing his dad and watching him, but he's pretty down to earth."

"So what's up with you two? You guys didn't do any work last Saturday, and now you're going to an art fair."

"I dunno. He just asked me to go with him."

"Asked you to go with him as his study buddy or asked you to go with him because he's desperately in love with you?" she asked.

I said we were just friends, but she wouldn't let it go.

"Okay, duh, obviously I like him, but let's be honest. He's out of my league. He's out of most people's league. It's weird because normally if I like a guy then one of two things happens—either he likes me and asks for my number...or I find out he's not into me and I cry in my pillow and listen to man-hating music for at least three days," I said. "But this time's different because he's, I dunno, not just 'some guy.' I mean, I'm not putting up a shrine to him in my room, and I haven't rooted though his garbage can, but I have as much chance of going out with him as Kirk does of getting an 'A' in this class."

"You listen to man-hating music?" she asked, and I narrowed my eyes at her. "Whatever. Anyway, Em, he's asked you out once already, and you are seeing him tomorrow. Plus, he's *always* staring at you."

I said he was probably just bored in class today, but she wouldn't let it go.

"I'm not just talking about today. When we watched the movie on Monday, he watched you instead, and whenever I see you guys, he acts like there's no one else in the room," she said.

I couldn't hold back the big, stupid smile spreading across my face. "He does? For real?"

She nodded. "You know, it's weird. Here you were all upset you didn't have a partner at the beginning of the semester, and then you ended up with like, Mr. Perfection, as your partner."

As I left, she made me promise to e-mail her when I got home tomorrow with all the details.

Chapter 5

IN THE MORNING, I went to see Grandma before meeting Brendon. I downloaded some meditations for lowering blood pressure, which was what the doctors said caused Grandma's stroke in the first place. The nurses had moved her to a different room, and she was agitated. I tried to get her to eat some applesauce, but she just wanted to know when she could go back to her old room. My mom went to talk to the head nurse, and Grandma got concerned about where my mom went.

"Where did she go?" Grandma asked.

"Just in the hall," I said. "Do you want me to turn the TV on for you?"

But Grandma wasn't listening to me. She kept craning her neck, trying to see Mom.

"She's just outside the door at the nurse's station," I said. "See? She's right there."

"Gabrielle?" she called. "Gabby?"

My mother poked her head in the room. "Yeah? Do you need something, Mom?

"Just wanted to know where you went," Grandma said.

I exchanged a look with Mom. She shrugged and went back to talk to the nurse.

"Gabby? Gabby? Where did she go?" Grandma asked, leaning forward.

"She's still right outside the door," I said. "Do you want some more water?"

We left at one o'clock, when she started falling asleep. I didn't want to go, but the nurse practically shoved us out the door, saying Grandma needed her sleep. It seemed like all she did was sleep, but I didn't want to cause problems.

I hated seeing Grandma acting out of it and so dependent. It was like she was a little kid. Grandpa was starting to be more reliant, too. It was beginning to scare me. They used to take care of me, and it made me nervous how suddenly I was the stable one who needed to be responsible. I couldn't even rely on myself, so how could my grandparents rely on me for anything?

When I got home, I tried to focus on other things, but it seemed stupid to worry about what I was going to wear when I went out with Brendon while my grandma was dealing with health problems. I knew she wouldn't want me to stay home and worry all afternoon—and honestly, it wouldn't help her—but why did she have to go through it? It wasn't fair. I tried to take my mind off things, and I went outside to see what the temperature was. It was cool and seemed like it was going to rain, which was good because I hated myself in shorts. I used to wear them all the time in middle school, but now I felt weird about it, even though a lot of girls wore them to class. I was thankful for air conditioning so I didn't look completely stupid wearing jeans to school.

After debating what to wear, I decided to put on my khaki jeans and a blue-and-red shirt, which was like a formfitting baseball jersey. I considered cute red sandals, but I switched to a more comfortable pair of sneakers. After all, I could barely walk in those shoes on a good day, and the last thing I needed was to trip over my own feet in front of Brendon. I still didn't feel quite right, so I put on the red lipstick Margaux gave me for Christmas, which always made me feel more confident. Brendon texted me to say he was in the driveway.

When I got in the car, Brendon told me to pick out something to listen to. It sounded easy except for the fact I had the worst taste in music. Everybody knew I loved any stupid song written for a six-year-old girl, but I couldn't help it. Margaux always made fun of me because I used to have a sleeping bag with a girl band called the Sweetie Gals on it. I still used it as a blanket when I got cold. However, I didn't want Brendon to know I counted the days until the Sweetie Gals reunited, so I tried to find a song I thought he'd like. Then I saw it—*Sweeties for Always*. He owned a Sweetie Gals album, too.

"Do you have a sister?" I asked.

"Nope, just an older brother. Why?" he asked, and I held up the phone showing the album. "Oh, I downloaded it when it was on sale for ninety-nine cents. It's not bad, though."

"I know, I have the same one," I said. "Oh wow, you have the same TV theme song album I have, and we have a lot of the same chick flick movie soundtracks. So weird. If I find a Paulo Estevez song on your playlist, I'm gonna start to wonder."

"I didn't even know the TV one was in there," he said laughing. "And I don't own any music by Paulo or anyone who wears leather pants, but I have to admit I do own another Sweetie Gals album."

"I went as one of them for Halloween once. I was Bridget," I said. I wished my mouth and brain worked together a little better under pressure, but luckily he laughed.

"She was my crush when I was thirteen," he said. "I had her poster on my wall."

"Seriously?"

"I wouldn't lie about something so important. Then she started dating a basketball player and broke my heart. I've never fully recovered."

"Her loss," I said, and he laughed.

He parked on one of the side streets, and we walked down to see some of the different art displays. I began to relax.

"Some of this stuff is super ugly," he said.

"The sculpture over there looks like someone threw macaroni and cheese on it."

"Fun fact: gluten-free, dairy-free mac n' cheese is Bridget's favorite food," he said.

"You're kidding?"

"Hey, the Sweetie Gals's Web site doesn't lie," he said, smiling.

"Is that how you knew she was your soul mate?"

"Soul mate is such a strong word, and no, considering she chose some athlete over me."

"In her defense, you're still in high school," I said.

"Hey, what happened to 'her loss'?" he asked.

"You're right. She should have waited for you."

He gave me that smile where his eyes shone and the world dropped away. "Exactly. I am worth the wait, aren't I?"

I swallowed. "I'm sure you are."

"That whole section of iron zombies over there is freaking me out," he said. "Let's have a contest of who can find the weirdest stuff."

"Okay, but I have to warn you, I'm super into art—even the odd stuff. I just feel like if someone put all their creative energy into something then we should—" I stopped. "You're laughing at me!"

"No, I'm not, I just think it's cute how, I dunno, idealistic you are...and sweet."

"Another way of saying, 'naïve'?"

He squinted. "Naïve? No. You don't strike me that way at all. Why?"

I shrugged. When I was dating John, he told me how much he loved my sense of humor. Then one day, in front of everyone, he said what he liked best about me was how funny I was and how I had this "adorable naïve quality." I felt so stupid and immature. Kylie told me to blow it off, but Margaux said she got a weird, controlling vibe from him. She said, "There's a reason he always dates younger girls." I tried to ignore it at the time, but there was something to what she said. Plus, his ex-girlfriend *always* followed him around like a little puppy, and he didn't like it when I questioned him or didn't go along with his opinion on something.

"All right, I think I found something even you'd have to admit is a little strange. It's a five foot tall, completely rusted rabbit. Looks like a tetanus shot warning sculpture," he said.

He was right—it was odd and seemed like you could take a layer of skin off just by touching it. But I wanted to mess with him a little.

"My great-grandparents used to have one," I said. I tried to look serious.

"Uh-huh…wait, for real?" he asked.

"Yeah, my great-grandfather bought it for a fiftieth wedding anniversary gift right before he died," I said. "We have it now in our backyard. I'll have to show it to you when you drop me off."

He didn't know what to say, so I took pity on him and told him I was joking.

"Not cool. You had me believing I insulted your dead great-grandfather's taste in lawn art," he said.

"Actually they did have lawn art," I said. "They had those little girls on a swing and the little Dutch boy and girl who lean over like they're going to kiss. I used to push them together so they could actually touch." Could I puh-lease just shut up now?

"But no five-foot rusted rabbits?" he asked.

"Sadly, no." It was getting easier to talk to him, and I almost felt relaxed around him. Almost.

"Oh man, there's a clown," he said.

"Yeah, cute."

"Seriously? I'm about to flee to the safety of my car, and you think those things are *cute*?"

I shrugged. "When I was a kid, my grandpa took me to the circus and got all the clowns to sign autographs for me. They were nice clowns, so I guess I never got scared of them. But are you? I mean, is it an issue?"

"Stop smiling!"

"I'm not smiling," I said, biting my bottom lip.

"You are *so* smiling. It's not unusual to be afraid of clowns," he said.

"It is a *little* unusual when you're, you know, the age you are," I replied.

"I wouldn't say I'm 'afraid,' in so many words. It's more like their presence makes me uncomfortable."

"Oh, much better. More mature than the whole I-wet-my-pants-because-I-saw-a-clown thing."

"You don't know the back story to my terror, okay? You wouldn't be so quick to judge if you knew what I had been through," he said. "You see one of those—"

"Cheerful bringers of joy?"

"More like terrors in rubber noses. Anyway, one of them scared me as a kid. My dad was on the campaign trail, and this clown was trying to make a point with him, so he came up and scared me, just to see if he could get a rise out of my dad in front of a crowd."

"How awful! I'm sure it goes against the clown code of honor," I said.

"Well, you might be right because later the company who supplied the entertainment claimed the guy was never on the list. He snuck in just to terrify me to prove a point. Ever since then, I think about who is hiding behind the makeup—the mask, you know? So that's what it's all about."

"What a crappy thing for someone to do to a little kid."

"And now I can't date girls who wear heavy make-up—I get flashbacks," he said, smiling.

I cracked up. "No wonder all your girlfriends have had the natural look."

He tilted his head. "You know who I've gone out with?" How did he not realize how many girls were into him?

"I'm joking," I said. Well, I sort of was. "You went out with Lauren, though, and she fits the look."

"Yeah, we dated for a while. Some people seriously were saying we'd end up married. So crazy." Everyone said those things because they were both high achievers with perfect looks and backgrounds. It was like the daughter of the peanut butter dynasty being promised to the jelly tsar's son.

"Yeah, insane. You're both in high school."

"I know, right? People always try to map out my life for me. They assume I'm going to follow in my father's footsteps: get married young, run for office, work my way up the ladder, have the perfect family—only unlike my dad, they assume I'll eventually run for President. Although I think my old man's still got designs on the Oval Office."

"So is any of that what you want?" I asked.

He blinked. "I don't even know *what* I want. It's hard to explain, but when you grow up in a family where your dad and your grandpa were known for something, it's like everyone assumes you'll pick up the baton and finish the race. I know it sounds like, 'oh, poor little rich kid crying because his family has connections,' but it's overwhelming."

"Wow, I never thought about it that way. I guess I just assumed you had all these doors open to you, and your life was, well, planned. But also like you had it made—you were set."

"That's what most people think, and in some ways it's true, but is it what I want? I honestly don't know."

"What would you do if you didn't have any family pressure on you?" I asked.

"You'll laugh at me."

"If I didn't laugh at the Sweetie Gals or the clown thing, then I think you're safe."

"True, you have proven yourself worthy of my trust," he said, smiling. "Okay, I would like to be a journalist. This sounds weird, but I am super into current events. Pretty much all of the apps on my phone are news. As a kid, I loved sitting with the press on the plane when there were big events. My dad wouldn't be into the idea, though. He hates the media with a passion."

"Does he know you're into journalism?"

"Nah. I mentioned something once after a negative story about him came out and said how they were just doing their jobs, and he cut me off. He said it used to be about reporting the news and staying neutral, but now everyone tried to make a name for themselves, and it was somehow okay for journalists to give their opinion. That is exactly why I want to do it. I want to go back to how it used to be, getting both sides of the story, staying neutral, and putting the facts out there. And yeah, I'd love to be a part of the big moments in history, too. See it firsthand and report so people know exactly what went down." His brown eyes were shining, and I had never seen him get so animated. There was something about seeing someone's face light up when they were passionate about a subject.

"Sounds like it's your calling."

"Yeah, well, when your family's into social causes, it's like you're meant to carry on the legacy, and they'd never understand—especially me siding with the enemy? No way."

"You should see yourself when you talk about it. Your voice changed; your face lit up. This is something you're seriously passionate about."

"For sure, but my dad would never pay for me to study journalism in college. He'd die first."

"What if you took an intro class? Just told him it was a requirement and went from there? Will he check your schedule every semester?" I asked.

"Knowing him, yeah. There's a path set for me. I'm not sure there's anything I can do to get out of it. I have three relatives who are in office, and my younger cousins and I have all done at least one government internship. My brother's the black sheep of the family for going off to a third world country to help orphans. I think my dad was okay with it because he thinks it looks good for Jayson to care about the needy. Don't get me wrong, my dad's a good guy, but he's always concerned with how we're coming off to the public."

"I bet he loved Lauren," I said and then slapped my hand over my mouth. Those words were not supposed to come out.

"Yeah, he did. Why?"

"Nothing, she just seems like the perfect first lady type."

"You aren't the first person who has said that, and it weirds me out."

"Oh, sorry."

"No, I mean, not you saying it, but the idea. You know, I've never told anyone other than my brother any of this, but I sit here with you and pour out my guts."

"Oh yeah?"

"I can't quite figure you out," he said. I prayed he didn't finish the thought with, "So glad I've found a therapist in you. You're like the little sister I never had."

"You were trying to figure me out?"

"All the time."

My heart flipped. "And? Any conclusion yet?"

"Nope, so I'm going to have to spend a lot more time with you," he said, moving closer. He put his hand under my chin and lifted my face to meet his. Then he kissed me, and I tried not to pass out. The smell of his cologne, the way he held my face—it was like a scene from a movie. This kiss was what romance writers wrote about.

"Any objections?" he asked.

"Huh?"

"To me spending more time with you."

"I think I might be able to work you into my schedule. Have your people call mine," I said.

"They told me they'd get back with me and never did."

"I'm firing my whole incompetent staff," I said with a smile. "So looks like I'm free."

"Perfect," he said, and we kissed again.

Chapter 6

THE NEXT DAY, Brendon called me about coming over to his house. I was still a little uncomfortable about the idea of hanging out at his place. After all, I had seen it online, and the idea of being around his older brother Jayson, the guy everyone talked about being Mr. Perfection, made me anxious.

"You know what? There's a ton of people here right now working on something for my dad, so maybe we could do something else," he said, and I exhaled. There would be no anxiety attack today.

"Oh, yeah, if it's busy. I don't want to get in the way."

"I go for a walk in our neighborhood every night. You want to go with me? I could pick you up after seven."

"Sure."

My neighborhood was nice, but his was gated. His area was also close to downtown Birmingham, so we could walk there if we wanted, or we could go over to the pond on the last street of the neighborhood. There was also a cemetery nearby, but we avoided it and stuck to walking by Sacred Heart, his old grade school.

"My brother wants to move out of the house and go

someplace more modern. My mom's the same way. She thinks our house is too old."

"Isn't your house a landmark or something?"

"Not quite, but it was owned by one of the old car guys in Detroit. Well, his son anyway. My mom is always talking about wanting someplace new and decorating it the way she wants, but I like this area. My dad calls it an 'established neighborhood.'"

"Huh?"

"Older houses and lots of trees. Seems like all the new areas have zero trees."

"Oh, I hate those new subdivisions, which are all open with no trees. I love those big houses you can't even see from the street because there are so many trees hiding them."

"Exactly. I hate the idea of everyone being able to see in—like living in a fishbowl," Brendon said, staring out at the pond.

"Is that kind of how you feel now?"

"Yeah, I think it's why my dad and I like the fact our house is tucked away. My mom's into that life. Big open windows, everyone watching. Not my thing to have people staring at me." He reached over and took my hand. "I love how I can tell you anything."

"Always."

He leaned his head against mine. "So how was your grandma today?"

"She slept the entire time I was there. The nurses said she had a rough night and to let her sleep. I'm going back tomorrow and praying she'll be more alert."

He dropped my hand and reached for his wallet. "Here. One of my dad's supporters gave this to me the night my dad was re-elected. It's a prayer card of the Divine Mercy. Sometimes when I'm anxious I repeat the phrase on the front, 'Jesus, I trust in you.' Maybe it would help your grandma to say it, too."

"Thanks. I've never seen this before. I'll take it with me tomorrow."

"What's weird is I remember the supporter's name—it was Emilia, but everyone called her Emme. Maybe it's a sign, huh?"

"Well, I do believe in signs."

—•—

AT FIRST I didn't think much of the Emme/Emilia thing until I was visiting Grandma in the hospital the next afternoon. She always kept a stack of worn prayer books and her rosary by her bed at home, so we had brought them to the hospital for her. She had gotten into this habit where she just liked to hold the rosary and the prayer cards.

"Emme, will you hand me my...my..." Lately she had problems finishing some of her sentences, which frustrated her. The doctor said she probably had a mini-stroke we weren't aware of, which had caused the speech problem. I always tried to figure out what she wanted because I hated seeing her get upset over not being able to get a sentence out.

"The rosary?" I asked, but she shook her head and sighed. Her big green eyes fixed on mine. I was the only one in the family who had any green in my eyes like she did. My mom and aunt took after my grandpa and had deep-blue eyes. "Do you want the devotional?" I picked up the book and about twenty little prayer cards fell on the floor.

"Sorry Grandma—" I stopped when I saw a card on the floor that said Divine Mercy. I had never seen her with one before, and I flipped it over. It said "St. Faustina" on the back.

"Where did you get this card?" I asked.

She tried to say "Faustina," but it wasn't going to

happen. She sighed and said, "It's Polish." She put her hand on mine and pushed it toward me. "Keep it."

"I brought you one from my friend. It's the same prayer, but it has a picture of Jesus on the front. See?"

She nodded smiling and said, "Oh yes, it's beautiful."

"He wanted me to give it to you."

She held it up to her heart. I noticed she was getting drowsy and decided to call my dad for a ride home. Just as I was about to dial, Brendon called.

"What's up? You busy?" he asked.

I said I was still at the hospital, and he asked if I wanted to go grocery shopping with him.

"I have to pick up stuff for my grandparents, and it'd be more fun if you went with me. C'mon, please? I'll even stop at the Milky Palace afterward for ice cream," he said. Grandma always took me there for a dipped cone after I went to the store with her, but I'd never told him.

"Sure, you want to pick me up in the front? Take the east entrance or else you'll end up in the ambulance zone," I said.

"New boyfriend?" Grandma asked as I hung up. "What's he like?"

"Well, his name is Brendon, and we do have different interests, but somehow we kind of seem in sync with each other. Sometimes I'm able to tell when he's about to call before the phone rings."

She nodded. "You had a different sort of smile on your face, so I knew it wasn't just a friend. Haven't seen you smile big in a while."

"He's thoughtful. He asks about you and what I'm in-to."

Grandma tilted her head to the side. "Don't all boy-friends do that?"

"John never did. I guess looking back it was all about him."

"Never liked him," she said, moving her hand to

dismiss the whole idea.

"Wish I could say the same thing," I said, biting my lip. John had had too much of a hold over me for way too long.

"You have fun. I'm going to rest now. So tired."

I went downstairs, and Brendon texted me he was in the parking lot.

"You're not going to believe this, but I read my horoscope today. It said a Leo would bring a sunny outlook into my life today, and my lucky number for the day is three," he said, pointing to my shirt, which was a yellow jersey with the number three on it.

"You read your horoscope? Since when?"

"Sometimes I glance over at the section while I'm reading the news. By the way, yours said a hot Cancer will sweep you off your feet and bring nothing but happiness and rainbows to your life."

"Interesting, because when I read it this morning it said to avoid misunderstandings and there could be a plumbing disaster waiting to happen. Maybe I missed the part about rainbows and the hot Cancer."

"You obviously didn't turn the page," he said, laughing.

"My mistake."

"But there was a plumbing disaster at *my* house. Jayson overflowed the bathtub, and my mom was furious. I think he was having another argument with his girlfriend while filling the tub, and he got distracted. Those two are either breaking up or making up—it's exhausting listening to them. That's what I like about you—you're not some high-drama girl."

"All the girls in your circle are, though," I said. "Not trying to be a jerk, but…"

"Oh no, you're right. They are, so I appreciate how you're different."

"Bored with your group now?" I asked.

"Nope, just…I was going to say, 'Looking to upgrade,' but it sounds horrible, doesn't it?" he said laughing.

I cracked up. "I get where you were trying to go with it, but yeah, it sounds bad. I'll pretend it's a compliment and not a sexist thing."

"I didn't mean it that way, like a trade-in for a car or a guy with a trophy girlfriend, I just meant…" His face got red, and he cleared his throat. "I've never met anyone like you before. The way you're so open about things. There's this vulnerability about you—"

"Naïve and immature like a little kid," I said, turning away. "Yeah, whatever."

"No, not what I meant. You're sensitive and caring—"

"Now I'm too sensitive? I don't—"

"No, Emme, I wasn't trying to say you were *being* too sensitive—I meant you're sensitive to other people's feelings, and when I said vulnerable I meant it as a positive thing."

I shrugged.

He put his hand over mine. "Being vulnerable is a good thing."

"Since when?"

"Well, for me it's nice to be around someone who is real as opposed to the fake people who have social media perfect lives when I know the real crap going on behind closed doors. You share what you feel—you don't hide it. It's an amazing quality to be open and show your feelings. I admire it since I grew up in a family who lives by the rule 'Put on a good face no matter what's happening.'"

"Yeah, okay."

"You know I'd never talk down to you or anything. I want to be clear. I meant everything I said in the best possible way. Emme, it'd kill me to think you thought I was trying to hurt your feelings in any way."

He squinted his eyes and bit his lip as he waited for my reaction.

"I know you wouldn't do it on purpose, but some people say stuff not realizing how it might impact the other person. Maybe I am a little naïve or whatever," I said.

"Did someone tell you that?"

"Yeah, my ex. He always made me feel so young and...whatever." I didn't want to drag out my whole past relationship and let Brendon know how I felt inexperienced and unworthy. Right now he didn't know what I was like last year, seeing as we didn't run in the same circles. He had no idea I had been cheated on and how my self-confidence had been trashed. I felt sick thinking about the time I asked John what was so wrong with me to make him go back to his ex.

"Well, he's an idiot," Brendon said.

"You don't have to say that."

"He let you go, so I'm guessing he's not going to be working at NASA anytime soon."

"Well, this is true."

"You know what's crazy? Your horoscope said something about misunderstandings. That's kind of weird."

"Yeah, it is," I said, although it's no weirder than the fact every time we hung up on the phone I had noticed the same number combination of how long we talked. But I'd never tell him because he'd think I was a weirdo.

"I guess we should head to the store, huh?" he said. "My mom's going to wonder where her stuff is."

"I'm so glad this is our last week of class," I said.

"Oh, right, I meant to tell you I get to miss the last week. It just got cleared with Mrs. Rae because I'm going with my dad to Virginia on Wednesday—right after class gets out."

I wanted to ask for how long, and I found myself feeling insecure. Would I sound clingy asking? After all, we had never defined what we were, so did I have a right to ask?

"It's just this thing he has to go to because a guy my grandpa worked with is having a library named after him. Grandpa can't go in his condition, so Dad is going in his place."

"Should be interesting."

"Will you miss me?" he asked.

I glanced over at him, and he was doing the crooked smile, which made every girl's heart melt.

"Maybe," I said and then wanted to slap myself for being so stupid. *Maybe?* Seriously? That was my answer?

"I am wounded. To the core. *Maybe?* Wow, okay. Now I know how you feel about me," he said as he pulled into a parking spot.

"Well, I'll miss having someone to play tennis with. Hey, is your friend Sam going to be around? He plays, right?" I asked, smiling to try and lighten the mood.

"Oh, ha ha. Great, my girlfriend and my best friend hooking up behind my back. Nice."

"Girlfriend?" I said and wanted to slap myself for the second time. Was it possible for me to be mysterious, or did I have to blurt out whatever crap came into mind? Lauren wouldn't have burst out without thinking or come off so needy, asking him to define their relationship. She always seemed in control.

"Yeah, isn't that what we are, or did I completely misread this whole situation, and I'm just so into you I assumed we were dating?" He glanced down and then back up at me and gave a shy smile. How did he manage to look unsure of himself while seeming confident? How was it possible?

"You never called me your girlfriend before."

"Actually, I do all the time; you're just not around to hear it." He smiled. "So, are you okay with it?"

"I love the idea," I said and then realized I had just used the L-word. "Well, I mean, it's fine or whatever."

He started laughing. "I liked your first response better. Not that hearing, 'it's fine or whatever,' isn't what all guys want to hear."

I put my hand over my mouth and laughed. "Sorry, I just...I didn't mean to. That word kinda made it seem so intense, and I wanted to lighten it up. I'm not smooth in the slightest. Stuff comes out of my mouth, and then I feel like I've said too much."

"You say what you're feeling, and that's what I love about you," he said, and then his eyes widened. "And now I've said the word, too. Wow, you bring out something in me—it's so weird. I'm normally not so open. This is kind of freaky for me. I just want to make sure we're on the same page because I thought we were, but...well, then you kind seemed shocked by me saying, 'girlfriend.'"

"I liked you saying girlfriend."

"Yeah?" His eyebrow arched. "Because I want to know how you feel. I know with my background it sometimes can seem like it's all about me, and I want to make sure you don't feel overwhelmed by all that. It's not what I'm about, but it *is* what I come with, if that makes any sense."

I nodded, and he reached over and put his hand on my shoulder.

"This all feels so new to me, and I normally don't talk about this stuff," he said. "But I guess I'm at the point where I'm feeling different things, and I've had so many relationships with people who wanted to be with the *idea* of me instead of the actual me."

"You don't think that's why I'm with you, do you?" I asked, feeling queasy.

"No, never for a minute, but I've been wrong before. But you and I—I dunno how to describe it, but it feels different. Like we click. It feels easy with you, although I do feel a little insecure sometimes."

"Must be a first for you," I said and then squirmed. "Sorry, I don't know where that came from."

"Um, I've felt insecure before, Emme," he said with a laugh. "I am human after all."

"Not going to lie to you—I avoided going to your house because the idea of your family is overwhelming. Sometimes I am a little quieter around you because I'm afraid I'll say the wrong thing, and I know you think some of the things I'm into are weird, but I love spending time with you...and I've said the L-word again. Whatever—it's true. I love spending time with you."

His smile made the corners of his eyes crinkle up.

"I've never seen you smile so big before," I said, and then wished I hadn't said something that made me sound like a creepy stalker.

"Not much makes me smile this big, but that did," he said and leaned over to kiss me.

We jumped apart when his phone got a text. He picked it up.

"It's from my mom asking where her groceries are since I left the house an hour ago. Somehow I got distracted," he said, smiling.

"We better get her stuff."

We got the groceries, and he dropped me off on the way home.

"Hey, I'll text you while I'm away and call when I can," he said. "So I'll ask you again, you gonna miss me?"

I leaned over and kissed him.

"Answer your question?" I asked.

"Definitely. See you soon."

Chapter 7

I HAD BEEN noticing more and more signs about Brendon and me. Even my horoscopes were surprisingly accurate, like when the paper predicted a person who was born under the sign of Cancer would call me from a far distance and "lift my spirits." Right after I read it, Brendon called my cell phone and said he had taken a last-minute trip to Washington, D.C., with his dad after their stop in Virginia, and he wanted to see how I was doing.

"Grandma was so tired today. She slept for almost our entire visit, and she's not eating much. I'm kind of worried."

"Did she say why she wasn't eating? Like, does she have no appetite? I'm just asking because last month they put my Grandpa on an antibiotic, and it made everything taste weird, so he wasn't eating. But when we figured it out, we just had to find what foods didn't taste metallic to him, and for some reason if he took some soda first—it had to be cola—it'd kill the metal taste, and he could eat a little bit."

"You know, they did put her on a strong antibiotic the other day. Maybe it's causing the problem."

"I was losing it when he wouldn't eat because sometimes people stop eating...you know...toward the end," he said. "It's scary thinking you might lose the one person who gets you. Actually, I kind of feel like I have two of those people in my life."

"Your brother?" I asked and then felt stupid. Had I ruined a romantic moment?

"Well, I guess somewhat, but I meant you."

My face felt warm. "I wish you were here right now."

"Me, too. I've missed you a lot this week. Normally, I'm busy with stuff and focused, but I keep thinking about you and wondering what you were doing."

"I was being bored and missing you. Now you're all caught up, so come home."

He laughed. "I hate when you're in class because I can't text you."

"Kirk texts all through class, and Mrs. Rae's stopped caring. She's given up on him learning anything."

"So like every other teacher he's ever had?" he asked.

"This is only my first class with Kirk, but I'm going to go with yes."

"Gotta run. Dad wants me to go with him to some meet and greet thing. I'll text you later."

I didn't hear from him the rest of the day. Normally I had my phone with me all the time, but today it was like I couldn't be more than two feet from it, and I kept checking the volume to make sure I didn't accidentally turn off my ringer and miss a call from him. Then I was checking my voice mail notifications just in case I missed an update. I was starting to feel pathetic checking it so much.

Brendon didn't call me until the next evening.

"Hey, what's up?" he asked.

I tried to act nonchalant like I was fine not talking to him all the time. John always said I was clingy whenever I called him instead of him calling me, and I was not going to make that mistake again.

"Nothing."

"Oh, well, anything interesting happen the last day of class?"

"Nope."

"Em, are you all right?"

"Fine."

"Okay, well I had a crazy thing happen this morning. Our plane hit major turbulence on the way back to Michigan. I hate to fly on a good day and this scared the crap out of me. Even Dad was panicking."

"Oh wow, are you okay?"

"Yeah, it was pretty intense though. The plane dropped at one point, and one of the aides had a full-blown panic attack."

"It must have been terrifying."

"Pretty much. Before I forget, my family is having a barbeque tomorrow. I meant to text you about it earlier, but I kinda got distracted with everything going on. Can you come?" he asked.

"Yeah, sure."

"Great, come over at noon, okay? See you tomorrow."

Meeting the Agretti family? On their turf? And now to pray for a barbeque-canceling thunderstorm for tomorrow afternoon.

Chapter 8

I CHANGED OUTFITS five times trying to figure out what you wore to a senator's barbeque. To anyone else's party, I would have worn shorts and a T-shirt, but I had a feeling this was going to be fancier. Still, I wanted to be myself and comfortable. I tried on a sundress, but it felt like I was trying to be something I wasn't—preppy. It was like I was trying to be a mini-Lauren. I changed into a pair of khaki capri pants and a red boatneck shirt dressier than my other casual tees. Then I decided that I'd dress it up a bit with a pair of red sandals instead of my usual sneakers. It was cute, but not too casual.

I thought I'd blend right into the crowd until I got there and saw every other woman in a sundress. And all of them seemed to be in a similar type of bright-colored print. It was like there was some store or designer they all knew about, and I was one hundred percent unfamiliar with it. As more and more women showed up wearing pink and green print dresses while carrying matching bags, I started to wonder if everyone but me was the member of some preppy cult. One of the servers dropped a stack of napkins near me, and I stopped to help her pick them up. I couldn't find Brendon so I texted him saying I was there.

"Hey, Emme," he said, coming over. "So happy you came. Come on, I want you to meet everyone."

He took me over to meet his brother Jayson, who was even better-looking in person. Jayson was a few years older than Brendon, and he had lighter brown eyes and cheekbones that reminded me of a ski instructor in the Alps. There was a blonde girl standing next to him in a yellow sundress and grasping Jayson's arm like it was a life preserver.

"Hey, I've heard a lot about you," he said. "This is my girlfriend, Brooke."

Brooke gave me a once over and a half smile.

Mrs. Agretti walked over to get Jayson, and Brendon introduced me to her.

"This is Emme, the girl I told you about," he said.

"Right, of course, Emily," she said, reaching her hand out like she was going to shake mine and then somehow getting distracted and turning away before we connected. "Brendon, your father is going to want you to greet the Steins. Go now."

"Yeah. I'll be back in a minute, Emme," he said.

I stood there like an idiot as they left me there alone. Glancing around, I tried to make eye contact with someone I could talk to, but it was like I was invisible.

"And you must be Emme Trybus."

Senator Agretti stood in front of me with his hand out.

"Yes, hello. It's nice to meet you," I said, shaking his hand.

"Well, I just had to come over and meet the girl who keeps my son on the phone twenty-four hours a day. You know Brendon avoids making calls if he can, texts and e-mails are his thing, so when I saw him making the effort to call you, I knew you were special."

"Oh, well...um..." I stammered like a complete idiot trying to figure out how to handle what he said.

Senator Agretti put his other hand on top of mine, and it was like he had laser focus as he asked me if I was enjoying the barbeque.

"Well, I just got here, but so far it seems great," I said.

"Did either of my sons offer you a beverage?"

"Uh, no."

"Kids today. No manners. Now what would you like? We have cherry lemonade, which is amazing. Made with homegrown Traverse City cherries. Would you like Jayson to get you a glass?"

I nodded, but it seemed like he was selling the lemonade on TV rather than casually offering me a drink. He was completely different from any other father I had ever met. He even smelled different with all the cologne he wore. Senator Agretti had this way of making you feel like you were the only person in the room as he zeroed in on you.

"Dale, come over here and meet my future daughter-in-law," he said with a laugh. A man walked over, and I recognized Dale as being the guy whose name was always being mentioned as a possible Presidential candidate.

"Emme Trybus, this is Congressman Dale Allington."

Congressman Allington shook my hand as Senator Agretti said I was dating Brendon.

"Apparently you have his father's approval since he's planning your wedding," Congressman Allington said, laughing.

"Brendon never likes to talk on the phone and suddenly he meets Emme, and it's like it is attached to his head," Senator Agretti said. "So far I like everything about her, but her one giant flaw."

I felt my adrenaline shoot up and then he said, "There's the unfortunate fact she is too young to register to vote."

Both the men laughed, and I pretended to join in, but the conversation wasn't like anything I had experienced before. His dad was being attentive, but it seemed a bit over the top. But at least he was paying attention to me, and he was friendly.

Brendon came over, and his dad slapped him on the back.

"Just talking to my future daughter-in-law here, and she is as lovely as you described," his dad said.

"Way to freak her out, Dad," Brendon said, but he was smiling.

"You two have fun."

"Well, you made a great first impression," Brendon said to me.

"I'm not sure how, since I didn't say much."

"Dad can tell right away if he likes someone. He takes in how people present themselves and how they interact with people. We were standing together when you helped the server pick up the napkins."

"It wasn't that big a deal."

"Three people walked past her, and Brooke almost stepped on her hand," Brendon said.

Jayson brought my lemonade over, and Brooke came with him.

"So you're Brendon's latest," she said with a big smile. "Just kidding. I always tease Brendon, don't I?"

She beamed up at him with her bleached teeth, and I was uncomfortable with how she was touching his arm. It was exactly what my ex-boyfriend, John's, ex-girlfriend used to do. At the time my intuition told me something was up, and I ignored it because I didn't want it to be true. And right now I was getting the same bad vibes from Brooke.

Senator Agretti came back over, and I almost puked when Brooke put her arms around his waist and started saying how "ah-may-zing" he was. Brendon didn't say anything, but I saw his mother roll her eyes behind Brooke's back. I couldn't imagine doing that with a friend or a boyfriend's father.

"Well, thank you, Brooke. If only the voters all shared those feelings," he said, and then moved away from her. He exchanged a raised eyebrow with his wife, and I got the feeling neither one was on Team Brooke.

"Emme, I'm sorry I rushed off when you first got here," Mrs. Agretti said. "And Brendon pointed out I got your name wrong—I'm so embarrassed."

"Oh, it's fine. Not the first time I've been called Emily."

"Well, you have a beautiful and unique name," she said. "Now let's get you a plate before all the men eat up the food. We're always outnumbered at these things."

I followed her to the table set up, and she handed me a plate.

"Would you like a hot dog bun or a hamburger bun?" she asked.

"Mom, Emme doesn't eat meat," Brendon said. I felt uneasy as I saw her try to figure out how to respond.

"Oh, well, what can we find for you?" she asked.

"I usually make a veggie burger with just lettuce and tomato and pickles on a bun," I said. It was my usual go-to at events like this, and I thought it'd look less weird if I pretended to be eating a burger in front of everyone.

"Problem solved," she said. "Do you like avocado? We have some in the kitchen I can get for you. Come with me."

We walked to the kitchen together. Their all-white kitchen was huge, like something from a decorating magazine.

"I'm sorry I'm so underdressed," I said. "Brendon said it was a barbeque, and I didn't think to ask what I was supposed to wear."

"You look fine," she said, and then I saw her look past me and frown. I followed her gaze and saw Brooke standing next to Brendon with hand on his bicep. "Emme, why don't you let me deal with this veggie burger, and you can get back out there with Brendon."

I walked back outside, feeling queasy as I watched Brooke laughing and putting her head on Brendon's shoulder. I couldn't see his face, but wondered if he was into her little girly helpless act. Then I saw him switch his lemonade to his other hand, forcing Brooke to let go of his arm while he took a drink. Was that intentional?

"Hey guys," I said, walking up.

Brendon gave me a smile, and he didn't look guilty, so maybe the flirting was one-sided.

"Where's your food?" he asked.

"Oh, your mom said she'd bring it out for me."

Mrs. Agretti walked out then with my plate. "Why don't you two go sit down?" she said. Brooke started to follow us when Mrs. Agretti asked her if she'd get her a bottle of water.

"I was hoping my grandparents would be here so I could introduce you, but my grandpa wasn't having a great day," Brendon said.

"Anything serious?" I asked.

"Nah, some days are better than others, you know?"

"Yeah. So how long have Jayson and Brooke been together?" I asked.

"They're off and on. I don't think he's ready to be serious, but somehow they always find their way back to each other. Who knows?"

I took a bite of my food while wondering if everyone else was aware Brooke was leeching onto what she saw as a meal ticket, or if it was just Mrs. Agretti and me who picked up on her vibes.

"She seems friendly."

He laughed. "I'm guessing you like her about as much as my mother does."

"Oh?" I took another big bite to avoid having to respond.

"My mom made Jayson tell Brooke there was a dress code of no shorts because last time she showed up in these ones that were so short. I mean, my mom *still* brings it up."

"Am I okay in this?" I asked.

"Trust me, you're fine. You could enter a convent in that outfit compared to what she had on last time."

Great, I dressed like a nun next to Jayson's hot, flirty girlfriend.

"I wasn't sure what to wear."

"You look great," he said.

My phone got a text just then, and it was from my mom saying the nurse gave Grandma some pain medication and she was going to sleep the rest of the day.

"Everything okay?" Brendon asked.

"Yeah, just an update on my grandma."

Brendon offered to take me home as the party was winding down and went to get his keys. Senator Agretti was talking to someone and the guy seemed to be pretty aggressive. I decided to walk over to thank him for inviting me and maybe give him a break. His face brightened as he saw me come up.

"Emme, did you get enough to eat?" he asked.

"Yes, I wanted to thank you for inviting me."

"This is our youngest's girlfriend," the senator said to the other guy, who couldn't have cared less.

"Now you'll be a sophomore this year, right?" Senator Agretti asked. I knew he was stalling to avoid his other conversation, but I didn't mind, seeing as I hated confrontation, too.

"Now, what are you taking?" he asked, and again he focused on me like I was the only person at the event. There was no way he, or any adult, could be that interested in a high school sophomore's schedule, but he acted like it was the most important thing in the world at the moment.

"American history, English ten, biology, creative writing—"

"Yes, Brendon said you were a writer," he said. "Who are some of your favorite authors?"

My mind went blank, and I stammered trying to think of even one writer's name.

"I am a Hemingway fan myself," he said. "Have you read any of his work?"

I nodded and then noticed how he brought the other man into the conversation about books, and pretty soon he had changed the whole tone between them. Slick.

"You ready to go?" Brendon asked, coming over. I nodded and then saw Brooke approaching us.

"So nice meeting you, Emme," she said, giving me a hug and almost gagging me with her strong perfume. "Who knows, maybe I'll even see you again."

Seriously? Then she went over and hugged the senator and asked him for a selfie for her social media page. She put his arm behind him, and I noticed he crossed his arms in front of himself. I wondered if that was so no one could say he put his arm around her.

Mrs. Agretti walked up then. "I want a picture of all of you together," she said. I handed her my phone and asked if she'd take one with mine as well.

Brooke got right in between the senator and Brendon, and I wanted to barf as she giggled. Mrs. Agretti took the photo and then said, "Honey, we need one with you next to Emme."

Senator Agretti moved over to me and put his arm around me for the photo.

"Everyone say, 'Six more years,'" he said.

He gave me a hug good-bye, and Mrs. Agretti handed me my phone. "I took three pictures since you're a blinker. I *always* make sure people get a good photo."

She hugged me, and as we walked out, I overheard Brooke complaining, "My head's cut off in the photo."

"So what did you think?" Brendon asked.

Of Brooke's leech-y ways? "What do you mean?"

"Of the party. I know it can be a bit much to come to these things, and you said it was intimidating to come here, but you did amazing. Some people get overwhelmed or act stupid, but I knew you'd be fine."

"Everyone was pretty nice."

"My parents both told me you were adorable."

I was hoping for elegantly brilliant and a riveting conversationalist, but adorable was okay. Of course, next to Brooke I'd never be an exotic goddess, but then again, I would probably seem reserved and classy next to her.

He pulled up to my house, and my parents were both outside, bringing groceries out of the trunk.

"You must be Brendon," my mom said, coming over.

"Hi, it's so nice to finally meet you."

Mom insisted he come in and meet Grandpa.

We walked in the side door, and Brendon saw our garden gnome in the maize-and-blue college football uniform.

"No way, that's my team, too," he said.

"Well, you're okay with me then," Dad said.

Mom made us sit down at the table and brought out some iced tea. I hoped Brendon didn't feel put on the spot as she started asking him questions about his family.

"Mom, he still has guests at home," I said. "He needs to get back."

"It's fine," he said. "How is your mother doing, Mrs. Trybus?"

"Oh, you're so thoughtful to ask," she said. Gross, she was gushing. I mean, yes, he was cute, and everyone at the barbeque had been a little gushy over him, but it was embarrassing to have my own mother doing it, too.

Dad acted more normal, and Grandpa seemed more alert as he joined in the conversation. When Brendon mentioned he was looking forward to football season starting soon, Grandpa spoke up saying, "Looks like we'll have a pretty good team this year."

I was thrilled Grandpa was following the conversation. Maybe I had been worrying about him for nothing.

"The quarterback looks promising, but then again, I say that every year and get disappointed," Brendon said.

Dad and Grandpa both laughed.

Brendon got a text from Jayson then, asking him to come home and save him from all the annoying questions about his future. I walked Brendon out, and he said he'd text me before he went to bed.

I walked back to the kitchen and thought my mom was going to do cartwheels.

"He's so darling and polite," she said. I had a feeling she was mentally planning our wedding.

"He's a nice kid," Dad said. "I worried he might be stuck up, but he seems down to earth. More mature than most kids his age, but he's probably used to being around adults more."

"Yes, he did seem more grown up. Polished," Mom said. "Did you like him, Dad?"

Grandpa nodded. "It was nice to see Dennis again."

"Dennis?" I asked.

"Yes, we should have him come over more often," Grandpa said.

Mom sighed. "Dennis was Grandpa's cousin. Dad, that wasn't him. That was Emme's boyfriend. Remember, Dennis has been gone for twenty years."

Grandpa just nodded and went back to reading the newspaper like it was completely normal to think a dead man had dropped by for a visit. I went to look over at my dad, who had a surprised look on his face.

"I'm starting to think it's more than just—"

"*Not* now," my mother said, cutting Dad off.

"Okay, but it's going to get worse before it gets better."

"Not now."

Chapter 9

BRENDON SPENT A week away with his dad, but was back in time for my birthday. He wanted to take me to the country club to have lunch and play tennis. When I walked out to his car, I found a tennis racket sitting in the passenger seat. However, Jayson and Brooke were also in the car.

"Hey, my mom just bought herself a new racket and wondered if you'd like her old one."

"Oh, wow. So thoughtful," I said. It had to be expensive.

"Her tennis coach said it will take your game to the next level. Promise," he said.

"You sure you can handle it, bro?" Jayson asked.

"At least this won't be a repeat of my humiliation on the miniature golf course last week," Brendon said as we walked onto the court.

"Hey, I told you not to swing like a maniac. At least they didn't make you pay for chipping the elephant's trunk," Jayson said.

"If I hadn't been losing by like, a billion strokes, then maybe I wouldn't have hit it so hard," Brendon replied.

"And then you had to win a free game so the stupid bill-board flashed our scores for the whole world to see."

"Were you embarrassed that I beat you?" Jayson asked.

"No, I was embarrassed I got a thirty-two at a par eighteen course that includes a bear wearing a tutu."

"I still have the tickets for my free game. When would you like to have our rematch?" Jayson asked as I served. The new racket was *way* better than my old one. It was like there was a new power behind my serve.

"What happened to just playing for fun?" Brooke asked, scowling. I hadn't even broken a sweat, but Brooke acted like she was exhausted. She seemed overwhelmed, and I thought maybe this was an opportunity to get to know her without all the weirdness. As we sat down for lunch, I told her about how worried I had been the first time I played tennis here at the club.

"Well, I, unlike some people, was honest about my game. I didn't say I played only once in a while and then turned into Venus Williams on the court," she said as she took a bite of her chicken salad.

I wasn't sure if she was joking or annoyed with me.

"I think it's great Emme's gotten into it. Usually I'd play with Sam, who kicks my butt, or Jayson, who you can clearly see isn't as good as me, but now I can play tennis with Emme. My equal...finally."

Jayson punched him in the arm, and Brooke laughed like Brendon was a stand-up comic. Lauren had been co-captain of the tennis team last year, and I wondered if they had played together a lot when they were dating. She seemed like the kind of person who would let him win, but then totally annihilate the next person who came onto the court.

"Okay, I will concede you are the better tennis player, but if only I could find someone who was my equal in miniature golf," Jayson said. "And might I add, both our parents golf regularly."

"I'm rebelling against the establishment," Brendon said.

"Yeah, you just keep telling yourself that," Jayson said.

"So Emme, do you want to do the movie in the park thing this weekend?" Brendon asked. "Or just hang out at my house."

"Whatever you want to do. I can't believe this is our last weekend," I said.

"There's still Labor Day," he said.

"They just give us that to keep us from killing ourselves the first week back," I said.

Brendon cleared his throat and looked away, and I wondered if I said the wrong thing, but then he came back to his usual self.

"Should I take your shoelaces away? You know, I better keep you away from miniature golf courses—you could do some damage with those putters," he said. "Anyway, I have one other present for you."

"What is it? A Faberge egg?" I asked.

"The mall was all out of those," he said, handing me a box.

Brooke was giving me the side eye as I opened it. It was a beautiful, stainless steel Riley Turner watch with a lavender face. I had seen the same one in a magazine, and I knew it cost a lot. I loved it and said a silent thank you my birthday had come before his because I wouldn't have had a clue what I would have bought him.

"Oh, cute," Brooke said with an expression that appeared like she smelled a skunk. "But, Brendon, are you implying she is always late?"

"No, I just noticed Emme always checks her phone for the time, and I thought maybe she'd like a watch."

"Yeah, you can wear it along with those hundreds of bracelets you have on," Brooke said. "Why do you have so many on?"

"They're crystal bracelets, and each one is for something specific," I said. "The jasper is for grounding, and the onyx absorbs negativity—"

"You seriously think your bracelets have magic powers?" Brooke asked, sneering.

I glanced over at Brendon, who seemed uncomfortable.

"No, of course not. Just trying to have my bases covered, you know?"

"Hey, we should get Dad an onyx one," Jayson said. "Do they make onyx underpants? Those could win him re-election the next time around."

I gave a little smile as they all laughed, but I wondered if Brendon's weird expression was because he was embarrassed over my bracelet thing. Looking around the room, I realized I was the only female there with an armful of bracelets. All the rest had on understated jewelry, if any. Even Brooke was wearing just a pair of diamond stud earrings and nothing else. I suddenly felt overdone—like some weird boho hippie chick. Brooke's whole look was simple, with her blue golf shirt and khaki skirt. Meanwhile I was wearing a dark pink T-shirt and matching gingham capris, and suddenly my outfit seemed loud. Everyone else had a classic or preppy look. I would have felt boring and unfeminine in Brooke's outfit, but somehow she managed to make a golf shirt sexy without being over the top.

"Okay, so I hate to bring this up on your birthday, but we need to go over our schedules for school and see when we'll be in the same halls and stuff," Brendon said.

I was hoping to have a least a week until I had to think about school starting. I didn't expect to have any classes together, but after we compared schedules, we found we didn't even have the same lunch period. Plus, they had assigned him a seventh hour and given him a study hour during the regular school day.

"It stinks we don't even get out of class at the same time. You'll have to wait a whole hour while I'm in my last class if you want to ride home with me," he said, frowning.

"I'm so disappointed," I said. "I thought we'd at least have lunch together."

"Do they make a bracelet to help with that?" Brooke asked with a fake smile.

"We'll find a way to meet up during the day," Brendon said.

He dropped me off first and walked me to the door—the first time all day we had without Brooke and Jayson around.

"I hope you had a great birthday," he said.

"It was great. Thank you so much for the presents—they're amazing."

"Just wanted to do something special for you."

"I didn't know Jayson and Brooke were coming," I said.

"Yeah, I was getting ready to leave, and Brooke insisted. She kept saying we all have to hang out more. She likes you a lot."

There was no possible way she liked me. Either she was looking for a way to spend more time with him or sabotage our dates.

"Thanks again for everything." I went to kiss him when someone honked the horn and we sprang apart.

"Brooke's such a kidder," he said. "I better get going. See ya tomorrow."

———

I PUT OUT my outfit for the first day of school and checked my e-mail before I went to bed. Brendon had sent me a reminder he'd pick me up at seven and said it was supposed to be cool tomorrow. He was obsessed with this new weather app and always had to know the exact temperature. He'd freak if he planned on wearing long sleeves and then it was hot, or if he wanted to do something outdoors and then it rained. I thought his weather obsession was weird, but he said it was no weirder than how I was always paying attention to which sign the moon was in. He'd tell me I was crazy when I'd say that I had no energy because it was an Aquarius moon day. Although once, on a Cancer moon day, he did admit he had a little more energy than usual, but he said it was probably the sugar rush from the three cans of soda he drank.

Brendon walked me to all my classes on the first day. Darren Ritts was sitting by the window in my creative writing class. We had been in the same history class last year, and he had been the only thing that had kept the class from sucking. I was happy to see someone I knew, since I knew I'd have to read my work out loud in class. Other than Rory, I didn't know anyone else in the room. Mr. Horowitz walked in and made us go around the room and tell the class our names and our favorite books. I brought my bloodstone crystal along for self-confidence and held it in my hand as he talked. I figured I'd just repeat the title of a book somebody else mentioned, but my brilliant plan failed when he called on me first.

"My name is Emme Trybus, and I'm a sophomore. My favorite book is *The Bell Jar*."

"Good, and why did you choose it?" he asked.

Crap, I was hoping he wouldn't ask. My hand was so sweaty the bloodstone almost shot out of my grip. I hadn't finished the book yet, and I only chose it because I thought it would make me look smart in front of all these brains.

"I recently read a Sylvia Plath biography and got into her work," I said.

He seemed satisfied with my answer and moved on

to the next person. The rest of the students named serious books they probably understood all the themes of, whereas I just read for enjoyment. Then I found out there was only one other sophomore in the class besides me. Everyone else was a junior or a senior. I wondered if it was too late to drop the class. Darren and I were catching up on what we had done over the summer when Brendon walked up. I told Darren to have a good weekend, but he didn't say anything.

—•—

I WENT TO Brendon's grandparents' house on Saturday. Each year his whole family got together for a big barbeque Labor Day weekend. Everybody decided to play volleyball, but I stunk at sports so I sat on the porch and talked to his grandparents. I could tell Brendon wanted me to play, but he didn't say anything. Since I was used to my own grandma being sleepy and not able to follow a conversation, I made sure to include his grandpa.

"Are you from Michigan?" his grandpa asked.

"Yup, my grandparents voted for you," I said smiling.

He and his wife laughed. His grandfather had some issues speaking and searched for words a lot, so I tried to follow him as best I could. He pointed a lot to the kids while smiling, and he'd clap his hands when someone did well during the game.

His family had a tradition where they took a big group photo, and Brendon made me sit in the front row with him. I wondered if they'd cut me out of the picture if we broke up someday. Brooke was there again with Jayson, and she sat on his lap for the photo. I bet Mrs. Agretti would cut her out of the picture, even if she and Jayson stayed together.

We were all standing by the table with the food, and

Brendon picked up a bowl of chips.

"Hey, Brooke left some for the rest of us," he said.

She winked at him, put her finger out, and tapped his nose while making this annoying, "boop" sound.

"He's always teasing me," she said to me like I was a complete outsider. "No one picks on me more than Brendon."

He shrugged as he took a bite of his hot dog.

"Did you tell her about the buffalo thing?" she asked while grabbing his arm.

"I don't think so."

"It was sooo funny," she said, rolling her eyes. "We were all at this fundraiser, and Jayson and Brendon had just been to South Dakota with their dad, and Brendon couldn't shut up about the buffalo burgers they had there. So he's going on and on about it, having no clue the guy he's talking to is like the number one guy for beef in the nation. So Brendon basically was talking up this guy's competition. How embarrassing! Major faux pas," she said with another wink at him. She was giving him flirtier looks than I did, and I was supposed to be his girlfriend. Yet Jayson didn't seem to be around whenever she did it.

Brendon and Jayson got called over to meet someone, and the second they were gone, it was like I was invisible to Brooke. She walked away, leaving me standing alone, and I felt stupid, so I went back over to sit with his grandparents. I tried not to enjoy it when Brooke fell while trying to play volleyball in flip-flops, but I couldn't help laughing when Brendon's grandma made a comment about not realizing they "made shorts quite as short as Brooke's."

Brooke tripped again, and I wondered if it was on purpose as she managed to fall right in front of Brendon. Unfortunately he caught her, and I thought she overdid it grabbing onto him.

"You saved me," she said to him. "Always the boy

scout, always the hero, huh?"

Rolling my eyes, I glanced over to where Jayson had been standing, but once again he was gone.

"I'm going to get something to drink," I said to Mrs. Agretti. "Would either of you like anything while I'm up?"

"Oh no, but thank you."

I ran into Jayson in the house when I went to get some water.

"Hey, there's only one piece of chocolate cake left," he said. "You wanna split it with me?"

I thought he'd cut it in half, but instead he handed me a fork so we could eat off the same plate. Obviously no one in the Agretti family cared about germs. Their immune systems must have been made of steel. We were almost done eating when Brooke came in to see where he was.

"Oh, hey *Emma*," she said as she wrapped herself around his arm. "Love your contacts. They almost look real."

Jayson's mouth dropped open, but I just said, "You're outfit is so cute, Brooke. I love it." Then I walked away. I love throwing people off when they insult me. I wish I had the nerve to tell her off, but I wasn't on my own turf, and I didn't want to look stupid. Margaux would have put her in her place though. In fact, Margaux once told off a girl who had been acting way too friendly with her boyfriend. I remember her going up to the girl, saying, "Oh, I'm sorry, did you just go blind? Because this is my boyfriend you've been flirting with, and you obviously lost your eyesight and confused *my* boyfriend with yours. Or else you're just completely pathetic. So did you go blind or are you just pathetic? Which is it?"

"Em, I wondered where you went," Brendon said, coming in. He put his arm around me. "Hey, everything okay?"

I nodded. No point in sharing my humiliation. I wondered if Jayson would tell him later that Brooke had insulted me.

—

BRENDON DIDN'T MENTION Brooke being passive-aggressive when he called me the next day. Part of me wanted to say something about how Brooke had been flirting with him, but I didn't want to give him any ideas and make him start looking in her direction. Sure, he hadn't encouraged her, but he hadn't sprayed mace in her face either.

"I have to run out to the pharmacy and get a prescription for my granddad. Want to come along? I haven't seen you in sixteen hours, and I'm starting to go through withdrawal," he said, laughing.

"Sure." I didn't look my best, but I would have gone to Antarctica if it meant getting out of the house.

Once we were out, neither one of us wanted to go home. Brendon hated seeing his grandfather get worse, especially when he'd start drooling without even realizing it, and I couldn't stand freaking out every time the phone rang, thinking this was another call saying Grandma had fallen out of bed again. Her falls were getting more frequent, and I couldn't understand why or how she kept falling out of her bed. They had gates on the side and a pad on the floor, and yet somehow she'd slip out and wind up on the floor. Then my mom would have to go down to the hospital while they did yet another scan to see if Grandma had broken anything.

Since my mom was consumed with Grandma, I was staying with Grandpa as much as I could. She felt she couldn't take him to the nursing home or leave him alone, so she'd leave in the evenings to see Grandma. However, it was getting harder for me to deal with Grandpa asking where she was all the time. It was one thing to know Grandma was now living in a nursing home full-time. It was another to be reminded Grandpa didn't know where *he* was half the time. Plus, it physically hurt having to show him where the bathroom was—every day. My gut felt like it was twisting when he'd ask, "Now where's the restroom?" like he had never been in my house before, when my parents had lived in the same house for over seventeen years. And hearing, "Where do I sleep?" every single night wasn't much better. At least he knew we were his family. And he called my parents by their names most of the time. Sometimes he'd call my dad by my uncle's name, but even that was better than nothing. Although he did call my Aunt Caroline, "Rudy," a couple of times, which was weird since it was his brother's name, and Uncle Rudy had died when I was nine. All I remembered about him was he was a bald guy who always gave me candy and he smelled like peppermint and foot spray. Sometimes when I smelled foot spray, it was actually sort of comforting because I always took it as a sign Uncle Rudy was watching me...in a protective way, not in a creepy from-beyond-the-grave way.

"So what do you want to do now?" Brendon asked.

"Don't you have to get the medicine back soon?"

He shook his head and said it was just a refill. "Do you want to hang out at your house?" he asked.

Yeah, great idea. It would be real fun when Grandpa thought Brendon was his dead cousin and then asked him where his wife was when even Brendon knew.

"I don't feel like going to my house."

"Wanna just drive around?"

Brendon wasn't the kind of guy who opened up and told you everything he was feeling, but sometimes he'd talk about how hard it was seeing his grandfather get worse. Today he didn't want to talk, and neither did I. I think we both just needed to be with somebody.

KYLIE CALLED ME later to find out how things went at the Agretti party.

"Okay, but his brother's girlfriend was way too flirty with Brendon. She did this thing where she literally fell at his feet, and he had to save her—so pathetic," I said.

"That Brooke chick?"

"Yup."

"Did he encourage her?" Kylie asked.

"No, but he didn't walk away either. She made me feel like such an outsider, and I was already irritated she crashed my birthday lunch."

"You know, you need to say something to Brendon about this."

"I can't because I'll sound like some jealous, paranoid girlfriend—everything John accused me of being."

"And you weren't paranoid or jealous then either. You were right on target."

"Yeah, but back then I had a gut feeling something was up," I said.

"Do you have one now?"

"Like he's cheating on me? No, it's more I feel like I'm being excluded, and she's pawing my boyfriend."

"You need to talk to him because I know you, and if you don't, it's going to come out in other ways. There's no way you can hold all those feelings in."

"Maybe, whatever. So how was your weekend?"

"Emme, seriously. Think about it. If you don't, you're going to be getting an attitude with him on the little things. He's not a mind reader, and I doubt he'd think you were being jealous. Just share what you feel."

Chapter 10

WHEN I GOT to class the next day, my usual seat next to Darren was taken.

"Way to save me a seat," I said, poking his book as I sat behind him.

"Where's your boyfriend?" he asked without taking his eyes off the page.

"Physics," I said. "So how was your weekend?"

"Worked. What'd you do?"

I dug in my bag to find a pen as I told him Brendon's family had a party on Labor Day.

"I wouldn't have thought you two would have anything in common," he said, still not looking up.

I asked him why, and he said Brendon seemed "pretty ambitious and driven."

"And I'm a slug on a log?"

"No, he just seems different than you. Like he's from a different world."

Mr. Horowitz came in then and began telling us about his weekend hiking near his cottage in Traverse City, while I thought about what Darren had said. Brendon *was* driven, but it was one of the things I liked about him. Sure, he set goals and was ambitious, but Darren had made it sound like a bad thing. Maybe it was my imagination, but I felt he meant I wasn't in Brendon's league. I was starting to get weird vibes about Darren, but I figured I was just being paranoid about my relationship.

Mr. Horowitz asked us all to write about something we had done over the weekend. My home life was a lot more chaotic than my friends' right now, so assignments that reminded me of this were not welcome. I went into my own little world as I wrote my essay, and I didn't look up until I felt somebody touch my arm at the end of class.

Writing about my weekend and feeling like I didn't fit in with Brooke put me in a funk. The more I thought about Darren's comment, or overthought about it, the more my self-esteem slipped into the gutter. I was not in a positive mindset by the time my guidance counselor, Mr. Murray, called me down to his office. Every September the counseling department makes all the sophomores and juniors meet with them for an "informal chat." Yeah, whatever. It was to make sure we could read and had some sort of plan for the future which didn't include being a "baby's mama" for some football player. Mr. Murray had the results from a test I had filled out last year. I remembered taking the test in homeroom on the last day of school, and my teacher saying it was "not a big deal, just a fun quiz to find out your interests." Yeah, now my "fun quiz" was being held up as my life plan for the future. Meanwhile, he had a poster above his desk that said, "Not Every Day is a Good Day." You're telling me, buddy.

Mr. Murray read off my results, which basically said I was a loser with no ambition. I had ambition. I wanted to be a writer, own a little boutique, and have my own organic skin care line. So then Mr. I'm-going-to-look-down-on-you-because-I-need-to-feel-like-a-big-man asked me patronizingly if I had a game plan for my store and organic skin care goals.

"If you want to start a beauty cream line," he said, coughing, "then you'll need to take a chemistry class. And if you're serious about owning a store, then you need to take some business classes."

Yeah, I barely got through the math for dummies class I took last year, so I was sure business classes weren't going to be a breeze for me. And chemistry? Was he joking? I only got through the intro to physical science class last year because Tyrell Johnston was my lab partner, and he did all the work since I told him I was afraid I'd blow myself up.

"Well, my main goal is to be a writer, and I'm taking creative writing—"

"That's nice, but those types of jobs are uncertain. You need to have a game plan to fall back on. After all, you don't want to end up bagging groceries," he said, touching his nasty goatee. "Besides, they have those U-Scan things now, so bagger jobs are down."

I walked out with my self-esteem now out of the gutter and into the toilet. And not even one of those nice TV remodeling show toilets, but the gross ones at the beach with no doors on the stalls, a ring of rusty water in the bowl, and the remains from the person who didn't flush. I should have known the day was going to suck when I saw it was a Taurus moon day, which was my irritating time. I thought the day couldn't get worse, but then Katia Muniz, the school big mouth, came over and started asking me about Brendon.

"I heard you guys are super serious. Is it true?" she asked.

No, I made it up because I have no life. "I don't know. We're just dating. Why are you asking?" I said.

"Um, no reason," she said, smirking. Now there could have been a ton of reasons why she was smiling all weird: maybe she thought of a funny joke, or she had food poisoning and she wasn't smirking, but having stomach cramps that gave her a weird expression; or perhaps she was just a jerk who was trying to let me know I was way out of my league. Margaux came over and stared Katia down until she walked away.

"What did Katia want?" she asked.

I said she was asking about Brendon and me, and Margaux rolled her eyes. "I hate how she's always trying to start drama," she said.

And Margaux would know all about drama. We became friends when I changed schools in sixth grade. Margaux was the first person who talked to me. My biggest fear about starting a new school was not having anybody to sit with at lunch. However, on the first day she asked if I wanted to eat lunch at her table with her boyfriend, Todd, and all their friends. Her friends didn't exactly welcome me, but Margaux always made sure to include me, even if Todd complained about me hanging around. He was her first boyfriend, and she told me they had been going out for six months, which actually was still the longest relationship she has ever had. I became part of their group until a few weeks later when Katia told Margaux this guy named Jeff, who she had a huge crush on, liked her. Margaux wrote Todd a note saying they should just be friends, and Todd was hurt, but he seemed to be okay with it—until Katia told him Margaux "dumped his butt for Jeff." The next day I got to Margaux's table before her, and suddenly everybody was being super nice to me. And then Margaux walked over with her tray, and Todd told her no one wanted her there. I remember her eyes watering as she stood there, not knowing what to do. When she went to another table, I got up and followed her. She never said anything, but ever since that day, she has always had my back.

"Just forget about her," she said, snapping me back to reality. "Are you going to Brendon's locker before class?"

I nodded, and she said she'd call me later. When I got to his locker, I heard Lauren telling him to check his e-mail because she wrote him back. *Back.* There could be a zillion reasons why he was e-mailing her, like they were on one of his stupid committees together or it could have been a homework question. But I didn't need my intuition to tell me nothing good could come from his ex and him e-mailing each other. I didn't e-mail my ex. Of course, partly because John had dated, like, fifty girls after me—and continued to talk to his ex while he was with me—and now he ignored me in the hallway like a complete jerk, but still. I tried to put it out of my mind and tell myself it was perfectly innocent, but all I could think about was how John had told me how "it was no big deal" when he was getting e-mails from his ex, and it had actually been a huge deal. And Margaux always told me exes who can't let go always get back together. As much as I tried to tell myself I was just paranoid and it was fine, Lauren's perfect little heart-shaped face kept popping into my head all day.

To add to my lovely day, Mr. Horowitz made us read our essays out loud in class. I felt a hot drip of sweat slide under my arm, and I tried not to make eye contact with him and clutched my bloodstone until it was all sweaty. As I hoped that he'd forget about me, he called on me right after some guy named Tom read his piece about the meaninglessness of life. Mr. Horowitz asked the class for comments when I finished reading. Silence. I hated how no one ever spoke up when I read something. It made me feel so unpopular. Everybody jumped right in when one of the popular juniors read something. If Rory read something, then half the class couldn't wait to tell her how amazing it was, but even when I thought I had written something good, no one cared. Finally, Mr. Horowitz had to call on someone to talk about my essay.

"Tom? Do you have anything to say?"

Tom's head snapped back like he had been in a trance. Rory whispered something to him, and he said he liked the part about me trying to get out of playing volleyball. Then Darren spoke up and said he liked how I wrote about sitting with Brendon's grandparents when they were left out because of their health. I hadn't intended to say it, but he had picked up on it. He went next, reading his piece on how he visited his grandmother in a nursing home. His piece described the weird, hospital smell in those places, and it made me feel like I was back in Grandma's room.

Later, I saw Darren sitting by himself in the lounge, so I decided to sit with him instead of waiting in the computer lab for Brendon.

"Working on our next assignment?" I asked.

"No, this is a short story I've been messing with for a while. Do you want to read it?" he asked.

I still wasn't used to how open everyone in our creative writing class was about their writing. Maybe they had all been taking classes where they had to read out loud so they were used to it. Or maybe they were more confident than I was because they were all better writers. His story was about a girl he had met on a camping trip. The part of the story he had written was basically a description of her. I asked if it was a true story.

"Sort of. I met her last summer, and she dumped me on the Fourth of July. Right during the fireworks."

"So sad," I said. I couldn't imagine anyone dumping him.

"Tell me about it. I can't stand fireworks now," he said. "Let me see what you're working on."

I handed him my essay on getting over my fear of horses. He read it and said he was impressed I was able to get on the horse after being so scared.

"Actually, I kinda added some stuff to make it sound better. I was actually riding one of those ponies that walk in a circle at a carnival. You know, the ones who are, like, sedated or something and couldn't hurt a fly?"

"Those can be scary for a little kid," he said.

"Uh, I was twelve at the time, and my mom had to bribe me with cotton candy to get on it. I was so scared, and I was probably bigger than the horse," I said.

He cracked up. "Well, you did a good job of making me believe you were brave...even if it was a fat lie," he said.

I glanced up at the clock and realized Brendon would be waiting for me at his locker, so I got up. Darren asked if I wanted to hang out again after school since we both had to wait during seventh hour for rides, and I thought it would be fun to have someone to talk to.

Brendon needed to stop at the public library downtown. I picked out some magazines to look at, but when I got back to the table, Brendon had already brought some books for me to read while he picked up stuff for his paper. The books were all mysteries, which he liked, but I wasn't into. He told me to pick out the ones I wanted and he'd put them on his library card. I didn't want any of them, but I grabbed two with interesting covers.

"What about this Hans Von Swiller one? I read a bunch of his stuff over the summer, and he's good," he said, adding it to my pile.

I hoped he wasn't going to quiz me on them. On the way out, he asked me if I wanted to look at the writing section. I was ready to go, but he was already halfway down the aisle, so I followed him. He picked up a couple of books on writing and handed them to me. They all seemed the same to me, but I said they were interesting, and we went to check out.

"Can we stop for something to drink?" I asked as we walked to the car. "There's a new juice bar on the next street."

"We could just go to Beanie Weanies," he said. "It's

right here."

If I wanted coffee, I would have said, "Hey, let's stop for coffee," but I wanted juice. However, I didn't feel like arguing—or walking home. He ordered an iced mocha, and I stood there trying to figure out what I wanted.

"How about a soda?" he asked.

"You know I don't drink pop," I said.

"Well, how about water?" he said as he checked his voice messages. "There *are* other people in line..."

Great, he cared more about the guy in line behind me getting what he wanted. I bet he would have gone to the juice place if Lauren wanted it. Of course, she probably only drank pure spring water flown in from the Alps. I finally settled on a bottle of apple juice, but I made sure everybody in line *and* behind the counter knew I wasn't happy about it not being organic. We sat down, and he automatically opened my bottle for me. I knew he was just trying to be nice, but couldn't I open my own stupid juice? I kept thinking about my numerology book and figured that my attitude change had something to do with my moving into the number six year, where I was supposed to get my life in order and break bad habits. Maybe I was just adjusting. Then his phone rang, and I *knew* he was talking to a girl. He gave one-word answers, and he didn't look at me once.

"Yeah. Okay. I'll call you when I'm done with this," he said.

Done with this? What the crap? I decided not to ask him about the call because he would just get defensive. I learned that the hard way last year when I asked my ex, John, who called while we were at the movies. I remember thinking it might have been an emergency because he got up and went into the lobby to take the call. Anyway, he almost took my head off and started accusing me of not trusting him. At the time, I had no reason to think something was up, but I had been getting weird vibes from him before the phone even rang. And, a few weeks after John flipped out about the call, I found out his ex-girlfriend, Brittanie, had been calling him a lot, and pretty soon the two of them were together, and I was alone. Sure, I was better off, but I was also hurt and humiliated to have to see them at school, making out near my locker. Margaux never said anything directly, but she hinted she might know something about an anonymous call to the school board complaining about people "going at it" in the halls because right after John and Brittanie hooked up, practically on my locker, the assistant principal made an announcement saying anyone "participating in any sort of lewd conduct or public displays of affection" would get an in-school suspension. She might not have been the most tactful person in the world, but Margaux was loyal.

I knew Brendon wasn't John, but there was a little part of me which worried all guys could be like that. Zach and Kylie's relationship seemed great, but Zach was also protective and sweet. Plus there was the fact Zach worshipped the ground Kylie walked on and would probably have given her a vital organ if she needed one to survive. I wasn't sure Brendon even came close to feeling that way about me.

Chapter 11

THE NEXT DAY, Mr. Horowitz told us about a local writing contest he wanted us to enter. He said we had to hand in one of our pieces for the contest, but we could choose which one to enter. I went through the stuff I had written in class so far, but nothing seemed good enough to enter in a contest. Darren already knew what he was going to enter, so he went through my class portfolio to help me find something.

"How about this piece you wrote about your grand-ma?" he asked.

I thought it was too personal, so I decided to hand in my essay about being scared on the horse. It was funny, and everybody seemed to like it when I read it in class. Mr. Horowitz stopped me as I was leaving class.

"Emme, this essay on overcoming your fear is good, but I was blown away by your piece on your grandmother's illness. I wish you'd consider entering it," he said.

It was the first time the man had said anything positive about my work. Normally he'd just sit back, put his fingertips together and say, "In-*ter-est*-ing," whenever I read something or participated in class, so I agreed to do it. I guess I wanted him to like me. Besides, the chances of my winning and having to read it out loud in front of a room full of people weren't good. Darren was waiting for me outside the room, and I told him I was submitting the story about my grandma instead.

"Good choice," he said.

I forgot about the contest until Mr. Horowitz mentioned it in class two weeks later. He announced that twenty students in the area had been chosen to read their work at Java Café and the judges would pick the winners that night. He said Rory, Darren, Tom, and I had been chosen. I couldn't believe it, and I overheard someone say she was shocked I had made it, too. It stung, but I tried not to let it bother me too much. After class, I couldn't wait to tell Brendon.

"Awesome. What did you write about? Your amazing boyfriend?" he asked.

"Not quite. Oh crap."

"What?"

"I'm going to have to get up in front of all those people and read," I said. "And the worst thing is Mr. Horowitz made me enter this sad story I wrote about my grandma. I'll probably be so nervous, and I'll start crying and make a fool of myself."

"You'll be fine, and I'll be there. If you start crying, I'll pull the fire alarm, and everybody will clear out," he said.

"What if you're not near the fire alarm?"

"Then I'll set the place on fire so it'll go off on its own. Problem solved," he said, smiling. "We have to go out and celebrate. What about going to the new Japanese place?"

I wasn't crazy about that restaurant, so I suggested we get takeout from the sandwich place and eat in the park like we had on our first date.

"We have to do something more special than just sandwiches. I know—there's this Italian restaurant right on the water. You'll love it."

I almost choked when we walked into the restaurant. It was exactly like the one I had imagined us at before we ever started going out. There were lights all over the trees and fake indoor vines and candles on all the tables. The glow from the flames flickered against the glass and gave the place a magical look. Brendon kept smiling at me as I ate my spaghetti.

"What? Do I have sauce on my face?" I asked.

"No. I was thinking about the scene from the cartoon—you know where the two dogs are eating spaghetti," he said.

"Are you implying I look like a dog when I eat?" I asked.

"You know what I mean, the part in the movie where they're slurping the noodles, and they get caught on the same noodle."

I picked up a piece of spaghetti with my fork, but apparently it worked a lot better with cartoon dogs because the noodle broke and sauce splashed in his face. He wiped it off as we cracked up.

When I was a kid, I used to have a coloring book my grandpa gave me where this teenage girl based on a doll did all these traditional date things like go to football games and have romantic dinners. Grandma was upset when he bought it for me because she thought the doll was an unrealistic role model, but she calmed down after my dad pointed out the doll had been an astronaut and a teacher, while all the boyfriend doll ever did was wear outfits that matched hers. As stupid as it sounded, I always hoped that I would have a similar life. Well, just with the fun dating stuff, not going out with a guy who wore clothes that matched mine. I had never had a coloring book moment before, and now it seemed like I was living that life. Sure, I didn't have a pink convertible or the plastic mansion, and my hair was far from perfect, but I was happy. It was the first time I had ever lived up to a coloring book moment, and I hoped it would last.

Chapter 12

I GOT MORE and more nervous as the day of the contest grew closer. Kylie and Darren said I would be fine, but I had visions of passing out in front of the crowd or puking on stage. I tried to convince myself they were just nerve-induced visions and not any sign of what was to come. To help calm my nerves, I started wearing my bloodstone crystal all the time for self-confidence. At first I thought it wasn't working, and then I realized I'd probably be in the psych ward without it. Brendon knew I was freaking out, so when we came home from school, he stopped and got a batch of my favorite organic peanut butter chocolate chip cookies from Leocadia's Bakery and gave me a card to cheer me up. As I was opening the envelope, he put his hand out to stop me.

"Okay, don't laugh, but I *might* have written you a poem. Why am I even telling you this?" he said and sighed. "Just read it by yourself when you get inside, okay?"

I was barely through the door when I started reading the poem. John, my ex, had given me a poem last year, but then I found out he e-mailed the same poem to every girl he went out with. Normally, he'd just changed the last line to rhyme with the girl's name, but he couldn't think of anything to rhyme with "Emme," so he left the last part off. Brendon didn't seem like the type to do something like that though.

To: Emme
Imagining a life without
Longing to be complete
Overcome by emotion
Venerated
Excited by the future
Young and old alike
Old memories awakened
United
Everyone thinks they know me
Most pretend to care
Many misunderstand my feelings
Everyone should be so lucky

Well, I guess it was romantic-ish. I wasn't exactly sure what he was trying to say, but I guess I couldn't expect something like, "I can't stand to be without you, and even if one of us should perish, we'll still be together, for our love is deathless, my darling, my sweet, my immortal beloved." However, I'm a romantic and would have settled for "Looky, looky, I like you more than cookies." I was just hoping for a more obvious "I like you" type of poem. I wasn't expecting him to use the L-word yet, but it would have been nice to have the word show up there. Of course, John used to say "I love you" all the time, but at least with John, I could tell they were just words to him.

It was a sweet gesture that he had written a poem for me. Although I was going to pretend it was too private to share if Margaux wanted to read it. She'd tear it apart and say it was all about him, which it kind of was. It was a weird poem to give to your girlfriend, but the fact he wrote anything at all was romantic.

The phone rang, and I knew it was him. "Hey, I just finished reading it," I said.

"And?" he asked. "I don't know what I was thinking giving a poem to a writer."

"I was completely prepared to lie to you and say it was good, but it actually is. I liked it," I said. He seemed to be waiting for me to say something else, so I added, "Super good."

He didn't say anything, so I started talking about my Shakespeare exam. I knew he was looking for me to say something more about the poem, but what could I say? I wasn't a hundred percent sure what he was trying to say, and I'd feel stupid if it seemed like I read too much into it. After all, I didn't want him to think I thought one poem meant he was obsessed with me. I wasn't going to make the same mistakes I made with John and take the "I love you's he used to spout off and make them out to be more than they were. Never again was I going to let my guard down. Brendon still hadn't said anything, so I figured changing the subject was the best thing to do.

At night, I went to lie down, and I ended up falling asleep, but I woke up with my heart pounding in my chest. My first thought was something had happened to Grandma, so I called the info desk and made them go check on her. The nurse sounded irritated, but then he always sounded sort of mad.

When I woke up the next morning, I realized dealing with Grandma's stroke was hitting me harder than ever. I was starting to feel like it wasn't worth getting close to anybody because it hurt too much when you had to deal with the fact they might leave you. And I didn't want to even think about what would happen if Grandma died. I snuggled deeper into my pillow and wished I had some-one to talk to about all this. Just then the phone rang, and it was Brendon.

"Hey, what's up? I went for a run at five a.m., finished my calc homework, and went to the bookstore to start researching my psych paper," he said.

He had accomplished all those things, and I hadn't even sat up yet.

"While I was at the bookstore, I saw they had a new book by the astrologer you like, Holiday King. I don't know if you'll be as into this book because it's about grief and dreams. Maybe it's too close to what you're dealing with, but I picked it up for you anyway," he said.

I didn't know she had a new book out. He said it was called *It's Better to Have Loved and Lost than to Have Never Loved at All.*

I didn't tell him that was what had been on my mind because I wanted to change the subject. Instead I told him he had perfect timing because I was freaking out over the reading in public.

"I'm going to have to get one of those meditation CDs or something because I am seriously on edge," I said. Even though I was thrilled he had called when I needed him most, I was still feeling anxious.

"Wait a sec, it's my other line," he said. "Hold on."

As soon as he clicked over, I started feeling like I was going to be sick. My stomach felt like it had rolled over, my heart started racing, and my anxiety shot up.

"Emme, you're going to kill me," he said when he got back on the line. "But Sam just called. He has pneumonia, and I have to handle the charity auction the night of your reading."

"What? But you *promised*."

"I know. I told Sam I couldn't go, but now he's sick, and there's nobody else who can do it," he said. "He said he called everybody he could think of, but there's a play going on the same night, and half the student council is either in it or working backstage."

I don't think he realized how upset I was since I didn't start screaming, but it was only because I couldn't even wrap my mind around what he was saying. My whole body was numb, and I felt dead inside.

"I'll make it up to you, I promise," he said. "Listen, I have to go make some calls now, but I'll talk you tomorrow."

I reached for my aromatherapy soothing lavender stick to calm me and sat there staring at the wall until Rory called asking me what I was going to wear to the reading. I hadn't even thought about it. I just wanted blend into the background so no one would notice me. Rory had it made because she always wore black, and she was so tiny she could wear anything and get away with it. Although maybe black wouldn't be such a good choice in case I puked on myself. Of course, how much would it matter, seeing as no one I knew would be there to watch me throw up? I called Margaux, who said Brendon was being a selfish jerk and offered to go shopping with me to pick out a new outfit.

"You'll feel more confident if you look good, and we can always find a weird outfit to distract everybody in case you wet yourself on stage," she said.

"Yeah, I guess."

"I was joking," she said. "You're not going to wet yourself. C'mon, we'll go to the mall, get you something cool, and you absolutely have to get new makeup. Nothing says confident writer like cat-eye liner. Kylie and I are both coming to the reading, but we'll sit in back so we won't freak you out."

ON THE NIGHT of the reading, Rory wore a sheer black T-shirt underneath a black jumper, with tights and clunky boots. The only color in her outfit was her bright-red lipstick. I wore an orange V-neck sweater I picked out with Margaux because I had read orange was supposed to be an energizing color. It was also supposed to be good for healing your love life, and seeing as mine was nearing the crapper, I needed all the help I could get. Plus, Margaux thought the glittery logo on the front would distract people. It didn't say "serious writer," but at least it was cute. Margaux felt women appeared more confident and powerful in red lipstick, so she picked out a lip gloss for me. It was a bright red, but sheer, so it wasn't too obvious, and you could put a shimmery white color over it to make it extra glossy. It was called "Romeo and Juliet," and I tried not to take it as a bad sign about relationships. Margaux told me to ignore the fact Romeo and Juliet's relationship didn't exactly work out and said, "They're famous characters, and you write, so look at it as a positive sign."

At the competition, they called Rory up on stage second to read, and she didn't look the least bit nervous. Neither did Darren. Meanwhile, I clutched my bloodstone, and I went to the bathroom five times before I walked on stage. The essay contest had proven to be an effective laxative. The lights on the stage were so bright I could only see the judges and not the crowd, which made me feel a little better. Kylie and Margaux were supposed to be sitting out there somewhere with my family, but I had no idea where. They called me up next, and I was so nervous about messing up (and throwing up) that I didn't even realize what I was reading. It was just a bunch of words on a page. It seemed like people clapped for me when I finished, but my legs shook so much I couldn't even focus on anything other than getting back to my seat without tripping.

Rory, Tom, Darren, and I sat there while the judges talked. The restaurant had given us free coffee, but I hadn't had a sip. I was afraid any caffeine would make me even jitterier, and I wanted to be calm because I had a strange feeling I was going to have to go back up on the stage. It wasn't like I saw myself winning first place, but somehow I knew I'd go home with some sort of prize. Rory put her arm around me when one of the judges got up and announced the two fifth-place winners, who were from a different school. Then she read off the two fourth-place winners and announced Rory and I had gotten third place.

"We did it," Rory said, hugging me.

Darren told us to go up on stage, and we both got twenty-five-dollar gift certificates to the bookstore next door. Tom didn't place, but Darren won one of the first-place prizes and got a hundred-dollar gift certificate.

Kylie and Margaux came over to congratulate us. "You should use that certificate to get *You Can Change Your Life Today*. It's like, *the* best book."

Margaux said I should see if they'd let me use it to get magazines. "What did I tell you? The gloss was perfect under the lights, and the shirt was cute. Everybody else was all in black, and you stood out—especially since none of the girls wore lipstick—well except for the goth girls, but black lipstick isn't quite glam."

My mom came up to me and said I did a great job, but all I could focus on was how she was alone.

"Where are Dad and Grandpa?" I asked.

"It wasn't one of Grandpa's better days, so Dad decided it might be better if they stayed home. He wanted to be here, but Grandpa got confused trying to find the bathroom and had a little accident. No big deal, but Grandpa was upset and embarrassed, and Dad worried he'd get more confused if we took him to an unfamiliar environment."

Darren came up and said we should go to the bookstore and spend our certificates. He offered to drive me home, so Mom gave me a hug and left. We went to meet up with Tom and Rory. Tom was complaining that

the judges didn't "get" his piece. I didn't think that anyone did. It had something to do with nature and death,
but so had everything else he had written in class. Darren
found a collection of short stories at the bookstore, but I
wasn't sure what to get, so Tom picked out a book of author interviews for me. We all went over to the music section, and Rory put on the headphones to listen to a new
release. Tom pulled me over to show me a CD he always
listened to when he was writing.

"Ready?" he asked, putting the headphones on me. I
nodded. He said it was Ingrid Gilberto. Rory started dancing in the aisle to an Anders Bortz song, and Darren
joined her. We went to check out, and Rory bought a volume of poems that she had wanted for a long time. Darren ended up buying the short story book, an Edgar Allen
Poe novel, and *Travels with Charlie*, and I bought the inter-
view book.

"I need some food—big time," Rory said. "What's
still open?"

Darren wanted to go to a diner, so we all got huge
plates of pancakes, and Rory and the guys shared some
bacon. Everything had worked out in the end, but Brendon hadn't known it would. Sure, I had a good time, and I
was thrilled I got third place, but I was still mad that
Brendon had gone to his stupid charity thing after he had
promised to be there for me. After all, I had gone to all the
parties he invited me to, and I never asked him to anything which had been half as important to me. He knew
how nervous I had been, and he still went to that auction.

Brendon called me the next day, but I didn't pick up
the phone. Later, my dad said he called on the house
phone when I went grocery shopping with my mom, but I
didn't call back.

On Monday, Mr. Horowitz congratulated us in class.
He gave the four of us each a book he had picked out especially for us. I thought that was sweet until I saw he had

given me an Edith Wharton book about a spoiled brat
who twisted mind games into an Olympic sport. Was this
some sort of message? Darren got *For Whom the Bell Tolls,*
Tom got *The Sound and the Fury,* and Rory got a book of
May Sarton's poetry.

"Our next assignment is sort of a book report, but I
want you to focus on when the writing works for you and
when it doesn't. We're not going to approach the book as
readers, but as writers," Mr. Horowitz said. "I was going
to have you present them in front of the class, but, ah,
well, we can just discuss them in groups instead."

Everybody knew it was because the last time we had
to get up in front of the class, this one guy got so nervous
he got a nosebleed, and I have never seen a room clear so
fast. I knew I'd have to work extra hard on my paper to
make up for my crappy participation grade. I always sat
there during class, nodding to show I was listening, but
avoiding eye contact so I wouldn't have to actually say
anything. Mr. Horowitz always threw around names like
Faulkner and made jokes only he could understand. Of
course, there were always some butt-kissers who laughed
like they understood him when I knew they didn't. Tom
used to cough, "Posers," whenever anybody did it, which
always made Darren and me crack up. After class, Brendon was outside waiting for me.

"Did your dad tell you I called?" he asked.

I nodded and continued walking.

"So how did the reading go?"

I told him I got third place.

"Congratulations! So were there a lot of literary types
there?"

"I'm not a literary type?" I said. He started to answer,
but I cut him off. "I have to go, Kylie's waiting for me." I
walked over to Kylie and Zach and glanced back in his
direction and saw he was still standing there. Maybe now
he'd realize he couldn't walk all over me and expect eve-

rything to be just fine.

Brendon didn't call me at night. Either he didn't feel like dealing with me or he just didn't care. Maybe he thought this would all blow over, or maybe there was something on TV that was more important. Or maybe Brooke had come over to see his brother and flirt with him instead.

I saw him in the hall the next day, but I managed to avoid him. Instead I sat down and shuffled through my bag looking for my notes, but I found my Riley Turner watch instead. At the time I thought it was so sweet he had given me a watch because he noticed I didn't have one. It seemed like he was being thoughtful and observant, but maybe he was just making fun of me for being late a lot.

"Hey, do you want to get some ice cream after class?" Darren asked, leaning over. I nodded, but I was curious whether Brendon would bother showing up after class. He did show up and said he needed to talk to me. Darren walked over and asked if I was ready to go. I motioned for him to give me a second, and he stared at Brendon as he walked away.

"Can we sit down somewhere to talk?" Brendon asked. I walked over to one of the benches and put my bag on the seat beside me so he'd have to sit across from me.

"Em, I'm sorry I missed your reading. I would have been there if I could have, but I had to fill in for Sam at the fundraiser. I know I messed up—big time." He handed me a box.

I stared at it, and he asked me to guess what it was. Did he think he could just buy me something and I'd forgive him? I opened the box and inside was a chocolate egg decorated to look like a Faberge egg. It was gorgeous.

"When I told you I had a present for you for your birthday, you asked if it was a Faberge egg. Now I actually give you one, and you don't—" He stopped when his phone beeped to let him know someone was texting him. Why was it okay for him to check his messages while he was apologizing to me? It seemed like the least he could do was look at me while he was talking to me. Maybe I was being too hard on him. After all, he had tried to apologize over the weekend.

"Sorry. Em. There's just been so much going on with—"

"Brendon? C'mon, everybody's waiting for you to get started," Lauren said, coming over.

Wait, he was going to be with her after school? Lauren had another of her two-hundred-dollar tracksuits on. Only she could wear diamond earrings with sweatpants without looking like a rapper.

"Did you get my message before?" she asked as she reapplied her lip gloss and then smacked her lips. Why didn't she just crawl on his lap and lick his face? "I wrote you right back."

"I have to go anyway," I said, getting up. "I'm meeting someone too, but thanks for the egg. I'll see you later."

My thoughts were spinning as I went to meet Darren. I knew I still liked Brendon, but I wasn't sure about our relationship. I was afraid if I forgave him too easily, he would think he could treat me like crap and I'd put up with it. And why didn't he make it clear to Lauren there was no chance of them getting back together? I felt like she was just waiting for him to dump me, and then he'd be with her—the way the popular people's nature intended.

"Ready for a sundae?" I asked Darren.

"What's in the box?" he asked.

"Candy. Come on, it'll be your fault if they run out of decent toppings," I said.

He asked what Brendon wanted to talk to me about as we got in the sundae bar line. I said he just wanted to apologize for not coming to the reading on Saturday.

"What'd you say?" he asked, pouring chocolate syrup on his ice cream.

"Not much," I said, concentrating on not getting caramel sauce all over me. I was wearing my cream-colored pants, and those things were like a magnet for spills. "He just gave me some candy, and I thanked him and came over here."

Darren took my bowl from me and went over to pay. I tried to give him money, but he waved me off. I promised I'd buy next time, and he made a joke about me assuming there'd be a next time. We sat down to eat and talked about the new story he had started for class. I hadn't come up with a subject yet for the short story, but he was already halfway through his first draft. He asked if he could see the candy Brendon had given me. I handed him the box, and he glanced at it and handed it back to me.

"Pretty showy for a piece of chocolate. Does he think he can just open his wallet and you'll come running back?" he said.

"No, it's not like—see, we have this joke because when he gave me something, I asked if it—"

"Emme, he thinks he's so great it doesn't matter what he says or does 'cause he's Mr. Perfect. But he left you to go to the reading alone so he could work the charity auction with Lauren." My face must have shown how shocked I was because Darren said, "You didn't know? My brother was there, and he said Lauren and Brendon were together the whole time. You deserve to be treated better."

I felt sick. Brendon never mentioned Lauren being there. Maybe it was because he didn't get the chance to tell me, or it was because he had been all over his ex all night and was hoping I wouldn't hear about it. Or maybe he didn't care if I found out. Maybe he thought I was lucky to get any of his time, so I should just be happy he decided to spend any time with him at all. I mean, I knew

I wasn't good enough for him, but did the whole world have to see it, too? I started to say something, but Darren cut me off.

"I'm sorry Emme, but it makes me mad. He treats you like dirt, and I hate it. You deserve better."

The more I thought about it, the more I felt he might be right. Darren was bringing up the exact things I had been worried about. I still felt like Brendon cared about me, but I couldn't ignore the times he had put other things before me. Like when we'd talk on the phone, and it would be obvious he was watching a football game at the same time, or when I needed his help with my French homework, but he didn't call me until eleven o'clock at night because he had been working on a paper.

I was still confused when Brendon called me after school and asked if I wanted to go to the mall. He hates shopping, so I figured he was trying to be nice. Besides, I just wanted things to go back to normal, and I wanted to feel he liked me the way I liked him. But things just got weird the second we walked into a store. First we ran into Cassie, the girl from the tennis court. I tried to smile at her, but she just stared past me.

"Brendon, I have got to stop instant messaging with you on nights when I have a test the next day. It's your fault I bombed my French quiz," she said.

Cassie didn't look like the type who cared what her grades were. All she cared about was letting me know she and Brendon had been writing to each other for over an hour the other night. Fabulous. It was probably the night I was up at the hospital feeling sorry for myself. It was also irritating me how he kept checking his messages. I always put my phone on vibrate when I was with him, but he never did with me. Then, we saw this girl at the perfume counter who ran over to hug him.

"Hey Bren-Bren," she said. "Lauren said you guys had so much fun at the charity thing."

"Em, this is Lauren's sister, Monique," he said.

I should have known. They had the same bouncy hair, same giant diamond earrings, and the same way of making me feel like I was about to get anxiety-induced diarrhea. I was trying to look past all of that when I was looking at shoes and saw he was texting someone. Even though I didn't know who he was writing to, I just felt it was a girl. Not like he was necessarily cheating on me, but I felt like I wasn't interesting enough so he had to have a standby or something.

"Sorry if I'm boring you," I said, throwing a pair of mules back on the sale rack.

"What?"

"You can't spend like, two seconds without having to text someone or check your messages."

"Look, I'm sorry a lot of people text me. It's not a crime to have friends," he said.

"I'm just saying you're with me right now, can't you put—"

"I do so much for you, but it's never enough. I said I was sorry I missed your reading, but geez, Em. You're so sensitive," he said.

Maybe we both should have stopped and thought about what we were going to say next, because the next thing I knew I called him a selfish jerk.

"I'm sorry, but it couldn't be helped. This event was major for my college applications. I couldn't blow off something which will help me get into the Ivy Leagues for some stupid little reading."

"Stupid little reading? Seriously?"

"I didn't mean for it to come out—"

"I think you did. Will you just take me home?"

"Emme, I—"

"Please. I want to go home."

We drove to my house, and we didn't say a word to each other. I kept waiting for him to apologize and say something that would make it all better. But he stayed silent.

"I didn't want to get into a fight with you, but can you see it from my point of view?"

"I'll go to the next reading."

It wasn't just the reading; it was the fact he was on his phone all night when he was supposed to be with me. And I was sick of the constant girls acting like I wasn't even there.

"I'm overwhelmed by everything, and I'm feeling—"

His phone started to ring just then. Had he ignored it, maybe I would have been okay, but his eyes darted to the screen to see who it was, and even upside down I could read the name, "Lauren."

"You know maybe I just need a break from—"

And then he cut me off and said, "Fine."

I hadn't meant for him to take me so literally, but there it was. And I wasn't about to say, "Hey, that's not what I meant, I was trying to share my feelings on everything with you," when he obviously didn't care. He was so quick to move on without even hearing me out.

My eyes filled with tears, and I didn't want him to see me cry, so I got out of the car. When I got to the door, I realized someone left it unlocked. I went inside and figured my parents must have forgotten to lock it. The only real items of value in the house, the TV and computer, were still there, but I had the chills. I went to the fridge to grab a bottle of water when I noticed a note for me on the counter. Mom had written that my grandmother was back in the hospital, and she'd call me as soon as she had any information. Oh crap, I had my phone volume down while I was out.

My first instinct was to call Brendon to ask for a ride to the hospital, but I didn't want to beg, and I was afraid he might give me some excuse and say he couldn't do it. I got desperate to see Grandma so I dialed his cell phone, but got his voice mail, so I hung up. Zach and Rory were the only close friends I had who were old enough to drive, but Zach was at work, and Rory wasn't home, so I decided to call Darren. He drove me to the hospital, and I found out what room Grandma was in. My mom was in the hall talking to a nurse. Mom introduced the nurse to me, and they told me my grandmother had suffered another stroke.

"Is she going to be all right?" I asked. Darren put his hand on my shoulder.

"She's conscious, but unable to speak. We don't think she's in any physical pain, but she's paralyzed on her left side," the nurse said.

As we walked toward her room, I realized he hadn't answered my question. Mom told me Grandpa had been with Grandma when she had the stroke.

"What happened?" I asked.

"We had dropped Grandpa off at the hospital to visit. Aunt Caroline called her room, and Grandpa answered and told her Grandma had passed out. The nurse came and called an ambulance."

Mom said she had talked to Grandma's doctor, and Dr. Anton didn't think we should bring Grandpa to see Grandma while she was in the hospital. Dr. Anton thought maybe all of this was too much for him, and she wasn't sure how he would react seeing Grandma hooked up to the machines. The doctor said we should only bring him if we thought he'd be able to handle it. For now, my dad had taken him to stay with Aunt Caroline and Uncle George.

Darren stayed in the hall as I walked into Grandma's room. She was sitting up in bed, but one side of her face was slack, and her eyes were darting around the room and not focusing on anything. I wanted to go over and take her hand, but I was scared. She was making this little moaning noise, and it seemed like she was in pain. Sitting down next to the bed, I tried to talk to her, but she didn't even look at me. I kept repeating she was going to be fine, and started bringing up things we could do after she got out of the hospital. I just wanted her to believe she was going to get out of the hospital—even if I didn't believe it myself.

"When you get home we could make those sugar cookies—remember when I tried to make the dough pink, and it came out all gross?" Her eyes darted around the room, and she didn't seem to absorb anything I was saying. I put my hand in hers and asked her to squeeze, and she gripped my hand so tightly I almost couldn't get it out of her grasp. I went into the hall to tell them how she responded, but the nurse said it was just a reflex and not to look too deeply into it. Mom suggested Darren and I go and get something to eat. I didn't want to leave, but she insisted and gave us some money.

"Emme, please. You need to have dinner, and I want some time alone with Grandma."

Darren asked where I wanted to eat, and I said I didn't care. He pulled into a parking lot and I followed him in. It wasn't until I sat down that I realized Brendon and I had eaten here before. Last time I was there, the waitress had basically hit on Brendon right in front of me. Darren and I had the same waitress, but I was sure she didn't remember me and just as positive she would have remembered Brendon. I ordered a salad even though I knew I probably wouldn't eat much of it. Darren tried to reassure me Grandma was going to be fine.

"There's so much doctors can do these days," he said. I nodded, but I knew she was in trouble. I could tell my grandma knew it, too.

After we ate, he dropped me off at home because he had to go to work. He offered to call in sick, but I didn't want him to miss work. However, I also didn't want to be in the house all by myself. I tried reading to distract myself, but I couldn't concentrate, so I put the TV on to break the silence. Why was there never anything good on? I lit every green candle in the house, and I even tried calling some friends, but no one was home. Darren called me on his break to make sure I was okay.

"You know when I get upset sometimes it helps to write about it," he said.

"I just want to go to sleep so I'm not conscious, you know?"

"Yeah. Listen, do you want me to stop by on my way home from work?" he asked.

"No, I think I'm going to just go lie down for a while, but thanks."

I considered calling Brendon to tell him I hadn't meant I wanted a break from him, but I was afraid he'd say he had plans or something, and he wouldn't be able talk. It would hurt even more if he said it *after* I told him about my grandmother.

Instead I called Margaux and told her the whole story.

"Oh man, I'd go nuts with girls constantly flirting right in front of me," she said. "But honestly, that's just part of what it's like to be dating the 'It Guy.'"

"What do you mean?"

"You know how magazines call models and those socialites the 'It Girl' all the time? Well, he's like the male version. He's the guy every girl wants to date and every guy wants to be. It's a lot to handle."

"You're telling me. So what do I do now?"

"I'd wait a bit and let him cool down. Maybe he'll call you. Personally, the way things were left, I wouldn't want to call him first and look desperate. I'm sure it'll work out."

"Yeah, thanks."

I decided to go to bed and get away from everything. I had never gone to sleep so early on a Friday night before.

Chapter 13

THE NEXT MORNING, my mom said the nurses thought Grandma seemed more alert. I wanted to go see her, but Mom said they were going to be running tests on her all day and we'd just be in the way. Turning my cell phone on, I realized Brendon tried calling me last night. I was about to call him back when Darren called and said he wanted to take me to the zoo. Well, I hadn't been to the zoo in years, and I had never gone in the fall. It sounded like a good way to distract myself until I could go see Grandma. While I waited for Darren to pick me up, I tried calling Brendon back, but my call went straight to voice mail. Was he busy or had he sent all my calls to voice mail to avoid me?

Darren picked me up to go to the zoo, and we rode the train and then walked around.

"Just so you know, we can visit all the areas except the reptile house and the elephant house," I said.

"I understand the snake house, but what do you have against elephants?" he asked.

"When I was little, I heard these kids on the playground talking about the Elephant Man, and I thought you could get it from elephants. It makes no sense, but

I've been scared of them ever since. You should see me at the circus," I said.

"Well, it's certainly..."

"Weird?" I asked, narrowing my eyes.

"I was going to say interesting. Maybe seeing the elephants up close would help you overcome your fear," he said.

"We're talking about something engrained in my subconscious. If I went and saw the elephants, you might as well call every dermatologist in the area because I would come down with the symptoms. I can catch a broken leg," I said.

"Just out of curiosity, what are the symptoms of ele—"

"Let's change the subject. Even talking about it freaks me out," I said. "Anyway, I don't know the symptoms, and no, I've never seen the movie."

"It's a good movie," he said.

"I don't care if they remake it and offer me a role—I'm still not going to see it."

"Okay, I got it. Let's get a snow cone," he said, pulling me over to the concession stand.

The bottom of his cone started leaking. I tried to help him soak up the juice with my napkins, but pretty soon we both had cherry syrup all over our hands.

"You can't take me anywhere," he said, removing little bits of napkin stuck to his arm.

"I've got to wash my hands 'cause I absolutely hate it when my hands get sticky. It's like chalk squeaking on a blackboard for me," I said.

"So no elephants, no elephant movies, and nothing sticky," he said.

"Unless you have an antibacterial wipe," I said as it started to rain. "I can't believe this—I wouldn't have worn a white, long-sleeved T-shirt if I knew it was going to rain," I said. "I mean what does 'clear skies' mean? I thought it meant it wouldn't rain. Why is Michigan

weather so screwy? I was wearing short sleeves yesterday, and today I'm freezing my butt off in the rain."

Darren shrugged. "No big deal." I glanced at his open
flannel shirt and the rock band T-shirt he had on underneath. It was so different from Brendon's V-neck sweaters
and khakis, but it fit Darren's personality. There was
something hot about a literary guy who worked out. He
caught me staring at him and smirked.

"What?" he asked.

"Nothing, just making sure you didn't have any more
snow cone syrup on your face."

"Ah, thought maybe you were admiring my beauty,"
he said, laughing.

My face got warm. "Nope, just looking out for you."

The rain got heavier, so we decided to leave. I wondered if he was going to suggest going to get food or
something, but when we got to the parking lot, he noticed
he had a bunch of texts.

"Oh man, they're all from my boss, asking me to
come in tonight," he said. "Hope he's not mad I didn't
pick up. It's just when I'm with someone, I'm not about to
keep checking my phone—it's a pet peeve of mine."

I thought of how many times Brendon checked his
phone when we were out.

"I was going to see if you wanted to get food, but I
feel like I better drop you off and go into work. Cool?"

"Sure."

He drove to my house, and I was kind of grateful he
had someplace to be so there wasn't some awkward good-
bye moment with him walking me to the door or anything.

"I'll text you later," he said. "And I promise—no elephant emojis."

"Thanks for being so understanding."

"Anytime. Now go wash your hands in case someone
at the zoo did touch an elephant right before you touched
the same door handle."

"Jerk. See ya later."

I WENT TO the hospital with my mom the next day. Grandma slept the entire time we were there, and the doctor didn't have the test results back yet. My cousin Carla had sent flowers, which should have made the room more cheerful, but I was so depressed. Not wanting to give up, I placed crystals all over the room along with some prayer cards, and I had downloaded a special healing meditation, which was supposed to calm you. I was hoping something would work for her, but I had a feeling like it didn't matter what I did because nothing was going to make a difference. Over and over, I kept reminding myself how important a positive attitude was, but I just couldn't shake the horrible feeling my grandma was never going to leave the hospital.

Meanwhile, my mom kept waiting for Grandpa to ask to come visit Grandma, but he never mentioned it. Three days went by, and he didn't even ask how she was doing. Finally, I brought it up.

"Aren't you worried about Grandma?" I asked him.

"Why? What's wrong with mom?" he asked, sitting up straight.

"She's been in the hospital. She had another stroke," I said.

"She did? Nobody told me. When did this happen?"

"Grandpa, you were with her when it happened," I said. "Don't you remember?"

"No one told me," he said, getting angry.

However, ten minutes later he was concerned with making me an ice cream cone, and he didn't bring up Grandma again. I checked my e-mail while he dished out the ice cream. There was a message from Kylie, but I didn't feel like writing her back.

Chapter 14

RORY WAS ABSENT the next day, so I ate lunch with Darren. He had a greasy fish sandwich, and it smelled so gross it made my grilled cheese sandwich taste fishy. I felt someone watching me and saw Brendon staring at me from across the room. He was sitting with a couple of his friends, and I wondered why he was there, since he had a different lunch period. I also wondered why Lauren was practically sitting on him. She was so obvious. He didn't seem to be paying attention to her, but she was helping herself to his French fries, when she had perfectly good fries on her tray. He gave me one of his lopsided smiles, which was the only time he ever seemed unsure of himself. Of course, Brendon looking insecure only made him look hotter. I decided to write him a note in fifth period. With Grandma's health so bad, I was starting to see you shouldn't hold grudges or hold back about how you feel. Besides, lately I felt so alone. I couldn't talk to Mom about everything because she was going nuts with Grandma in the hospital and Grandpa not knowing where he was half the time. I needed Brendon now.

Hey,

I'm sorry about getting mad about the reading. I know you couldn't help how your friend got sick. And I'm sorry about the whole thing at the mall. I miss you.

Love,
Emme

It was just three sentences, yet I had poured my heart into them. I felt so vulnerable. I asked Sam to give it to him, and Brendon was waiting at my locker before sixth period.

"Hey. I'm so glad you gave me the note," he said. He brushed my hair back and slid his arm around me. "Wait for me after seventh period, and we can hang out, okay? I'm going to lie and say I'm sick so I don't have to go to the homecoming committee meeting."

"You're on the committee? I thought there were mostly girls on it."

He laughed. "Anything for the transcripts. The college I want to get into only takes the top students, and you have to be well-rounded. My dad only reminds me daily."

"So aren't you going to ask me to homecoming?" I asked, standing up on my toes to kiss him.

He pulled back. "Crap. I already said I'd go with Lauren."

"What? When?"

"She just asked me on Sunday, and you and I were broken up, and the co-chair has to go to the dance—"

"We were not broken up!" I said.

"You said you needed a break!"

"Did it even occur to you to try and work things out with me? Or did you run straight to Lauren the second I got out of the car?"

"You mean the way you run to Darren every time

you get mad at me?"

"Don't make this about—"

"It's perfectly okay for you to hang out with him, but I can't have female friends—"

I started to say something, but he cut me off. "I know your ex-boyfriend got back with his old girlfriend, but not every guy is like that. Why does everything have to be so complicated with you?"

"So not the point!" I said. "The point is you said you'd go to a dance, like, five minutes after—"

"Could you please lower your voice?"

I couldn't believe he was more concerned about me making a scene than the fact he had basically crapped all over our relationship. And I was too shocked about the dance to even start crying. Moving past him, I ran into the girls' bathroom, went into the big stall in the back, and stared at "Randi's a loser" until the bell rang. I couldn't believe he had said he'd go to a dance with another girl without seeing if we were going to work things out. As I walked to class, I told myself I shouldn't care about what he did since he obviously didn't care about me, but it hurt to think I could be replaced so fast.

After my class, I decided to walk past Brendon's classroom. I don't know if I was hoping to find him devastated and crying, but what I saw was Lauren waiting for him. He didn't look upset at all as they walked off together. I followed them, and he stopped at the vending machines to get a soda. He took a drink, and she reached up and took the bottle from him, her raspberry-colored nails clutching it. I watched her drink out of his bottle, and then I walked away. I was angry, hurt, and trying hard not to care. Maybe some part of me had wanted Brendon to think there was something more between Darren and me, but now I was afraid he thought I had moved on and it was okay for him to move on, too. Then I wondered if I wanted him back because *he* had moved on. I had forgotten how thoughtful he could be and how he shared things with me he could never tell anyone else…and his big brown eyes and the way he'd focus them on me.

I went to class and tried to concentrate as Mr. Horowitz told us he had decided we should start writing journals. "We'll write about different things, like a book you wouldn't normally pick up, or a public spot and write about the people walking by," he said. "And we're going to go on a field trip to the art museum to write about the paintings next week, so get these permission slips signed—and no forgeries. Tom, I'm looking in your direction. Real signatures, people."

"What's wrong?" Darren asked, leaning over.

"Nothing," I said.

"You sure?" he asked. "Well, I'm here for you, if you want to talk about anything."

Margaux and Kylie came over after school when they heard about Lauren going to the dance with Brendon.

"She, like, pounced on him in a weak moment. She was waiting for an opportunity, and then she just went for it," Margaux said.

"It sucks he said he'd go," Kylie said. "But it's not like he said he was going as her boyfriend. I mean, you said he seemed happy when you gave him the note—"

"*Hello!* He agreed to go to a dance with another girl," Margaux said. "He's obviously not into Emme enough to turn Lauren down. I'm sorry, Em, but seriously, what's he gotta do? Wear a sandwich board saying, 'Emme, I've moved on. See ya?'" Margaux grabbed a rice cake. "What the crap? This package says they use natural fertilizer on the rice? Does it mean animals are, like, pooing on the rice cakes?"

Kylie and I put our rice cakes down. "See, this is why I don't eat organic," Margaux said, getting up. "Don't you have any junk food around here? I know your mom eats Cheeze Puffies; don't even lie. Ooh, score. Corn chips."

Kylie said she saw the same thing happen on *Sunset Falls,* and the couple on the show realized it was all a big misunderstanding, and they got back together.

"Of course, Angelique had amnesia at the time, so that was a big factor, but whatever," she said. "Anyway, I just don't get why Brendon would think it would be okay to go to the dance with another girl."

Margaux rolled her eyes. "Did he even wait until you were out of the car to ask her? Besides, he'd lose it if you were going with someone else."

"Lauren asked him—"

"That's what he wants you to think," she said, as Kylie smacked her arm.

"But it's not just *anyone* he's going with," I said. "It's his ex. His perfect, annoying, stupid ex."

"Lauren's an honor student, she's not stupid—oh, you were being sarcastic...yeah, sorry," Margaux said. "Anyway, the only way to deal with this is to let Brendon see how it feels. Turn the tables so he can see what it's like to be completely humiliated—"

She stopped when I glared at her. "Thanks. Makes me feel so much better," I said.

"If there was any hope for you guys to have a relationship, then Brendon would have to make a clean break from Lauren for it to work—*if you* even had a relationship left. I mean, would you even want him back if he's just going to keep running back to her? And now Lauren knows if you're out of the picture, then she can have him."

"True," I said, and Kylie nodded.

"If you guys get back together, then you've got to let him know you won't put up with it," she said. "And you need to make him see he's not the only guy in the world interested in you. Trust me."

She was right. After all, I had felt like crap for days because of him, and he needed to see what it was like to be pushed aside. I had always been sort of worried about Lauren because of what had happened with John and Brittanie, but deep down, I thought Brendon and I had some deep connection. It felt like we were meant to be, and he wouldn't want to run back to her, but I guess I was wrong.

The next few days were a blur. In the back of my mind, I kept thinking about how crappy things always came in threes. My grandma's stroke was one, and the breakup/dance thing was two, so what would the third thing be? I'd get attacked by rabid squirrels? Or maybe the escaped killer from the Samson prison would find me. Maybe I'd get run over or something. I just hoped it was quick and painless. Sure, I knew I needed to focus on positive stuff, but the only silver lining was how at least Brendon's date with Lauren had taken my mind off my grandma's condition for two seconds. How did people go on with their lives when crap happened to them? I wasn't the only person in the universe who had bad stuff going on, so how did those people get out of bed in the morning? Because if it wasn't for my school's militant get-your-tush-to-class-or-fail policy, I would have stayed locked in my room and watched soaps all day. At least I had the field trip to take my mind off things.

On the day of the field trip, Mr. Horowitz had us spilt up into groups of five when we got to the museum and let us wander around. We were supposed to write down our feelings while we were there. Rory and Darren were in my group, and we went through the rooms and made fun of the exhibits. I had a sinus headache from the stupid weather, which couldn't decide if it wanted to rain or not. I tried to hang back so I could be by myself, but Darren wouldn't leave me alone. Normally, I thought he was cute and funny, but today he kept bumping into my shoulder, and it was irritating. I wanted to ask for some space, but I didn't want to be mean, so I decided to sit down and start writing. I found a bench away from everybody else and started to work.

Instead of writing about the artwork and the people in the museum, I started writing about my grandma. I wrote about the time everyone in the family went to get a Christmas tree, and she and I stayed back and made Christmas cookies. I was getting into it when Darren sat down next to me.

"Whatcha writing?" he asked, nudging my leg.

I covered my pad with my hand and shrugged. I wasn't ready to show it to anybody yet, so I said we should go join the group. As we walked out, I noticed he kept trying to get me alone. He had a way of muscling everybody out with his shoulder, and pretty soon he and I were the only two walking together.

We got back to school, and Darren walked with me to my locker. Before we had the fight, Brendon used to leave his physics book in there because it was closer to his class. I hadn't run into him at the locker in a while, but today he was there getting his book. I could have sworn his book hadn't been in there for a week, but maybe I hadn't been paying attention. Out of nowhere, Darren started asking me how Grandma was doing.

"Do you want me to go to the hospital with you again?" Darren asked. I felt weird, since Darren was now acting like he was my boyfriend or something. After all, he had only gone to the hospital once, yet he was making it sound like it was a regular thing. But I didn't want to get into it in front of Brendon, so I just shook my head. Then Darren put his arm around me and gave me an awkward hug before he walked off.

"Hospital? What's going on?" Brendon asked.

"Grandma had another stroke. Darren gave me a ride to the hospital, which is how he knew about it."

"Oh man, Em, you should have called me. I would have gone with you," he said, putting his hand on my arm. "I had this feeling something was wrong, and I was going to call you, but—well, how is she?"

I shrugged. "It's not good this time. I'm not sure she can come back from it."

"Can I drive you home?"

"My mom is already on her way to pick me up."

He walked me out and told my mom he was sorry to hear about Grandma.

"I'll call you," he said and gave me a hug before walking away.

"How come he didn't know about Grandma?" my mother asked. I told her I didn't feel like talking about it, but she wouldn't let it go.

"It's no big deal. We've just been having some issues since he bailed on coming to my reading," I said, but left out the dance part.

"You owe him a second chance at least. You think your father goes to every event important to me? And think how many events of your dad's I blow off? I've gotten out of reunions, company picnics—"

"Mom, can you please leave it alone? I don't want to think about guys right now." And I didn't want my mom to know I was such a loser my boyfriend had moved on less than thirty-six hours after we split up.

I was so confused about my feelings for him. At times, I felt like we had this deep connection where he knew when I needed him and he understood me, but then I felt like he had let me down and didn't care. I had enough to worry about with Grandma, and I didn't want to let Brendon in again and then have him leave me, too. Besides, how could I be completely sure he even wanted a second chance? Just because he was nice to me at my locker didn't mean he wanted to get back together.

We got to the hospital, and the doctor said Grandma was now in a semi-coma, but she didn't "appear to be in any physical pain." Why couldn't doctors ever talk like normal people? Even the simplest things sounded clinical and cold coming out of their mouths. The doctor said Grandma had thrown up right before we arrived. Mom tried talking to Grandma, and she seemed to respond to her voice. Grandma would sigh or scrunch up her face when we'd ask her things. I was anxious, and after a while, mom took me to get a cup of tea.

"I know Grandma's scared too, but I'm so uncomfortable in her room. And I get freaked out when she makes those noises," I said, taking a sip of my tea. "Great, I just burned my tongue."

My mother blew on her cappuccino. "I wasn't going to tell you this, but yesterday, she rolled over, and I almost knocked a nurse down running out of the room. Honestly, I'm just not good in hospitals. I tried volunteering once at a hospital, and I passed out when I walked in a room where they were taking blood."

I felt better knowing I wasn't the only one getting weirded out. Mom said my Aunt Caroline and Uncle George were coming on Friday to see Grandma. She asked if I'd stay with Grandpa while they were at the hospital.

"By the way, Grandma said something last time I was here about a bracelet she wanted you to have. The pink and silver charm one you used to play with when you were little. I put it on your dresser," she said. "Grandma said something about how you might need it. I don't know exactly what she was trying to say because she was kind of out of it and slurring her words together."

"It's rose quartz," I said. "And she's right—I do need it now."

"Why?"

I didn't want to tell her rose quartz was considered the "heart healing" and love stone, and since my love life was in the toilet, it just might help. Instead, I just said I wanted something of Grandma's to make me feel better. I wondered if Grandma somehow sensed I needed it or if it was a weird coincidence.

——

THAT NIGHT, DARREN invited me to a party. I didn't want to be around people, but he insisted.

"It'll take your mind off things," he said.

I said okay and wore Grandma's bracelet. It became obvious the night was going to suck when we walked into the party and some guy stared at it and said, "What's with the weird bracelet?"

"It's my grandma's."

"Yeah, it looks like something an old lady would wear."

I held back my urge to smack the guy and fought off tears. Darren introduced me to a bunch of people who I couldn't have cared less about meeting. I had a quart of organic dairy-free mint chocolate swirl ice cream waiting for me at home, and I would have rather stayed home, watching TV and eating.

"You want me to get you some pizza?" he asked. I shrugged, and he brought back two lemon-lime sodas and a slice of pepperoni and sausage pizza. I wasn't a huge fan of lemon-lime soda, but I kept drinking it to avoid talking to anyone, and *hello*, I didn't eat meat. I picked off all the pepperoni and sausage and managed a bite of pizza. His friend, Greg, took a look at my plate and said there was cheese pizza in the kitchen. I said this was okay, but I could taste the sausage grease on my slice.

"Sorry, let me get you a different slice," Darren said. "I wasn't thinking."

Unlike most guys, Darren actually stayed with me all night. Usually, guys walked in with you, and then went off with their friends while you sat there wondering what to do, but he made sure I was okay, and if I needed anything, he jumped up to get it.

"Are you okay?" he asked. "I was hoping this would take your mind off things, but I guess it would take a lot more than a party, huh?"

"Yeah, but thanks for bringing me," I said.

"I just didn't want you sitting home and worrying about your grandma. If I could do anything, you know I would, right?" he asked. He leaned forward like he was going to kiss me, but then he pulled away. On the way home, I tried to figure out why he pulled back. Was he afraid I wasn't over Brendon? And did I *want* him to kiss me? Part of me was so hurt over Brendon and Lauren and didn't want to date anyone, and part of me wished Darren hadn't pulled away.

When I got home, Dad told me Brendon called, but I just wanted to slip into my sweatpants and curl up in bed with my ice cream. I had just gotten underneath the covers when the phone rang. It was Darren wanting to know if I had heard anything about Grandma.

"Nothing's changed." I didn't feel like talking about it—it hurt too much, and I also wasn't sure about my feelings for him. It didn't seem right to have these heart-to-heart talks if he was going to think I was leading him on. I just wanted to get off the phone and think for a little bit.

"Oh, hold on, I'm getting another call." I clicked over, and it was Brendon. Since he had called before and I had just spent the last two hours with Darren, I switched back and told Darren I had go.

"Who is it?" he asked.

"Kylie," I said, not wanting to confuse him—or myself. "Thanks for taking me to the party. I'll call you tomorrow, okay?" I switched back over to Brendon.

"How's your grandma doing?" he asked.

"She's in a semi-coma, and the doctors are running more tests."

He offered to go with me to visit her, but I didn't

want him to have to go through it. Besides, he was just offering to be polite. Nobody in their right mind would want to sit in a hospital room—especially when someone in their family had also suffered a stroke. Who'd want to relive that?

"How are you dealing with everything?" he asked.

"Not well. I feel like I'm underwater half the time and super tired."

"I'll let you go so you can get some sleep," he said. "Just wanted to know if there was anything I could do. So...let me know if you need anything, okay? Anything."

The next morning my mother called the nurses' station, and they said Grandma seemed more alert, but I had a bad feeling. I tried to ignore it, but I couldn't shake it. My parents went to meet Aunt Caroline and Uncle George, and I stayed with Grandpa. The four of them were exhausted when they came home. Caroline was crying and holding Grandpa's hand. He asked her what was wrong, and she didn't answer. Later, Mom told me Dr. Anton didn't think Grandma was going to improve, and they were going to move her to hospice care in a few days.

"What does that mean?" I asked.

Mom cleared her throat. "Well, it's where people go when they're not expected to improve."

"Do they know for sure, or are they just giving up on her?" I asked as tears rolled down my face.

"She hasn't come out of the semi-coma, and her latest scan showed there's...well, a lot more damage from this latest stroke."

My body felt ice cold. "But some people are in hospice for months, right? Margaux's great-aunt is in hospice, and they went to a baseball game with her a couple weeks ago."

"Emme, every case is different. I know it hurts, but we have to think of what's best for her," she said as she wiped her eyes.

"I don't want to be selfish, but I just want her here," I

said.

"I know. Honey, I need to talk to you about how 'out of it' Grandpa has been lately. You know Aunt Caroline had called Grandma's room on the day she had her stroke. Grandpa had picked up the phone, and he was confused."

"What do you mean?"

"Grandpa said she couldn't talk, and Caroline asked where she was, and he said, 'On the floor,' and Caroline said, 'What do you mean on the floor?' So she called the nurses' station from her cell phone, and they came running."

"But all you have to do to alert the nurses is hit the blue thingy on the phone, and they come right away. Why didn't Caroline just have Grandpa call them?" I asked.

"Well, Caroline couldn't believe Grandpa hadn't done it himself," she said. "When he didn't react, she knew something was wrong. Grandma said he had been slipping lately, but I don't think we realized it had gotten so bad. I was hoping him not asking about Grandma was about being in shock or denial, but it's more serious, and it's not going to get any better. Em, I don't know what we're going to do. We have to keep a closer eye on him, okay?"

I nodded.

That evening I went downstairs to get a glass of apple juice. Grandpa was getting ready for bed, and he came over to give me a kiss.

"Good night, sweetheart," he said. "Now where do I sleep?"

"You're sleeping in the guest room, remember?"

"Oh, right, right, right. The guest room." He nodded.

I knew he didn't remember where the room was, so I walked him to the place where he had slept every single time he had ever stayed at our house. He climbed into the bed, and I put the blanket over him.

"Where's Mom sleeping?" he asked.

I didn't feel like getting into it and upsetting him, so I said she was in the other room. He seemed satisfied with my answer, and I switched off the light. My parents were in the family room, and I sat next to my mom.

"What are we going to do?" I asked.

"About Grandpa?" she asked, and I nodded. "He's going to stay here for a while, and then he's going to stay with Aunt Caroline until we can find something more permanent."

"Like a nursing home? Mom, the place Grandma was in made me want to kill myself. Plus, Grandma had a lot of issues with walking and needed around-the-clock care—for her it was a safety thing, but you can't put him in there. We can take care of him."

"Emme, it's getting harder and harder the more confused he gets, and it might be best for him to be someplace where there are others more—"

"He's not like those people. Some of them don't even know where they are," I said.

"Does he?" my dad asked.

"*Yes*, he just gets a little confused sometimes."

"Em, he doesn't even know what's going on with your grandmother," he said. "We need to take him back to the doctor because I think he has Alzheimer's—"

"Clint, his doctor, said it's hardening of the arteries, and it's just gotten worse," my mother said.

"Well, I think they're wrong," he said. "Let's just take him in for a checkup anyway."

"Fine." My mother got up. "Good night."

Chapter 15

GRANDMA WAS STILL in a semi-coma the next day. The nurse came in, and I told him she had squeezed my hand.

"Probably just a reflex. I wouldn't read too much into it," he said.

"But the morning nurse thought she seemed more alert."

"Mara is young. I don't want to give you false hope," he said as he walked out the door. I made a face at my mother.

"He's a disciple of doom. He should not be around sick people," I said. "Grandma could get up and salsa dance, and he'd say it was a reflex and oh, *don't read too much into it.*"

My mom cleared her throat. "He doesn't want you to get your hopes up."

"Whatever. How can Grandma get well with someone like him around? Kylie says your attitude has a lot to do with your recovery, and he's just a big, stupid —"

"Yeah, well, your dad's not much better these days," she said.

Dr. Anton came in, and I got up and asked if we

could talk in the hall. My mom followed me. I didn't want to talk in front of Grandma in case she could hear us because I only wanted her to hear positive things.

"They're moving her to hospice tomorrow," Dr. Anton said.

"So you don't think there's any chance she'll recover?" I asked.

"Not unless she wakes up, and even then, as you know, the test results showed she wouldn't have her sight, and she probably wouldn't be able to speak either," Dr. Anton said.

"What?" I stared at my mother, and when she nodded, I realized she already knew. "Mom, why didn't you tell me?"

"We didn't think she'd come out of the coma and didn't see the need to upset you," she said.

"So what are they going to do for her at hospice?" I asked. "She can't feed herself, so what do you do then? A feeding tube or something?"

"Her living will allowed for the tube, but it said nothing extraordinary, so there will be no ventilators if she should require one," Dr. Anton said. "There's nothing more we can do. Now we just want to make her comfortable."

"Emme, Grandma would be terrified if she woke up and she couldn't speak or see," Mom said. "And the doctors don't think she's going to wake up at all."

"But she's trying. She's been making noises and squeezing my hand like this," I grabbed Dr. Anton's hand, which made her jump.

"I know it seems like she could wake up, but she's not going to. This time the damage was too severe," Dr. Anton said.

"You're all giving up on her, but she's strong. She's going to wake up. I know she will." I was crying, and my nose was running.

I wiped my face and tried to get calm before I went back into the room. After all, I didn't want Grandma to know how bad things were. If she didn't open her eyes, they were going to send her someplace where she'd fade away and not even have a chance to get better. I walked over to the bed.

"Grandma, if you're ever going to wake up, you've *got* to do it now," I said.

She shifted slightly, but didn't open her eyes. Aunt Caroline came in, and I could tell she and my mom wanted to be alone with Grandma, so I went to the cafeteria. I bought a bottle of water and sat in a booth by myself. Looking across the room, I saw a girl sitting by herself. She was obviously upset, and I wondered if I should go over and say something to her, but I figured she'd probably tell me to mind my own business. It was a good thing I didn't go over there because a guy came in and sat with her. He moved to her side of the booth and put his arm around her. I wished somebody was here with me. I could have asked Kylie to come with me to the hospital, but I knew she'd be uncomfortable. Darren had asked if I wanted him to come with me, but I said no because it would have been weird for me. Brendon knew how much hospitals weirded me out, but I couldn't ask him to come with me. Part of me wished somehow he knew I needed him to be here, and he'd just show up. I even daydreamed about it, but he obviously wasn't reading my mind.

Mom and Aunt Caroline had each other to confide in, and I had no one but Grandpa. Lately it felt like he didn't even know where he was half the time. It wasn't like my mom and I didn't get along, but we weren't super close the way some girls were with their moms. Even as I kid, I was never running up to her getting hugs like the rest of the kids on the playground because she wasn't that type of mom. I knew she liked to think of herself as being a "cool mom," but sometimes I just needed somebody to make me hot chocolate and sit with me while I cried. She was a great mom, but she was never going to be that person. Grandma was the one I went to when I needed to talk things out and be my shoulder to cry on. Right now I needed someone for a heart-to-heart more than ever, and I didn't know who I could turn to.

I tried talking to Kylie early on when my grandma first got sick, but Kylie's own grandmother wasn't doing well, and I could tell this whole thing freaked her out. Margaux wasn't exactly a sympathetic shoulder because you didn't know what she might say, and I hadn't known Rory long enough to unload on her. I had friends, but I didn't have anybody who I could have a deep conversation with. This was the sort of thing I would have been able to talk to Brendon about, but there was no way I could call him now. I just wished I didn't feel so alone.

Darren called me when I got home. He was concerned about Grandma and asked me all sorts of questions. He asked how I was holding up, and I said I was tired.

"Em, I just want you to know I'm here for you, okay? Do you want me to go with you to the hospital tomorrow?" he asked.

"No, but thanks," I said. It was nice to have him offer, but I didn't feel like I could open up to him about all this just yet. I got out my math book and tried to start my homework, but I couldn't concentrate. I checked my cell phone to see if I had any new messages and saw Brendon's number. Crap, the one person I would have wanted to talk to, but he didn't leave a message, and I felt weird calling him back. What would I even say? "Saw your number and wondered what you wanted?" No, I'd wait and see if he messaged or called me again.

Brendon e-mailed me on Tuesday, but it was just a reminder about some stupid student council thing. I kind of wished he had put a "hello" or even a "you suck" in it.

At least then it would be more personal. I was glad I hadn't called him back after seeing his number on my phone because I would have felt stupid if he was just calling about the fundraiser. Then I noticed the e-mail wasn't a forwarded one, which was weird, but maybe I was just hoping he had only e-mailed me about the fundraiser.

Later, I was walking to my locker after class when I saw Lauren walking with Brendon. She was holding onto his arm, and they appeared like the perfect couple. They both had the same dark hair, and they both had green golf shirts on. It was so cutesy it made me want to throw up. Lauren stood on her toes to whisper something in his ear. He put his arm around her and leaned over to hear her. There was a time when I had let Darren put his arm around me because I wanted Brendon to think there was something between Darren and me to make him jealous. Now watching him do it was making me ill. Margaux kept telling me I only wanted to get back with Brendon because I was jealous Lauren and the redhead were interested in him.

I watched Brendon walk to Lauren's locker. Apparently, he had been keeping some of his books in her locker since he and I weren't together anymore. I tried not to let it bother me, and I focused on putting my stuff in my bag. Just as I shut my locker, I saw Lauren stop almost in front of me, and she reached up and kissed him on the cheek. The worst part was she had done it right in front of me, and I couldn't pretend I hadn't seen it. He seemed surprised, but probably because I was standing there. I went straight down the hall and into the bathroom and locked myself in a stall.

I was late to creative writing, but Mr. Horowitz was late, too, and I scooted in right before he came through the door. Rory leaned over and whispered that Brendon had been waiting outside the room when she got to the class. I passed her a note asking if he was looking for me. She nodded. Mr. Horowitz told us to get into groups, and Darren moved his desk around to face Rory and me. We were exchanging papers when Mr. Horowitz called Darren over.

"Did Brendon say anything to you?" I asked Rory as soon as Darren was out of earshot.

"He wanted me to tell you he was looking for you. What's going on with you guys anyway?" she said.

Darren came back to his seat then and said he was going to have one of his stories published in the school's literary magazine. I was excited for him, but a little jealous, too. His work was exactly the sort of serious stuff the editors of the *Litzine* liked. My writing didn't have the edge Darren's did, but I thought it was good, even if my classmates didn't throw praise my way. After class, I took my time packing up in case Brendon might show up again. Darren kept telling me to hurry up, but I told him I had to go to the library and he didn't need to wait for me. I hoped Brendon would tell me Lauren was trying to make me jealous, and he didn't want me to misunderstand, but he didn't come back to the room.

I went to the library and went to the computer to look up books on *To Kill a Mockingbird* for my paper. I wrote the call numbers down and went to look for my books. I went around the corner and saw Brendon talking to the redheaded girl, which was weird since he should have been in class. I didn't want them to see me lurking in the shadows like a freak, but the books I needed were down the same aisle, so I stood behind a bookshelf and waited for them to leave. From where I was standing, I couldn't hear their conversation, but I did see her link her arm through his. They left the aisle, and I got my stuff. I was heading to a study room when I walked right into Brendon and dropped everything. How suave.

"Hey," he said, leaning down to pick up my stuff.

"Hi." I tried not to look at him because I was sure he

would be able to see how upset I was just by looking at my face. He brushed my hand as he picked up one of the books, and all my emotions rose in my chest. I felt like I could just let go and pass out.

"Thanks."

"Is everything okay? I tried to call you last week. I had this weird feeling—I dunno, anyway, are you okay?" he asked, putting his hand on top of mine.

"Brendon, c'mon, we're going to be late," the redhead said, coming around the corner. I jumped to my feet and walked away with my face burning. I thought he seemed sort of sad, but maybe I just wanted him to look depressed. It upset me so much, I ended up blurting the whole thing out to Darren on the phone.

"Emme, guys are different," he said. "We don't wait around to see if the girl still likes us. If we say we're sorry, and she doesn't accept it, then we deal with it and move on. And it sounds like he's definitely moved on since he has two girls hanging all over him."

"So *you* wouldn't wait around?" I asked.

"Well, *I* would, but guys like Brendon don't," he said.

What did he mean? Because Brendon was good-looking and had a little money, it meant he didn't have to have to follow the same decency codes as the less attractive guys? Were there different rules for hot guys?

My stomach hurt as I got into bed that night. My face felt hot like I had been crying, but I was too numb to cry. Darren was right. Brendon had moved on, and I was stupid for thinking he still felt anything for me—if he ever did. I just couldn't believe he could get over me so easily. Could I have meant so little to him? It had taken me months to get over John, and I hadn't even been in love with him. Of course, part of the reason it took me so long to get over John was the betrayal and the fact I had to keep seeing him and his ex around school, which made me cry for weeks. But maybe I wasn't in love with Brendon, either. Maybe my feelings were hurt, and I'd get over it just like I did with John—the stupid spiky-haired jerk who only got back with his ex because she'd sleep with him and I wouldn't. I wonder if Brittanie regretted it because he ended up dumping her for another girl.

I asked Margaux the next day if she had heard if Brendon was dating either Lauren or the redheaded girl who I now called "the Little Mermaid." She hadn't heard anything, but said Lauren was definitely into him. All she knew about the redheaded girl was her name was Nicola, and she used to do fashion shows at the mall. Fabulous. Margaux tried to make me feel better by saying one of her new boyfriend's friends thought I was cute. Unfortunately, it was the one who had a collage of half-naked girls in his locker. Lucky me.

My day only got worse when I found out I was making a D+ in geometry. My teacher suggested I stay after school in the math lab for help. Tyrell came over and sat in the desk next to me.

"How did you do on the last quiz?" he asked.

I rolled my eyes. "I would have done better if I had handed it in blank," I said. "I thought you were a math whiz, though."

He laughed. "I just need to make up a quiz because I was gone all last week."

I had been so wrapped up in my own junk I hadn't even noticed he hadn't been in class. I asked what happened, and he said he hurt his shoulder playing football and had surgery on it.

"How are you feeling?" I asked.

He was telling me about the operation when our teacher came over to work with us. Afterwards, my parents came to pick me up, and I asked Tyrell if he needed a ride. He shook his head, and I walked to the car. Grandpa was sitting in the back, and my mom was in the front seat with my dad.

"Sorry we're late. Grandpa's appointment ran over," Mom said.

"How did it go?" I asked.

Dad sighed. "The doctor still says it's senile dementia and hardening of the arteries, but I still think he has Alz—"

"Clint, I think the doctor is a better judge than you are," Mom said. "Anyway, the doctor explained Alzheimer's is when a person does irrational things like frying your purse on the stove, and he doesn't do things like that. He just has problems with his short-term memory."

Grandpa just sat there, looking out the window. I asked if there was any medicine he could take, and my mother shook her head. It didn't take any intuition to tell that she and my dad had been arguing before I got in the car. We went home, and my mom went into the bathroom and slammed the door. Grandpa stood in the doorway like he didn't know where to go. He was just waiting. My phone rang, and I led Grandpa to the living room.

"Grandpa, I have to get this call, but go sit down, and I'll bring you a snack, okay?"

It was Darren, wanting to make sure I was okay. I thought it was sweet of him to call, and I told him I had to go do something for my grandpa, but I'd e-mail him later. I went to the living room, and Grandpa was still sitting there, wearing his hat and coat. It made me sad he hadn't bothered to take them off, so I hung up his stuff and poured him a glass of fruit juice. Then I cut up some carrots and celery for him to eat. I decided to bring my laptop downstairs so I could be with Grandpa as I did my homework, seeing as my parents had both disappeared as soon as they walked into the house. Grandpa didn't say anything as he ate, and I wondered if he realized anything was wrong.

"When's Mom going to make dinner? I don't want to get too full for supper," he asked. I knew he meant my grandma when he said "Mom," but I pretended he was referring to my mother.

"You mean Gabrielle? She's going to heat up the spaghetti from last night," I said.

"Oh, Gabrielle's cooking then," he said. "Why not Mom?"

"Because she had a stroke, remember?" I asked.

"Oh, right. I just forgot for a minute," he said.

Mom and I went to the hospice after dinner. Grandma's hospice room was pale green, and it had an ethereal feel to it. It felt like I could close my eyes and be transported. I didn't know how Grandma could ever get better in a place which made *me* feel like death was coming for me. I was afraid of the way she was in the hospital with all the tubes stuck in her, but now there was something so scary about the way she seemed in a trance deeper than sleep. As much as I wanted to give her a kiss, I just couldn't do it. Her skin had a waxy look, and I was terrified to touch her other than to hold her hand.

Mom came back in the room and said we should get going. She went over to the bed and leaned down to kiss Grandma, so I went on the other side and leaned over too, but I pretended to kiss her because I couldn't do it. My heart felt heavy as I was walking out of the room, and I realized I would always regret it if I didn't give Grandma a kiss while she was still alive. Saying a prayer for strength, I ran back and gave her a kiss.

Chapter 16

BRENDON WAS WAITING at my locker after school, and he asked me how things were going. Maybe it was because the moon was in Taurus, which was always a bad time for me, but something inside of me just let go.

"Like you care. You didn't even take a minute before you started seeing someone right after we got into an argument, so *excuse* me if I don't take you seriously when you ask how I am," I said.

"Seriously? *You* didn't return my calls. *I* tried."

"That was you trying?"

"Oh please, I tried to talk to you again and again. I threw my dignity away, but I could never do anything right—"

"—I'm sorry you feel being genuinely sorry ruins your dignity. You never got it at all. You didn't understand why I was mad. How was I supposed to be okay with you saying you'd go to a dance with another girl?" I said.

"I know *exactly* why you were mad, and I had no idea how to convince you I wasn't with Lauren—" He stopped and ran his fingers through his hair. "I tried to make it up to you a million times, and you just wouldn't let me.

Emme, I can't talk about this right now because I have a meeting. I have to go," he said, walking away.

I had wanted him to turn around and tell me every day without me had been awful and to swear he'd never take me for granted, but he didn't. Instead, I went to meet Kylie and Zach.

"Emme? Where were you? C'mon let's go," Kylie said. "Geez, what's the matter with you?" she asked after I brushed past her.

"Nothing," I said, and we walked out to the parking lot. She switched the radio on in the car and flipped through the stations. She stopped on a Sweetie Gals song. What were the chances I'd hear a four-year-old song that reminded me of Brendon today? I leaned across the seat and changed the station. She raised her eyebrow at me, but didn't say anything. She didn't speak to me until we got to my house.

"So what's wrong? I'm sorry I was such a jerk before, but I've been PMS-ing today," she said.

"Trust me, she's yelled at *everyone* today," Zach said.

"It's okay. I was late because I ran into Brendon and he—ugh! I mean you realized you were rude and apologized, so why can't he ever apologize? Why are guys so insensitive?"

"I thought he did apologize," Kylie said.

"Only because I got mad at him," I said. "He doesn't even get why I'm still upset. He thinks he can just say 'sorry,' and I'll forgive him because he's cute."

"Did he say it like, 'oh well, sorry,' and then expect you to just forget about it, or did he say it like he realized he had messed up and wanted to fix it?" she asked. "The dance thing—yeah, it's major, but maybe he wasn't thinking."

"He *claims* he tried to make it up to me, and I wouldn't let him. He said he wasn't seeing Lauren, and he put it all back on me."

"Wow, he wants you to know he's not with Lauren? Sounds like he's trying. But can I just say maybe he's right because you do tend to get kinda defensive—see? You're doing it now, Em. I make one tiny comment, and you give me that look," she said.

"What look? I don't have a look," I said.

Kylie rolled her eyes. "The one where you look like you're going to turn me into an ice cube. Would it be so bad to give him another chance?"

"He obviously doesn't want another chance because he walked away from me in the library."

"Maybe he was upset and needed to get away. You should call him," she said.

"And let him hang up on me? He's moved on with the Little Mermaid."

"You don't even know if he likes her. Call him or else you'll wonder 'what if' forever," she said.

I don't know if it was because I had gotten another D on a math quiz and I felt the need to add to my crappy day or maybe it was because I heard yet another Sweetie Gals song on the radio and took it as a sign, but I called him at night. At first, I thought he didn't recognize my voice on the phone because he had no emotion in his voice, but it didn't change after I said, "It's Emme."

I realized it had been a mistake to call because I thought he'd do the talking, but he didn't. We sat in silence, and I had no idea what to say because I didn't know what he was feeling. I didn't want to look desperate, like I was trying to get back together if he had moved on. Maybe it wasn't a big deal to him.

"I just wanted to see how you were doing," I said. "And to say I was sorry I got an attitude with you earlier."

"I'm fine…and you?" he asked.

"Okay. How are your classes?"

"Good. Yours? Just a minute." He put the phone

down, and I could hear him talking to someone and the TV on. Then I heard a girl's voice. Here I thought there was half a chance he was home upset over me and instead he had a "friend" over. He came back on the line, and I told him I had to go. I hung up feeling worse. Sure, he didn't hang up on me, but he didn't sound thrilled to hear from me either.

Rory and I ate lunch together the next day. She told me she had been in love with Tom ever since the night of the writing competition. He still thought he was better than the rest of the class, and now he'd only work with her or Darren, the ones he considered the "serious writers," if we had to work in groups.

"I know Tom comes off kind of jerky, but he's sensitive and deep," she said. "He said he liked the way I tipped the ends of my hair purple. Most people don't even notice because my hair's so dark."

I nodded, even though I thought Tom was an arrogant poser. Most of the guys in the class were depressing, and I was sick of hearing all the poems on death. It was more like a therapy group than a writing class. One guy had written a poem about how it would feel to be dead, and a girl wrote a poem I thought was about birds, but Rory said it was actually about suicide.

"If I wanted to deal with death, I'd hang out at the hospice full-time. I go to class to get away from death talk, you know?" I said. "I thought it was supposed to be a fun class."

"Yeah, fun for people who like to cut themselves," she said. "So do you like Darren?"

"He's sweet, but I suck at relationships. I have, like, trust issues, but I don't even think it's just me being paranoid because both times I was right. Anyway, I do like him, but I'm not sure if I want a boyfriend right now."

"Plus, you still got a thing for Brendon," she said.

—•—

MARGAUX AND I went to have coffee the next day, and she asked me to go to Lauren's party with her. I didn't want to spend the evening hanging out in the house of some girl who was always trying to date my ex. Instead, I wanted to veg on the couch and watch *To Catch a Thief* on TV. Was Margaux trying to get me out of the house to cheer me up, or was she was too self-centered to realize I was going through a lot right now just because she didn't want to go to the party alone?

"You don't even talk to Lauren at school," I said. "So why would you want to go to her house?"

"Puh-lease," she said in her annoying baby voice. For some reason, she thought it made her look cute. "I'll do your math homework for a week."

"You don't even do your own homework," I said.

"Well, I was going to let you copy Tyrell's when I was done with it," she said. "Please go with me? You can see what Lauren's like in her...crap, what's the science term? Natural habitat? C'mon. Don't you want to see what her house looks like?"

"Okay, but you totally owe me," I said. "And we're doing signals. If I want to leave, I'm going to say something about having to babysit early tomorrow morning, and then we leave, all right?"

She said her brother, Dominick, would give us a ride to the party, and then we could call him to pick us up. Rory walked into the coffee shop and sat next to me at the counter. She was in a bad mood because she had seen Tom walking with his on-and-off again girlfriend.

"I think I'm going to straighten my hair for Lauren's party," Margaux said.

"I'm going to it, too," Rory said. "But only because Tom's going."

—

DOMINICK DROPPED US off at the party, and the second we walked into the living room, Margaux walked over to three junior guys and started flirting with the taller, blond guy. My house was nice, but Lauren's house didn't just beat it, it kicked its butt and took its wallet. My house was white with dark wood, but her house was warm shades of yellow and brown. It was also spacious. The kitchen opened into the family room and living room, and even the downstairs had one of those walkout apartment things, which meant Lauren had her own little part of the house with a family room and flat-screen TV. Rory and I met up downstairs and saw Lauren's perfect, yellow bedroom, which had a sitting room with a huge chaise lounge. It was like something you'd see in a magazine.

"Can't you just see some actress sitting on chaise lounge, posing with, like, her journal for *In Style*?" Rory asked.

"Would it be weird to look in her bathroom?" I asked, peering in.

"No, but don't open any cabinets," she said. "I read in this magazine how some girl opened up the medicine cabinet and the owners had put marbles and stuff in there so they'd know if anybody snooped."

Crap. I had wanted to see what kind of makeup or, more importantly, shampoo Lauren used. It irritated me that even her hair was the opposite of mine. Her straight, dark hair always fell perfectly into place and stayed bouncy. Mine was never straight or curly—just wavy, and it was a weird shade of dark brown that got a red tint from all the minerals if I washed my hair in hard water.

"Look at her tub," Rory said. "I love these claw-foot ones. Like something out of an old movie."

I shrugged, but I was dying inside. She had the exact tub I had always wanted. Whenever I got stressed during an exam, I'd always go to my "happy place" in my mind, which was a claw-foot tub full of warm water and bubbles. Now my "happy place" had been invaded by Lauren and her tub of evil. I decided to take a chance and opened the cabinet under the sink. No shampoo, but I did find out her "natural look" got a little help from several makeup counters.

"Look at these pads," Rory said, looking over my shoulder. "Aren't those for people who wet themselves? Does Lauren pee in her pants at school? Dude, I will never be able to look her in the eye now, knowing that."

"I dunno, she could have a medical condition," I said.

Rory moved the package, and then I saw it, sitting in the little container that held her lipsticks and compacts. There was a plastic disk, which could only be one thing.

"Oh wow, Lauren's on the pill?" Rory said, as my stomach felt like it was dropping fifty stories.

"Do you think that means...?"

"Probably just for cramps, you know, another medical condition," she said, closing the cabinet.

Rory wouldn't look at me as she stood up. Was this the reason Brendon was so quick to go back to Lauren? It was like John and Brittanie all over again.

"Crap, somebody's coming," Rory said, pulling the bathroom door shut. "If someone tries to come in here, we'll just say we had to pee."

"Together?" I whispered.

"We're super close—now shut up."

I stood at the door listening and realized Lauren was in the room with her best friend, Madison.

"So what's going on with you and Brendon?" Madison asked.

"I dunno. He's being weird," Lauren said. "He calls me and stuff, but something's off."

"Is he still into that Emme chick?"

Lauren sighed. "I checked his phone the other night,

and her number was on it. So I don't know if he called her or if she called him, but it was definitely her. It was probably her calling him. She's *so* pathetic. I wish he'd just get her out of his system. They have *nothing* in common, so I have no clue why he's not over her."

Rory put her hand over my mouth in case I was tempted to scream. We waited five minutes after we heard Madison and Lauren leave before we opened the door.

"So he's not her boyfriend, and she's aware you're still 'in his system,'" Rory said. I nodded, but the part about me being "pathetic" was echoing in my mind, and what I had seen in her bathroom was making me queasy.

We went upstairs just in time to see Lauren walk up and slide her hand up Brendon's arm. Meanwhile, Tom was over in the corner with his girlfriend.

"Well, this is fun," I said as I watched Brendon talk to Lauren. He started to walk away, and she pulled his arm back.

"I know. I want to go, too. I'm going to find Katia," Rory said. "Come with me." She started to head toward the hall when she noticed Brendon and Lauren in deep conversation. "Let's try the kitchen."

I tried motioning to Margaux I wanted to go, but she wouldn't look in my direction, and I didn't want to go up to her since Brendon and Lauren were over there. Rory came back and said Katia wanted to stay.

"Tom and his girlfriend are making out, and I just want to get out of here. Do you want to go to a movie or something?" she asked.

Margaux kept ignoring me, so I decided to leave without telling her. I was glad Rory had her car because I don't think I could have stood one more minute of watching Lauren hang onto Brendon.

We went to the theater, which was filled with a bunch of little kids who were sticky from who knows what. The only movie not sold out was *The Cutie Pies' Big Adventure.*

"I hate the Cutie Pies," she said. "My little brother watches the show, and it makes me physically ill."

"Well, we could walk the mall until the nine o'clock showing of the new Ally Patterson movie," I said, and she groaned. "I know you hate Ally *and* mall walkers, but I'll buy you some licorice at the candy store, and we can go to the bookstore."

"Okay, but if I get run over by any strollers—"

"I'll protect you," I said.

We went to the candy store and stocked up on licorice ropes and gum for the movie. Then we had blueberry-peach smoothies and read magazines and tabloids until the movie started. I had completely forgotten about my problems until the grandfather in the movie was diagnosed with Alzheimer's. I wanted to leave, but I didn't want to have to go into why I wanted to with Rory. She just sat there, chewing her licorice. I finally lost it when the old man in the movie wandered away from the home and got hit by a car.

"Hey, do you mind if we go?" I asked.

"It's almost over," she said.

"I know, I just feel sick all of a sudden," I said. I got up and walked out of the theater as Ally was asking the doctor about her grandfather's condition. Rory followed me out of the theater and asked if I wanted to stop in the bathroom before we left. I assured her I wouldn't puke in her car, and she took me home. My dad was sitting in the kitchen when I came in.

"How was the party?" he asked.

I shrugged. "We ended up going to a movie. Any news on Grandma?"

Dad shook his head. "We went up there, but nothing's changed. I'm glad you went out tonight."

"Why?" I asked.

"Your mom and I are concerned over how much time you've been spending in the hospital and at the hospice, along with watching Grandpa, too. I know you want to be there for your grandparents, but we worry it might not be healthy for you. Sometimes I forget how young you are to go through all of this. I was in college before I dealt with anything like this, and I know how it impacted me. You're mature for your age, but you are still a kid—sorry, teen," he said, smiling. "You have been so strong for everyone, and I don't think your grandfather would be doing this well without you. Still, I don't want to put too much on you."

"I want to be there for them, and I feel like Grandpa is calmer if I'm there."

"Yes, but I don't want you to sacrifice your high school years either, including homework or going out with friends. Your mom and I realized we might have leaned on you a little too much, so just know we appreciate it, but you get to have a life, too."

I nodded, and Dad gave me a hug.

"This is your way of saying it's not going to be okay, isn't it?" I asked.

He squeezed me tighter. "You can always read between the lines, can't you?"

"Please don't put Grandpa in a home. I don't mind sacrificing going out if it means he can live with family."

"Honey, we're not there yet. No decisions have been made, but I appreciate your willingness to help. Not many teenagers would offer."

Tears were running down my face now. "Promise you'll—"

"I promise you we will consider every avenue possible and do what's in his best interest, okay? Because it might come down to it that staying with us *isn't* in his best interest."

I wiped my eyes and nodded. Dad went to work in his office, and my cell phone rang. It was Margaux, wondering if I got home okay. I was still so emotional from my talk with Dad, and it showed.

"A lot you care. I could be dead in a ditch since you abandoned me," I said.

"Someone said you left with Rory. Nice of you to tell me you were leaving. Seth took me home," she said.

"Nice of me? Excuse me, who took off and left who now?"

"We just went to get some soda," she said.

"For an hour? Which one's Seth? The skinny one who looks like the chemistry teacher?" I said.

"He does *not* look like Mr. Carpenter. Anyway, he wanted me to meet his friends—"

"While I sat waiting like an idiot? I just—you knew I was anxious about going there in the first place, and I wish you could have been more sensitive and understood when I wanted to leave."

"I'm *sorry*, okay? I'll buy you lunch at the mall to make it up to you tomorrow," she said.

Well, I would have gone anywhere to get away from my house and all my problems. Her brother came over to pick me up in the morning. Margaux and I went to Sami Boutique's first, and we both found stuff to try on. I called her over to my dressing room to show her the dress I tried on. She came over with her cell phone.

"I'm leaving a message for Seth," she said.

"Do you guys have plans later?" I asked.

"No, he just wanted me to check in," she said, putting her phone away.

"For real?"

"He likes to know where I am," she said, walking back to her dressing room. She was acting like they were a couple now, when they had just met last night.

"So you guys are going out now?" I asked, struggling to stuff myself into a pair of size seven jeans. Why did I always try to force the issue when I was actually a size nine?

"We're just hanging out," she said. She always used

to complain guys only said "just hanging out" if they thought somebody better was going to come along. "Don't you think he's cute?"

I knew Margaux needed my approval because she couldn't go out, or "hang out," with anyone her friends didn't find hot. I could have ended the whole relationship there with one "Eww," but I said he was cute so I wouldn't have to listen to "What's wrong with him?" all afternoon. It was just easier to go along with what she wanted to hear.

I didn't end up buying anything, but Margaux did buy me a lip gloss, so I knew she wanted me to forgive her. We decided to eat, and she mentioned she was craving pizza. I knew she was trying to get me to go to the cheap pizza place in the mall since she had offered to pay, but I wanted something healthier and said I had been dying for a salad from Hill's. We got a booth and ordered iced teas and breadsticks while she checked out the menu. She told me she had invited Seth to go horseback riding tomorrow and asked if I wanted to come along.

"I could invite one of his friends to come, too," she said.

"No thanks," I said as the waitress came to take our order. "I get anxious around horses."

"I wish you'd come. It won't be any fun without you." She was slipping into baby talk again. How did she flirt with guys if she drove *me* crazy with the baby voice? I wondered if Seth was deaf or something.

We finished eating, and I decided to ask Margaux what she thought about the whole pill thing I saw at Lauren's house.

"I need to ask you about something—"

"Let's go to the candy store," Margaux said, grabbing my arm. "I need some gum."

While I wanted to get her advice, Margaux just wanted to talk to the guys who were in the candy store, and, of course, they came right over and started talking to her. One of the guys, Steve, said he was a senior at a nearby school. He was a little shorter, had a mustache, and was one of those guys who actually wore their class rings. Not my type at all. She was giving him her cutesy voice, which was just a step away from her baby voice. He ended up buying us gum, which made me uncomfortable, but we were out of there before he had a chance to ask for any phone numbers. Margaux was all about getting a guy to ask for her number, but she rarely wanted to date the guys. She just wanted them to ask her out. It made me uncomfortable because these guys would go out of their way for her, and I wished she just let them know she wasn't interested. We were walking to the makeup counter at the department store when I saw Brooke, Jayson's girlfriend, walking with some guy.

"That's Brendon's brother's girlfriend," I said. "I wonder who she's with."

Margaux shrugged. "Probably just a friend. What do you think of this liner? Is it too plum? I want it to be plum, but not *too* plum, you know?"

I said the liner was fine, but my instincts told me Brooke was cheating on Jayson. She wasn't holding the guy's hand or anything, but I knew something wasn't right.

We went to a few more stores, and I noticed Margaux kept checking her phone for texts when she thought I wasn't paying attention.

"I thought you two didn't have plans for tonight," I said.

"Nothing planned." She bit her lip. "I just thought he might want to do something tonight."

I was planning to ask her if she wanted to come over later tonight, after I got home from visiting Grandma, but I didn't feel like being second choice, so I said I needed to get home. Margaux called her brother to pick us up, and we waited in silence. She kept trying to start a conversation, but I wasn't in the mood to talk. We used to have so much fun together, and now she was acting all stupid over a guy. Her cell phone rang, and she almost dropped it in her frenzy to answer. It was obvious it was Seth.

"Hmmm? Just a sec, Em, did you want to do something tonight?" she asked. I knew she'd freak out if I said "yes," but at least she pretended to care.

"I have plans already," I said. She was busy making plans when her brother pulled up. Normally she and I sat in back and had Dominick play chauffeur, but this time I got in front with him. Margaux was still talking to Seth, and Dominick asked if she was annoying me half as much as she was him. I nodded.

"I want to throw her stupid phone out the window," he said. "Hey, do you guys want to stop and get some ice cream?"

Margaux had told me once before Dom liked me, which was why he didn't mind driving us around. He was a nice guy, but it would be too weird to date my friend's brother. I would have stopped to get ice cream, but Margaux said she had to get home to meet Seth, so Dominick dropped me off.

"Hey," I said, coming into the kitchen where my mom was making a smoothie. "What time are we going to see Grandma?"

"I went earlier, and she was agitated."

"She was conscious?"

Mom sighed and shook her head. "Like she's been, but they gave her something to calm her. So we decided not to go back tonight. It's what's best for her, Emme."

I wanted to ask questions, but my mom appeared so tired and older than I had ever seen her look. As she moved a strand of hair out of her face, I saw how lifeless her eyes were. As much as I wanted to talk about what was going on with her, I didn't want to add another burden on her, so I went to my room to check my e-mail.

To: tryBus
From: Rsegwick
  Hey! Are you doing anything tonight? I was thinking about going to a psychic fair and maybe seeing another movie or something. Interested? Call me when you get home because I've got some BIG news.
  Rory

We made plans, and I got my dad to drop me off at her apartment. Rory was waiting in the hall when I got there.

"Do you want to do the psychic fair? I cleansed my chakras so I'd be open for a reading," she said.

As we drove to the fair, she told me her big news. I thought it was about Tom, but Katia had called her this morning and told her Brendon and Lauren got into an argument after we left the party.

"Katia said she only heard part of it, but it was over you. Lauren wants you completely out of the picture, and Brendon's obviously still into you," she said. "Katia said Lauren was in her math class last year when they were dating, and she was always coming in late because of him. If he wrote her a note, she'd make a huge deal of reading it so that everybody could see, but they used to fight all the time," she said. "Basically Katia said when they broke up last year it was because Brendon told Lauren she was too clingy, and he didn't want a girlfriend right now. But then he started dating you, and Lauren was super annoyed."

"I don't know why she's mad at me," I said. "She's the one he's going to the dance with, and it's not like he's throwing himself at my feet."

"He still checks up on you though, right?"

"Yeah, but I think he doesn't want things to be weird

between us, and he kind of knows what I'm going through, so it makes sense he'd check on how my grandma's doing," I said. "Trust me, I wanted to read more into it, but I didn't want to get my hopes up."

We got to the fair, and there was a list of all the different types of readers who were there.

"I'm going to the woman who deals in karma and past-life stuff," Rory said. "What about you? There's guardian angels stuff, numerology, auras, past-life regressions, astrology—anything sound good to you?"

I decided to go for a reading with a woman who seemed like a younger version of my grandma. She handed me her tarot cards and told me to think about my question while I shuffled them. Even though I had a million things I wanted to know about my future, the first image that popped into my mind was Brendon, so I thought about our relationship as I shuffled.

"I'm going to do a past, present, and future reading first," she said as she pulled out a card. The Death card came up first. Great, I ask for guidance on my relationship, and I get the death card. Lovely.

"This means your thoughts and beliefs will change as you let go of old habits. You might question what you're doing, but there are new opportunities on the horizon, so you must move forward and let go of the past. Open yourself up to what the future can bring you," she said. I wondered if it meant I had to let go of my relationship with Brendon or all my feelings about relationships.

"The present card is the Lovers card, which means a relationship has recently come into your life or you need to make a decision regarding love soon. Your intuition is going to be strong now, and you will be using your heart rather than your head to make decisions. There's a strong emotional attachment toward someone," she said as she flipped over the next card. "Your outcome card is the Universe, which means you must focus on changing something in your life in order to succeed. This card is about having confidence and success."

I didn't say anything, and she continued. "It's all telling you that you need to let go of old negative habits and be willing to change and open yourself up. If you do it, then success is imminent. But I don't need the cards to tell there's something on your mind, so let's try this. Pick a few cards from the deck." She put the cards face down as I picked a couple.

"Okay, King of Cups reversed," she said, nodding. "This means there are some questionable dealings in your life right now. Also loss, suffering, sickness. It also represents a man who cares only for his personal welfare. There is deceitfulness around you."

All I could think of was a cartoon character running around saying, "There's treachery afoot." Of course, it was cute when a cartoon toddler said it, but not so cute when someone was telling you how someone was trying to deceive you.

"The next one you picked was the Tower. Right now, soul searching will save you a lot of trouble. If you don't listen to what your intuition is trying to tell you, then you might as well prepare for the worst. We all need to forget our ideas on how things should turn out because there are bound to be surprises, and I'm getting you'll definitely have an unexpected revelation soon, but I'm sensing it'll be positive—if you open yourself up to it."

The next card dealt with the stereotype of the broken-hearted lover, and she said I was to ignore the stereotype because it was all about holding onto the past and not moving forward. She said I wasn't missing what was in the past, but it was an excuse to avoid new relationships.

"Wait, I'm confused. Does this mean I *don't* want my old relationship back?" I asked.

"Do you think you were over-romanticizing it?" she asked. I shook my head. "Maybe the past you need to let go of isn't the relationship itself, but the events which led up to the relationship going sour."

She flipped over my next card. "The Nine of Wands is warning you about looking for trouble. How much of the fears are based on the pain of the past? You need to see each situation for what it is and not apply things from other areas to it. If there is trouble, then you'll be able to rise to the challenge. You're prepared for whatever comes your way. Don't use all your energy into protecting yourself because you can't experience life this way."

The next card she flipped over was the Ace of Cups, which was about love. She told me the card's appearance "proclaimed a time of great connectedness," and the walls I had built up were coming down. I didn't say anything, and she told me to pick another card.

"The Four of Swords represents recuperation, healing, and leaving a stressful situation behind in order to clear your head and reevaluate your plans."

Well, it certainly fit with all I had been going through at home.

"Do some soul searching to gain direction. This card is telling you to trust love and don't let fear keep you away," she said.

Rory came over to me when my reading was over. "My reader practically said Tom and I were soul mates," she said. "Of course, she did say my soul mate could be like my grandpa or my hamster or whatever, but she did say I had met my soul mate already and it had male energy. It's gotta be Tom. I don't even own a hamster."

Rory decided to get an aura reading, and I went to an intuitive reader, Layla, who also worked in picking out crystals for you.

"I'm sensing three cords around you. One you need to let go of because it's tethering you to someone who needs to be released. It might be a loved one who is ill, and you're worried they might die." I didn't say anything, but I could tell I didn't need to because she put her hand over mine. "It's okay to let go for both your sakes, but only do what is comfortable for you. There's another cord, and I feel someone is almost suffocating you. You need to cut this one for certain. There's another one holding you to a person, but I don't feel any negative energy behind this. I just feel there's something holding you two together, but it's more on his end," she said. "He wants to stay connected."

I wondered if it was either Brendon or Darren. She noticed my bracelet and asked if I knew about the healing powers of rose quartz. I told her Grandma had given it to me and asked her what else would help Grandma's condition and my situation with Brendon and Darren.

"Well, for your grandmother, pink calcite helps us release old fears and is good for grief and unconditional love. You said you gave her lapis, which is also good for strokes and bringing emotional baggage to the surface," she said. "Your bracelet is also for relationship stress and comfort when you feel sad. Peridot's good for grief, too."

"What about like dementia? My grandpa—it's not Alzheimer's, but—" My voice broke.

"My father had Alzheimer's," she said. "Agate is good for it and so is rose quartz. It looks like your grandma knew what she was doing when she gave you the bracelet. Here, I'm going to give you an agate and a polished rose quartz you can put in your grandfather's room."

I asked her how much I owed her for the crystals, and she said shook her head. "I've had to deal with dementia and Alzheimer's before, so this is my little way of helping. What we put out, we get back."

Thanking her, I got up to look for Rory. I had an unsettled feeling about everything. It felt like the readings brought up more drama than I expected and made me feel sick. This fair was supposed to give me peace and answers—wasn't that the whole reason people got into stuff like this? Enlightenment and peace? Instead I felt anxious and uncomfortable with knowing too much was coming around the corner. As I went searching for Rory, I saw a woman sitting at a table with the banner *Life Coaching with Cheryl*, and it was only ten dollars for a session. Well, what did I have to lose?

"Hi, I want a session or whatever. I'm not real sure what a life coach does, but I felt like this was where I needed to be," I said, sitting down.

Smiling, she asked me to share what was troubling me. This was different, seeing as the rest of the people at this fair had told me what my problems were.

"Where to start? Well, my relationship is in the toilet, my grandmother is in a semi-coma and no one seems to think she'll recover, my grandpa apparently has dementia, and I'm losing it," I said.

"So a lot on your plate right now," she said.

"I feel like I don't know what I'm doing, and every time I think I know, I do something stupid."

"What do you mean?"

"Well, I want to get back with my boyfriend, but it seems like every time we're around each other and things are going well, we suddenly get into an argument."

"Does he seem to start it or you?" she asked.

"I guess I do, but it's in reaction to things he's done."

"Do you think it's unresolved feelings coming to the surface or self-sabotage?"

"Why would I sabotage something I want, though?"

"Do you have any reason to fear getting close to him? A fear of intimacy or perhaps mistrust?"

I swallowed hard. "Well, my last boyfriend did cheat on me, and with this new guy—well, I'm uncomfortable with the way his ex is around him so much, and honestly, it's like every other girl seems to flirt with him."

"Okay, but does he give you any reason to not trust

him? Does he encourage these other girls and is anything shady going on you know of?" she asked.

Shifting in my seat, I had to admit Brendon hadn't done anything outright.

"I guess not. Maybe my ex is making me question everything, and well, I feel like I'm numb over this whole thing with my grandma. I'm not sure if I'm in denial or what, but it's like I feel torn between going to see her and staying with my grandpa, who is confused all the time now."

"Dementia is difficult," Cheryl said. "I had two grandfathers with it and a great-aunt. It is a game changer for a family."

"Does it ever get better? The dementia, I mean," I asked.

She patted my hand. "Not health-wise, but you learn to love them a little deeper. You see them vulnerable, and for some people it can change the relationship in a good way. I can tell you care a lot about your grandfather, and it will strengthen your bond. With my grandfather, I became the caregiver as I watched him when I came home from school so my mom could go out and do her cleaning jobs at night. Grandpa and I got closer, and although it hurt he sometimes called me by his sister's name, I knew deep down he loved me. And there was this innocence to him which made me want to be there for him and help him feel less confused."

"I get it," I said as my eyes watered.

"This might sound strange, but I get the feeling you're blocking your own intuition and common sense and relying on things like New Age things and crystals to make decisions for you."

My back straightened. "What do you mean?"

"Intuition can be a gift or something negative, depending on how you use it and where it's coming from. All of the tarot cards, aura readings, etcetera—it shows a lack of faith in the future. I'm not trying to knock what others are doing here, but my purpose is to try to get people on the right track and not just buying yet another crystal to try to solve a problem which talking things out would help."

I tried to move my left arm, which had a stack of crystal bracelets on it, out of her sight.

She laughed. "You can wear your bracelets as long as you don't rely on them to give you superpowers. I used to be so into numerology and wouldn't make a move unless my horoscope said it was okay. Now I come to these events to try and help others who were like me and afraid to make their own decisions. Sometimes I find someone who realizes their chakras didn't need to be opened, but their emotions did. I did turn to New Age stuff when things weren't going right in my own life, and it did way more harm than good. It's dangerous to open your mind to occult things, so I come here to try to help people sort their own stuff out."

"I think that's what I've been doing," I said. "It seemed more reliable to add up numbers than to…I dunno…"

"Trust your own reasoning and instincts?"

"But lately it feels like they're always wrong," I said. "And right now I can't get hurt by another guy—especially with everything else going on in my life."

She nodded. "So often people go to get their cards read because they're running from something, and they want someone else to be responsible for making the next decision. But it's okay to make a wrong decision because it's how you grow as a person. What you're going through now with your grandparents is uncertain and scary, and I want you to know anyone in your position would be scared, so it's okay to admit. And after what you went through with your first boyfriend, it makes sense you'd have trust issues, but you should stop and look at this new guy and not put any of the old guy's stuff on him."

"Makes sense. Numerology-wise we do fit, and I thought I was getting signs about us, too."

"Do you think you're relying on those things instead of your own feelings because you don't trust yourself?" she asked.

My stomach did a flip, and I knew she was right.

"Sometimes it feels like my intuition doesn't work when it comes to this kind of stuff—like I'm too close to the situation. I can sooner pick basketball game winners than I can a decent boyfriend," I said.

"Take a step back and just look at the facts and look at who these boys show you they are—not what their birthdates show you, but what they reveal to you through their actions."

"Makes more sense than what I've been doing."

"I'm not telling you to take off your bracelets, I'm just saying rely on your own good judgment instead of a card or a horoscope, okay? New Age stuff often tells you what you want to hear, and it's not a healthy way to live."

"This was so not what I expected, but exactly what I needed," I said.

Cheryl got up and hugged me. "You remind me so much of me when I was your age. Someone set me on the right path, and now this what I do in trying to make up for all the tables of people promising to change your life with a chakra cleansing. I know these people mean well, but sometimes it's easier to put a bandage on something, rather than fix it from the inside. When people are lost, they need more than a crystal or reading, and some of this stuff can be dangerous."

"Thank you," I said, and Cheryl squeezed my hand and gave me her card.

Rory was waiting for me and showed me her aura picture. "Did you learn anything interesting?" she asked.

"Definitely."

"Ooh, you got some crystals," she said.

"One of the readers gave me some for my grandpa."

"You mean your grandma?"

"Well, he's going through a lot right now, too," I said. My parents had been so secretive about Grandpa's condition and not wanting anyone other than my aunt and uncle to know. It made it seem like it was something to be embarrassed about, even though it wasn't. I mean, maybe Grandpa wouldn't want the whole world knowing he couldn't remember his wife was in the hospital, but it was nothing to be ashamed of.

"He has dementia," I said.

"I didn't know. My great-grandma had it, too. Is this why you wanted to leave the movie the other day?" she asked. "You should have said something. The movie brought back some stuff for me, too. I wish you had told me because I was getting a little upset during it. I didn't want to look like a dork crying, so I just kept stuffing food in my face."

"This time let's go see a comedy," I said.

She drove us to the theater, and as soon as we walked in, she asked me, "You wanna just forget the movie and go get coffee or something?"

"Why?"

"Okay, fine, Brendon's here and I didn't want you to freak out in case he's with Lauren," she said. "I'm pretty convinced he's into you, but if I could read guys, then Tom wouldn't still be with his loser."

I just saw the back of his head as he walked into the theater. He was with a group of people, but I couldn't tell if Lauren was there. We sat in the back, and I stared at the backs of heads, trying to figure out which one was Brendon. I finally picked him out and realized he was sitting next to Lauren, and I spent the whole movie watching the two of them. My hopes went down the toilet. I wished I had never heard Lauren was jealous of me because it just got my hopes up, and in the end it didn't matter. She was with him and I wasn't.

When I got home, I saw I had an e-mail from Darren, asking me to call him.

"Hey, what's up?" I asked.

"Do you want to go to homecoming with me? I mean, we could just go and make fun of people."

"Seriously? I'd love to. It'll be fun."

I called Kylie the second I got off the phone, but I got her voice mail, so I called Margaux.

"Cool. We'll all go together," she said. "Seth, Kylie, Zach, and I are all getting a car together, so you can ride with us. Oh, and Kylie and I are getting our hair done together before the dance, so I'll call and see if they can fit you in, too."

When school started, I pictured myself going to homecoming with Brendon, but going with Darren would be fun, and after all, he was always there for me when I needed him.

Chapter 17

MARGAUX CAME INTO class and sat down with a dramatic sigh. She was waiting for us to ask what was wrong, and I prayed no one would because it'd just encourage her with this Seth guy. Plus, I was still annoyed she picked hanging out with Seth over spending time with me.

"What's wrong?" Kylie asked her.

"Seth didn't meet me by my locker this morning, so when he came to my locker now, he's all, 'What's your problem?' And I wouldn't tell him what was wrong because he should just know, right? Then, get this," she said, flinging her hair back. "He starts to walk away, so I grabbed his hand, and he was like, 'What?'"

"Why don't you dump him?" I asked. I was sick of hearing about him.

"I *like* him. I just hate when he tries to act cool around his friends," she said. "Besides, I already have my dress for the dance, and Maxie's won't take it back once they start doing alterations."

If I were ever involved with somebody who required my presence at their locker at specific times under penalty of cold shoulder and had to spend every waking moment paying attention to them—oh wow, I think *I've* dated Margaux.

"What are you so mad about, Em? Everybody's talking about the fight Brendon and Lauren got into at the party over you. He's so not over you," Kylie said. She started to say something else when Ms. Cruz came in, and we all faced forward. She passed out the lit assignment, and the room got quiet as everyone began reading. My mind wouldn't focus on the page, and I passed Kylie a note about how I had seen Brendon sitting with Lauren at the movies. We spent the entire hour passing notes. Margaux bolted out of the room when the bell rang, and I saw Seth waiting for her at her locker. Tomorrow we would hear how great he was once again. I went to Rory's locker, and we walked to the lunchroom and got the hot lunch special. Rory picked up her burnt roll and pulled it apart, eating only the soft middle and leaving a little charred pile on her tray.

After school, Kylie walked me to my locker. I made sure to walk extra slowly past the hallway where Brendon hung out. He had his head in his locker and didn't look up as we walked by.

My dad was waiting for me so we could go to the hospice to check on Grandma. She appeared like she was in a deep sleep when we saw her. Sometimes she acted like she was sort of awake even though she was in a coma, but today she didn't seem aware we were in the room. On the way out, Dad and I stopped and lit a candle for her in the hospice chapel. There was a big painting of Jesus standing on a cloud and hugging someone who had just come to heaven. I knew most of the people in the hospice were terminal, but did the whole place have to reek of death? Shouldn't there be some glimmer of hope they might get better and get to go home?

I was so depressed I forgot I had promised to go shopping with Kylie after dinner. She showed up at the door, took one look at me in my sweatpants, and asked if I forgot we had plans.

"Sorry, I did. Things have been crazy, but let me get my bag."

I ran over to my mom. "I forgot I was supposed to go look for a homecoming dress with Kylie tonight."

"Well, you've had a lot on your mind. It's understandable. There's some cash in my upstairs desk drawer. Just don't get anything too expensive—or low-cut. And Emme, just hold everything up to the Sweetie Gals test—if one of them would wear it, then I won't pay for it." Like I could have pulled it off even if I wanted to.

In the car, I listened to Kylie talk about the dress she wanted. It was pretty warm for late October in Michigan, so she wanted something short, strappy, and cute. However, I couldn't get into dress shopping. I always heard the best part of going to dances was shopping with your friends for the dress, so I tried to act like I was having fun. Kylie even called Margaux and told her to meet us at the mall, which was a huge sacrifice on her part since she hated shopping with Margaux. We went to Maxie's first.

"Okay, do you guys like this one in blue or red?" Kylie asked, holding up two hangers. "Is the print weird?"

"No, I like the flowers. It's different. I like the red, but try them both on," Margaux said. I picked out a couple of black dresses, but Margaux said I shouldn't wear black to the dance. "Besides, it would look weird next to my dress since mine's more summery—like the ones Kylie's trying on."

I sighed and pretended to look through the rack.

"Do you want me to help you pick something out?" Margaux asked. I shook my head. A long time ago Kylie and I had talked about whether or not you could trust Margaux when it came to shopping. Sometimes she'd tell you something was pretty on you when it actually wasn't. At first, I didn't get what she was trying to do, but then there was this time when I tried on two sweaters. One of the sweaters fit me well, and the other made me look like I was swimming in it. Yet Margaux said she liked the bigger one on me. It was obvious which one fit me better, so Kylie and I never trusted her judgment when it came to clothes. Probably why Kylie ended up buying the blue dress even though Margaux swore that the red one was prettier.

"Okay Em, now we're on a mission to find you the perfect dress," Kylie said.

I found a dress, another black one, which was a little different than the usual homecoming dresses. It was black and knee-length, but with long sleeves that had a slit so it revealed part of your arm. It was more sophisticated than the strappy dresses everyone else would be wearing.

"No black," Margaux said. "Em, you always say what color you wear affects your mood, so why would you want a black dress? Plus, long sleeves for a dance...I dunno, I just don't think it's a homecoming dress."

"It's kinda like the awards show dress the actress Tina Carlsen wore," I said. "I love it, but is it *too* different?"

"Well, it would definitely get you noticed. It's gorgeous and I loved it on Tina, but I'm not sure it's a homecoming dress," Kylie said.

I ended up trying on a bunch of dresses Kylie picked out. The first one was green, but a little tight. On the plus side, it gave me cleavage, but I could barely breathe in it. I didn't like the blue shimmery one Margaux picked out because it was long and it made me look too tall.

"What do we have left?" Margaux asked. "Okay, there's the navy strapless one, but it might be hard to keep it up all night. What? Don't glare at me. Even I couldn't hold up a strapless dress all night."

"Give me the red one," I said. I came out in it and Kylie nodded.

"Not too short, not too tight. Perfect," she said.

"The three of us won't match," Margaux said. "But maybe we can put the guys in between us for the pictures so it won't matter. Hey, is it okay if Seth and I meet you guys at the game instead of going all together?"

I had invited Darren to go to the game with us, but he had to work since he had taken Saturday off for the dance. As I paid for my dress, I noticed Margaux and Kylie standing on the side looking worried and talking. I knew it was about me and how they had been looking forward to dress shopping. I had put a damper on the whole thing. How did people go through the motions of life when things got crappy? I mean, I couldn't be the only high schooler dealing with stuff like a grandparent in hospice and one with dementia, right? It sure felt like I was alone right now.

Chapter 18

I SPENT THE next few nights at the hospice with my mom. Grandma never woke up or even stirred while we were there. Mom made me bring my homework, but who could focus when I knew my time with Grandma was getting shorter? Every second I spent at the hospice made me feel guilty about leaving Grandpa on his own at home with Dad where Grandpa would ask him over and over where Mom and I were. But then when I'd get home and stay with Grandpa, I'd feel guilty that I wasn't at the hospice.

On the night of the homecoming game, Kylie came over after school and went through my closet to find me the perfect outfit to wear to the game. She kept holding things up for my approval, but I wasn't in the mood.

"C'mon, put something on, slap on some lip gloss, and let's go," she said.

"I've decided to just sit here and let life pass me by," I said.

"Lovely. Now move your butt."

Kylie managed to get me to put on some jeans and a red top. I told her it didn't matter what shirt I had on because I was going to wear a coat, but she ignored me. I put on some makeup while she curled my hair. When she was done, I had to admit she did an amazing job. We went to the kitchen where my dad and Grandpa were eating pizza.

"Glad I bothered with the lip liner," I said as I twirled a string of soy cheese around my tongue.

Dad dropped us off at the game, and we saw Margaux standing by the fence with Seth who, as always, seemed bored with life and like everything was beneath him. She gave us a little wave and tried to move closer to Seth to show what a fabulous couple they were. Brendon was over in the bleachers with Sam and some other student council people.

"Somebody thinks she's cool," Kylie said as she pointed to Lauren, who was coming down the path.

Lauren was waving to someone in the stands. She was wearing a pair of furry, pink mittens which matched her sweater and scarf perfectly, and she acted like she was Miss Popularity as she bounced around laughing and waving.

"Who does she think she is?" Kylie asked. "The homecoming queen?"

Actually, Lauren's name had come up as a possible candidate for junior princess, and I had panicked thinking she could have made it on the homecoming court. I would have died if I had to watch Brendon walk her down the aisle and hear her mention him in her speech. I had only been to one homecoming assembly last year, but every court princess or nominee had gone up there saying, "My mom's my best friend," and started crying, and then listed every single one of their friends and how "ah-maz-ing" they were. Gag. Luckily, Lauren's stuck up attitude kept anybody from voting for her. However, I had been afraid one of the girls who had been nominated would drop out before the actual homecoming election and Lauren would still get on the court. However, unless one of the girls got struck by lightning in the next ten minutes, it seemed there was no chance of Lauren getting on the court.

Lauren went to sit in the bleachers with the people from student council and sat right next to Brendon. Somebody had brought a stadium blanket, and I was getting sick watching Lauren and Brendon drinking hot chocolate with their dumb blanket. It reminded me of my stupid coloring book where the couple goes to a football game. Except the girl was never an obnoxious jerk who draped herself over the guy.

Kylie told me to ignore them, and she bought me a box of chocolate-covered caramels, but I couldn't concentrate on the game. Instead, I watched Lauren rub Brendon's arm with her stupid pink mitten. When we first started going out, in the back of my mind I guess I had worried maybe he had slept with her, but nothing had prepared me for how I felt when I was looking in her bathroom cabinet. I couldn't handle it.

"I'm freezing," Margaux said as she sat down and took the candy box from me. "Can I have some?"

I passed her the candy as I watched Lauren and Brendon leave their seats. Kylie suggested we get some hot chocolate to warm us up. We walked over to the concession stand, and Lauren and Brendon were there by the restrooms. They were standing super close together, and I felt embarrassed and shifted my eyes away. Kylie poked me and told me to look up, and I saw Brendon walking away from Lauren.

"So they're fighting. Big whoop. They argue, like, five times a day," Margaux said as she popped another candy.

"He's by himself now," Kylie said. "You should go talk to him."

Sam walked over to Brendon, and I felt dumb going over there, so we got our drinks and went back to watch the game. A few minutes later, Sam came up to sit with us.

"Hey, how's it going?" he asked.

"Good." I hadn't talked to him since Brendon and I had stopped going out, and now he suddenly has this undying urge to find out how I am?

"Great. So, how are your classes?" he asked.

"Fine. How are yours?"

"Good, anyway, Brendon wanted to know how you were doing."

"Why doesn't he ask her himself?" Margaux asked through a mouthful of caramel.

Sam seemed surprised.

"Well, I'm fine," I said. No one else said anything, so he left.

"Well, it's a good sign he asked about you, Em," Kylie said.

Margaux narrowed her eyes. "Pretty weak he was looking for a new girlfriend five seconds after he got into a fight with Lauren."

I started to ask Margaux if I should at least go over and talk to him, but then Seth came over, and she was too busy giving him attitude because he had left her for his friends.

"Fine, forget it," he said, getting up.

Margaux grabbed his arm, and he sat down again. Kylie rolled her eyes. Seth took out a pack of gum, and Margaux reached over and took a stick. He shoved the rest of the pack into his pocket without offering us any.

"Em, let's go walk around," Kylie said. As soon as we were out of earshot she said, "Sorry, I couldn't take another minute of those two. Explain this to me—why does Seth always smell like ham and rubbing alcohol?"

"I know, what's up?" I stopped when I saw Brendon talking to Lauren. "I cannot believe this. They're back together already."

"You don't know for sure," she said. "She could be groveling or telling him she hopes he has a nice life with you or—"

"You know, maybe I should have gone after Sam," I said. "He's nice, funny, smart, and not half as cute as Brendon, so I wouldn't have the whole school lusting after him."

"You've got to get over your self-esteem thing," Kylie said.

We watched Lauren and Brendon leave together, and then we tracked Margaux and Seth down for a ride home. I went to my room and sprawled out on the bed. The phone rang, and I sat up and listened. Lately, whenever the phone rang, I thought it was the hospice calling.

I ran into my parents' bedroom. My mom shook her head at me, so I went downstairs and sat with Grandpa.

"Hi, sweetie. How are you?" he asked.

He had been calling me "sweetie" and "sweetheart" lately—something he had never done before, and I hoped it wasn't because he couldn't remember my name. I told him I went to a football game, and he asked if I had a good time. I nodded. It was so hard to have a conversation with him lately. He'd just said "mm-hmm" when you asked him something, and it was hard to deal with. I switched on the TV, and we watched a movie until my dad came in to tell us to get ready for bed. Grandpa stood up and immediately my hand went over my nose. My first thought was, "Why does it smell like a dirty diaper in here?" And then it hit me where that smell was coming from. I didn't want to ask him if he had an accident and embarrass him, but that's exactly what it smelled like had happened. I was afraid to go and tell my dad because then he'd say we had to put Grandpa in a nursing home.

"Grandpa, why don't you go to the bathroom and start getting ready for bed," I said, and then I ran upstairs and told my mom. She went into the den and leaned against the wall.

"We'll have to get him some adult diapers tomorrow," she said. "I'll use some spray cleaner on the cushion and see if it helps."

"Are you going to tell Dad?" I asked.

"He thought he smelled something yesterday, but I took care of it before he saw the stain," she said. "Maybe these are just isolated incidents. We'll keep an eye on it. I'm not going to say anything unless I absolutely have to."

Chapter 19

IN THE MORNING she "absolutely had to" when Grandpa wet the bed. My dad didn't say anything and took Grandpa upstairs to shower.

"I'm going to wash his sheets, and then run out to get some adult diapers," Mom said. "Keep an eye on Grandpa when Dad brings him downstairs, okay?"

However, after lunch, Grandpa stood up, and we realized the diaper leaked, and he had wet another couch cushion.

"Mom, I asked him, like, fifty times if he had to go to the bathroom," I said, getting nervous. "He said he was fine. In fact, he seemed a little irritated I asked."

Mom sighed. "I know. He's from the generation where you don't discuss bathroom matters—especially with your teenage granddaughter. He probably didn't even realize he had to go."

That scared me. How did he not notice he was sitting in a wet adult diaper? And how long had this been going on? Was this his life now? Asking me where he slept every night and not knowing when he needed to use the bathroom? It broke my heart to see him getting more confused, and I didn't know what to do to help him.

"Emme, put these plastic dry-cleaning bags every-where Grandpa usually sits," Dad said. "This should help protect the cushions."

We told Grandpa to sit on the bags, but he kept for-getting. In fact, he stood up and removed the bag even as I said, "Remember, you need to sit on that right now?"

"Why? What's wrong?" he asked, concerned.

My eyes filled with tears as I saw his confusion de-spite the fact I had just explained it to him ten minutes ago.

"Um, I spilled something on it, and I don't want your pants to get wet," I said. I didn't like to lie, but I wanted to preserve his dignity. I saw my dad watching us, and he cleared his throat.

"Maybe we should move the recliners out of the fami-ly room," Dad said. "I can bring up an old chair from the basement. Might be easier."

He brought the chair in, and we moved the coffee ta-ble right in front of the loveseat. That way we could crawl over the table and sit on the loveseat, but Grandpa wouldn't be able to get to it.

Margaux texted me they were on their way to pick me up to get our hair done for the dance. Her dad drove up and took us all to the salon. Kylie decided to have her hair professionally straightened for the dance, and it was so silky and long. She kept running her fingers through it as she watched herself in the mirror. Margaux said she didn't want "dance hair" all pulled up and sprayed to death, so her stylist cut it in choppy layers and styled it around her face. Since I always wore my hair in a bun or long and loose, the girls talked me into doing something different for the dance. My stylist curled the ends and pulled it back in a low ponytail with a piece left out on the side.

Margaux offered to do my makeup. I told her nothing too extreme and let her do my eye makeup. She put on a sheer peach shadow. It was a little light for a dance, so Kylie added smoky eyeliner with lots of mascara.

"Em, I've never seen you with your eyes outlined," Margaux said. "I like it."

Kylie and I exchanged a look. "I think she meant it," Kylie whispered.

Zach, Darren, and Seth were waiting in Margaux's living room while her mom took pictures of us. I felt a little weird when it was my turn with Darren to have our "couples" photo.

We arrived at the restaurant for dinner. Seth had made reservations at a Japanese seafood restaurant, but Darren was allergic to fish so he couldn't eat anything there. All he had was a little dish of rice. They didn't have any chicken, steak, or even a salad on the menu for him. I asked if he wanted us to take the limo through a drive-through, but Margaux said she wanted to get to the dance before the backdrop for the pictures got messed up.

"Last year at the spring fling, the paper on the floor had shoe prints and crap all over it, and it ruined my pictures," she said.

"I'm fine, Emme," Darren said.

When we got to the dance, the photographers had messed up the number order, so to make up for it, each person could get two pictures taken. Darren and I had our picture taken, and then Kylie, Margaux, and I posed for one together. Margaux went over to talk to some junior guy named Cris, and Seth was not happy.

"Darren and I are going to go outside with Seth for a minute," Zach told Kylie and me. "He's super mad at Margaux right now."

I saw Margaux surrounded by guys going, "Cris, come give me a hug!"

"I guess you're my date then," Kylie said to me. "Let's dance, but I'm warning you—if a slow song comes on, you better watch your hands."

I cracked up. "I'll try to control myself."

I was having a lot of fun...until I saw Lauren walk by. She was wearing the black long-sleeved dress I wanted. She appeared way older and more sophisticated than anyone else at the dance. Plus, she had her hair up in a high ponytail like one those vintage sixties dolls.

"You looked better in it," Kylie said, just as a group of girls ran over to Lauren to tell her how "gorgeous" she was. "Are you mad at me for talking you out of it?"

"Probably wouldn't have been able to pull it off anyway. I always feel like such a kid next to her," I said.

"If it makes you feel any better, I saw Brendon watching you while we were dancing," she said. "Speaking of guys, where are our dates?"

We found the guys hanging out with Darren's brother, Matt, and some other junior guys Seth knew. Seth reeked of alcohol. So much for the assistant principal's threat of checking everyone's breath all night. We managed to pry Margaux away from all her admirers, and we all went to sit at one of the tables. It was just my luck Lauren and Brendon were at the next table—and she was almost sitting on his lap.

"Brendon, give me your jacket. I'm freezing," she said as she leaned in closer to him.

Kylie leaned over. "Who's going to puke first: you from watching Lauren or Seth from whatever he drank in the parking lot?"

"I'd say me. Although Darren seems like he had some, too," I whispered back.

"Zach said Seth's friends brought it, but he didn't have any," she said. She leaned over and grabbed Margaux's arm. "Hey, I thought you said we were only going to stay for a half-hour."

Margaux shrugged. "If you guys want to go, I can get my own ride home," she said as she got up to dance with Tyrell. "Just let me know what you want to do." Seth got up—well, he attempted to, but he fell over a chair. Zach glanced over at Kylie and raised his eyebrows.

"I better get Seth home," he said.

"Call me tomorrow," Kylie said, sighing as they walked away. "Well, at least I got to dance with him twice. Darren, do you want to go?"

We found our limo, and Kylie called Margaux's cell to tell her we were leaving. "So do you want us to wait for you or—" She stopped when Darren opened the limo door to throw up. "Gross, Darren just spewed every-where. Well, he did drink on an empty stomach."

I stuck my head out of the limo. "Are you okay?" I asked.

He nodded. "I think I'm going to find my brother or something—" He moved his head and threw up again. I offered to call his brother's cell, and we waited around until he found us. Darren stayed outside because he didn't want to get the limo dirty. Kylie exchanged a look with me.

"Is this how you expected your homecoming to go?" she asked as I rolled my eyes. "Well, on the plus side, at least *you're* not puking."

"Because I'd never drink at a dance, although I al-most did throw up when I saw Lauren on Brendon's lap," I said.

"Well, at least you have a hot date," she said. "Me."

I laughed. "Yeah, and you didn't even puke on me."

"*And* I didn't have to beg you to dance with me. Crap, I danced with you more than Zach. Poor Zach. Seth ended up being his date."

"Zach was still a better date than Margaux," I said as Kylie's cell phone rang.

"Hey Margaux. Yeah, we're still here. Darren's broth-er just came over to get him. We'll wait for you."

Margaux came into the limo holding her shoes. "My strap broke," she said. "Is there anything decent in the mini-fridge?"

Kylie passed around sodas, and Margaux told us that at the restaurant she saw Seth text messaging someone in the lobby. She asked him whom he was writing to, and he wouldn't let her see.

"It was this junior who likes him, and he's totally been encouraging her. It doesn't mean anything when you tell someone you aren't into them, and then you constantly e-mail, text message, and IM them," she said. "It's not like they're just friends. I mean she's made it obvious she likes him and…whatever. He's a jerk."

"How long do we have the limo for?" Kylie asked.

"My mom had paid for the whole night," Margaux said. "Want to get takeout and drive around?"

"Perfect," I said.

"You pick the place, Em," she said.

Even though I didn't eat meat, I was obsessed with the mushroom gravy at this southern fast-food chicken place. The girls were on board with it, and we all got combo meals.

"So this is how the night ends—just the three musketeers," Kylie said.

"Ooh, I could go for one of those right now. Let's get the driver to stop at a drugstore," Margaux said.

"I want it noted, for the record, my date didn't puke," Kylie said.

I laughed. "Not exactly something to brag about to your grandkids fifty years from now, but you do have us beat. Crap, I just got gravy on my dress."

Kylie told me to be grateful it was just gravy after the night we had. We went into a convenience store to get snacks. I had a funny feeling I shouldn't go in, seeing as my dress was stained, my face was greasy, and my hair was messed up from leaning my head back on the seat, but I ignored my intuition because I was afraid Kylie wouldn't get the potato chips I wanted. Ignoring my intuition proved to be the wrong thing to do because who did I run into? Brendon, Lauren, Sam, and his date. I couldn't turn around because they saw me walk in. Plus, Margaux had her hand firmly pushing me into the store. "Say 'hi' and act like you're having fun," she said in my ear.

"Hi guys," I said, smiling so hard I probably cracked my makeup, and I put my purse in front of the stain on my dress. "Getting some snacks?" No, stupid, they were paying for chips and candy bars because they wanted to feed the birds. I'm so dumb.

"Yeah, we're going to sneak it into the hotel," Lauren said. "See ya."

As soon as they cleared the doorway, the three of us said, "Hotel?" at the same time.

"Maybe they rented a room, and they're just having a little party or something," Kylie said.

"Or maybe after they leave their little party, Lauren and Brendon are going to stay in the room, and she's going to sleep with your man," Margaux said.

Kylie told her to shut up, but Margaux was probably right. Brendon wasn't my boyfriend anymore, so it wasn't like he was cheating on me, but it still felt like he had ripped my heart out, shoved it back down my throat, and then made me throw it back up.

"Em, you want to see if the driver will take us for frozen yogurt? Hmm? You want a little raspberry swirl to make you feel better?" Kylie asked.

Margaux pointed out the yogurt place closed at nine. She said the fast-food drive-through might still be open, and we started to leave when Brendon came back inside.

"Hey, I forgot to get some ice," he said.

Margaux moved in front of me to block the view of my dress.

Brendon picked up the bag of ice and said, "You guys can meet us at the hotel if you want. A bunch of us rented a room just to hang out. We're at the Ainsley Inn on

Woodward—it's right across from the Marcus restaurant, and we're in room one-thirty-one."

"Like hotels don't have ice?" Margaux said as soon as he left. "He came back just to let you know he and Lauren weren't hooking up."

"And I think we should go to the Ainsley to make sure they don't," Kylie said.

"I look too gross to go anywhere."

Margaux went over to the guy behind the counter. "I know the sign says customers can't use the bathroom, but take pity on her," she said, pointing to me. "Her ex just invited her to a party with his girlfriend and look at her dress. Please let her try to make herself look decent."

The guy leaned over the counter and said, "Nasty. Okay, but just for a minute."

The three of us tried to scrub the stain, but the gravy was not coming out.

"I can't hold my purse in front of my dress all night," I said. "Let's just forget it."

"This isn't over. Come on, let's trade," Kylie said. "We're about the same size, and I already have a boy-friend, so I'm not out to impress anyone there."

I hugged her, and we switched dresses. The driver took us to the hotel, and I had to do deep breathing exercises before we knocked on the door. I don't know what I was worried about, seeing as Brendon knew we might show up, but maybe I was afraid Lauren would answer the door wearing just a sheet. Instead, Sam answered the door and let us in. There weren't a lot of people there yet, but Lauren was clinging to Brendon like a static-y sock. Sam offered to get us something to drink, but then he saw the stain on Kylie's dress.

"Or maybe you just want water or something," he said.

"She was, um, helping a sick friend," Margaux said.

"It's just gravy," Kylie said. Sam raised his eyebrows

and nodded as he went to get us sodas. The three of us didn't know what to do, so we sat on one of the couches, huddled together like freaks.

"Why are we here again?" I asked.

"Because you're not over your ex, dummy," Margaux said, rolling her eyes. "But I'm not going to sit here all night when there's chocolate in the limo, so go talk to him or something."

Like I could walk over to where Lauren was sitting in the same oversized chair with him, almost on his lap. How obvious could you get?

"Why doesn't she just pee on him like a dog with a fire hydrant?" Margaux whispered in my ear. Out loud she said, "Hey, Brendon, do you have any other songs other than this album?"

He had to stand up, which got him away from Lauren, but did he want her so close by in the first place? I had this feeling he still wanted to be with me, but what if it wasn't intuition but just some pathetic desperate thing?

"Em, come here and help me pick one," she said.

"I don't have any Sweetie Gals ones on here," he said, smiling. Margaux went over to the side to give us room to talk.

"I wanted to ask you to dance tonight, but I didn't want to upset your boyfriend," he said.

My face got warm. "He's not my boyfriend," I said.

"So would it be okay to—"

"You guys, I want a group shot," Lauren said, holding up a camera. "Sam *finally* figured out how to use the timer. Let's go over by the couch."

I stood next to Sam and Kylie for the picture until I felt a hand in my back and found myself falling into Brendon after Margaux elbowed me. "Sorry, new shoes," I said after I almost knocked him over. I glared at Margaux, while Lauren and Sam set up both of their cameras. However, I couldn't stay mad at Margaux when Brendon put his arm around my waist for the picture. I moved closer to him and put my arm around his waist so Lauren would have to look at us in the picture for the rest of her life…or until she deleted the shot.

More people started showing up, and Sam got worried we were going to get kicked out of the hotel.

"Hey Emme, will you go out on the balcony with me?" Brendon asked.

We walked out, and there were a few people sitting there, but Lauren was inside with her friend, Madison. A couple of people slow danced.

"So did you get to dance with anyone other than Kylie?" he asked.

"Were you watching me?" I asked.

He bit his lip and glanced down as his shoes. "Maybe, so…do you want to dance?"

"Sure," I said. However, Kylie's dress was shorter than mine and a little wider, seeing she had a slightly curvier figure than me. It was a touch big on me, and I hoped it wouldn't slide down too far and take my strapless bra down with it. It was hard for me to completely relax while I was dancing because I could feel my bra moving south. I wanted to pull it up, but there was no subtle way to do it without looking like a weirdo. I hoped he didn't think I was tense because of him.

We started swaying with the music, and then he kissed me. Had he been drinking like the other guys? He didn't seem like the kind of guy who would, but then again I didn't expect Darren to either. What if Brendon had been drinking and didn't even know what he was doing? Maybe I could be any girl as far as he was concerned. What if he didn't remember any of this tomorrow? But yet I felt he wanted to be with me. Still, I knew it would look bad if people started talking at school about how he got drunk, and we were making out at a hotel. So I pulled back. If he wanted a relationship with me—

something more than just this moment on a balcony—then he was going to have to stop seeing Lauren, or whatever he was doing with her. I wasn't going to be the girl he ran to when he got confused, and I wasn't going to put up with her in my life anymore.

I was about to ask him what was going on with him and Lauren when he surprised me.

"Do you want to hang out tomorrow afternoon?" he asked. "I could pick you up around two."

I nodded, and Margaux, who appeared out of nowhere, suddenly grabbed my arm and said we had to leave.

"So I'll be at your house tomorrow then, okay?" Brendon said.

"Yeah, see ya then," I said over my shoulder since Margaux was leading me out the door.

"What's your problem?" I asked as we walked to the parking lot.

"I was standing nearby when I heard him ask you about getting together. You didn't look too eager, which was good, but you have to leave him wanting more," she said.

"Margaux, have you been reading, like, your grandmother's dating books or something?" Kylie asked. "It's not the olden days, ya know."

"I know what I'm talking about. Right now Brendon knows Emme's still interested, but he also has Lauren all over him, so Emme needs to be a little distant so he doesn't feel like he can have any girl who walks by," she said.

Kylie sighed. "I hate when I find myself thinking her messed-up logic makes sense. Makes me feel so...dirty."

———

BRENDON CAME OVER the next day, and he said he had

won a gift certificate to the Elistair Café, so we drove into downtown Detroit to have lunch there. He said Sam and his girlfriend might meet up with us, and I prayed they wouldn't come. Sam's a nice guy, but I tended to get nervous in groups when I'm the outsider. Of course, unless I knew everybody there, I *always* felt the outsider. Sometimes I wondered if anyone else felt that way or if it was just me. Brendon's cell rang, and I relaxed when I heard him say, "So you're going to hang out at her house instead?"

The waitress brought our food, and I couldn't help but notice she only talked to Brendon. I might as well have been invisible. She had already refilled his water and his iced tea twice, while I had to remind her I needed a tea bag to go with my hot water, and she never brought the glass of ice water I asked for.

"I'm going to go to the bathroom," Brendon said, getting up. "Be right back."

As I watched him walk away, I noticed he had left his phone on the table. I wanted to badly to check and see whom he had called recently. It would tell me a lot if Lauren's number was there. It was one thing if she was calling him, but another altogether if he was the one calling her. I was afraid he'd come back and catch me, but I had to know. I picked up the phone and checked the last sent calls. I saw Sam's name five times, some other guy's name, his dad's number, but not Lauren's. However, he had received several calls from her. I put the phone back and started eating and trying to look innocent.

"How's your sandwich?" he asked.

"Great. So did you have fun with Lauren last night?" I asked. He gave me a startled look—like I wasn't supposed to talk about it, but I wasn't going to pretend it didn't happen. I was still mad, and I wasn't going to act like it hadn't happened. I didn't do anything wrong, after all.

"It's always the same at those things. You spend a

fortune at dinner, get to the dance late, and then every-body winds up back someplace listening to music and watching TV, which I could have done without paying hundreds of bucks," he said.

Seemed like a safe way of answering without saying, "I was bored with Lauren," or saying, "Lauren was all over me after you left."

"How was your night?" he asked.

I could have said my date puked, and I spent the night either stuffing my face or getting anxious over him, but I pulled a Margaux and pretended I had the best time. She would never let a guy know he spoiled her night.

"We had so much fun at dinner," I said. "And the food was amazing."

"I saw you dancing with Kylie a lot. Didn't your date dance?"

I didn't want to point out it was hard to dance when you're puking in the parking lot. Instead, I said she and I were having a blast out there and avoided the question. He was about to say something else when Sam walked in.

"Hey guys. I thought I'd drop by for a second," Sam said. "Can I bum a fry, man?"

"So I heard your friend got suspended for drinking at the dance," Sam said to me.

Brendon raised his eyebrows. "You guys were drink-ing?" he asked.

And there was the answer to my question about whether or not he had anything to drink yesterday.

"No, the guy Margaux went with had some and so did one of the other guys in our group," I said, not letting on my date did, too. "Who got suspended?"

"Seth. Someone else was seen throwing up in the parking lot, but they couldn't confirm who it was, so he got lucky."

Brendon was staring at me. Did he look disappoint-ed?

"So are you friends with Seth?" he asked.

"No, Margaux likes him, but I'm not a big fan myself."

"She's lucky she wasn't with him at all last night or else she might have gotten in trouble, too," Brendon said. There was obvious disapproval in his voice.

"She doesn't drink. You saw her at the after party. All she had was soda."

"Yeah, I know. She needs to be more careful of who she hangs out with, though," he said.

"Well, she's not planning on running for office any time soon, so I think she's okay."

"Dude, I had my brother drop me off," Sam said. "Can I get a ride home?"

We left the restaurant, and I wished I hadn't gotten so defensive when Brendon brought up the whole Seth and Margaux thing. It was like I had gotten too carried away defending Margaux when all I needed to say was, "She'd never drink at a school dance or anywhere else," and leave it alone. But it wasn't actually Margaux I was defending—it was all of us because I felt he was looking down on us for not living up to some standard.

We were all quiet in the car as we drove back. Brendon dropped me off, and I wanted to say something like, "Sorry I got a little heated back there," but all I did was thank him for lunch, and then he drove away. Why was I always messing up my chances with him?

WE WERE SUPPOSED to go to the hospice at night, but my parents were too tired from moving furniture around for Grandpa to go. I thought about calling Darren for a ride, but I didn't want to start up anything with him. Instead, I called the nurse at the hospice, and he said Grandma was sleeping and hadn't touched her dinner.

"But she's not supposed to have real food. It could get in her lungs and kill her," I said.

He said she hadn't had anything, and I got the feeling he thought it didn't actually matter because she wasn't expected to recover anyway. I asked to speak to another nurse, and the head nurse who got on the line assured me it was a simple mistake and no one got hurt. Angry, I got off the phone and insisted we go over there. Mom agreed, and we drove to the hospice. Someone must have alerted the head nurse because she came in and started fluffing Grandma's pillows and tucking in her blanket.

"Has she started the therapy yet?" Mom asked.

"Pardon?" the nurse asked.

"The therapy exercises you told me about when my mother came here," my mom said. "Like having her squeeze a rubber ball and stretching her legs."

"Oh, yes. Well, we kind of felt in this case it wasn't going to, um, be necessary, and we didn't want to cause her any discomfort," the nurse said. She offered us some coffee and then disappeared.

"Why didn't you complain?" I asked. "She told you they'd do exercises with Grandma when you brought her here and now they basically said, 'What's the point?'"

"Well, I guess in her eyes what *is* the point," Mom said.

"But she lied," I said. Mom sighed. "Everybody's g-i-v-i-n-g up on her," I said, hoping Grandma wouldn't understand what I was spelling out. "But people recover all the time from these things."

"Yes, on TV shows, but we have to be realistic," Mom said. "Don't you think if there was any hope at—"

I cut her off because I didn't want Grandma to hear her own daughter had lost faith in her.

"Remember, we said no negative energy around Grandma," I said.

"Fine," Mom said.

"You know, eighty-five isn't old," I said quietly. "Great-aunt Lucille is ninety-five, and she goes out all the time to play bingo, and she has a boyfriend."

Mom laughed, "She's doing better than you."

"So funny," I said, rolling my eyes.

We went home, and the family room still smelled a little like urine. Dad said he had cleaned the couch the best he could, but we'd have to have it done professionally. I helped them cover the mattress in the den with plastic sheets meant for toddlers who were potty training. It took forever, and it made weird noises when Grandpa lay down on it. Mom asked him if he needed to go to the bathroom again before he went to sleep.

"I think I know when I have to use the restroom, Gabrielle," he said, getting annoyed.

"Okay, good night, Dad," she said.

We closed the door, and I went to my room. I hadn't finished my geometry homework, but I couldn't concentrate. I wondered if Ms. Atkins would do one of her random homework checks in class, but decided to go to bed and hoped I'd have time to do it in the morning. So what if I got a zero on the assignment. After all, I had bigger problems to worry about.

LUCKILY, MS. ATKINS didn't check our homework because I didn't get the final two problems done. Mr. Horowitz handed back our short stories in creative writing. He didn't believe in giving us grades since "you can't grade creativity," so he just wrote comments on our papers. Darren always got great remarks like "innovative" and "introspective," while I got comments like, "Where are you going with this?" but mine were staring to get better. This time Mr. Horowitz wrote he liked the subtle humor in my story and the twist in the ending. Darren read it and said I should submit it to the *Litzine.*

I shook my head. "It's not good enough. Besides, they print these deep, meaningful pieces, and mine would be too…you know, just not what they're looking for."

"I know you're not crazy about Lauren, but my friend Nathan works on it, and I bet he'd want to print it," he said. I hoped Nathan didn't laugh in his face and tell him I was a no-talent loser. Or worse, he would show it to Lauren, and they could both have a good laugh.

"So what's going on with you and Darren?" Rory asked, leaning close to my ear.

"*Nothing.* We've hung out, but just as friends," I said quietly.

"Does he know?"

I asked her what she meant, and she said she didn't think he would go out of his way to help me if he wasn't interested in me as more than just a friend. Part of me wondered if she was just jealous because Mr. Horowitz thought her last piece "lacked spark."

Our next assignment was to write about the first place we could remember as a child. I wrote about going to my grandparents' house back when my grandmother was still well. I wrote about the dark, glossy, wood furniture and the smell of chicken soup. I wrote about the lemon poppy-seed cakes, and I could almost smell them as I was writing everything down.

However, Mr. Horowitz said we were going to read our essays out loud when we got to class the next day. I tried to avoid looking at him, but I knew he'd call on me first.

"Miss Trybus? Will you read for us?"

I hated how teachers ask you to do something when you knew you had no way out. Like he'd be okay with it if I said, "No, I think I'll pass this time, but thanks anyway."

I was afraid I'd start crying and make a fool of myself

if anybody criticized me, but everybody was nodding when I finished. One of the girls said she could picture the kitchen. Nobody had spoken up to say they liked something I wrote in the longest time. Darren and Rory got it all the time, but I never did.

Darren called me that night to say his friend liked my story and was going to put it in the next issue coming out tomorrow. I was surprised it had gotten past Lauren's desk, but maybe she didn't see me as competition. It would be the first time anything of mine was published.

The next day I refreshed the online *Litzine* page a million times waiting for the new issue to go up. Then found my story on the third page. They had misspelled my last name, but my story was in print. Darren had an essay in there, too, and he congratulated me when he saw me.

"I think we should go out and celebrate," he said. "How about a steak sandwich, and we can watch a preseason hockey game on the big screen at Anthony's?"

"I have a ton of work in my other classes so I don't think I—"

"Are you sure? It'll be fun..."

I nodded, and Rory gave me a look from across the room.

I ran into Brendon at the vending machine, and he said he read my story. "It was great."

"Thanks. How have you been?" I asked.

"Busy, already started working on Dad's next campaign. His race is still over a year away, but with the next election coming up he wants to keep his name out there. It's a good way to see how things work in politics. Anyway, your story was good," he said. "I was thinking about you last night. It was weird because right after, a Sweetie Gals' song came on. Who knows, maybe they'll get back together or something."

"Anything's possible, right?"

He gave me a smile which always made my—and the

rest of the female student body's—heart melt.

"So the student council is sponsoring a fair. We have different tables set up where you can get information about the different clubs at school. Most people only go to get the free stuff they hand out. You should stop by after class," he said.

I tried to get Kylie to go to the club fair with me, but she didn't want to stay after school if she didn't have to. However, Rory said she'd go with me. Darren wanted to go, but I lied, saying we were going to be hanging around at the pom squad table because we might try out next year. Rory gave me an "are you crazy" look, but didn't say anything.

"Okay, fine. I can see where I'm not wanted. Just wanted to get some free pens and candy," he said as he walked away.

"Have you lost your mind, or do you want to dance in short skirts in front of the whole school?" Rory asked. I shook my head. "Oh, is Brendon going to be there?" she asked.

"Maybe. Come on. We'll be late, and they'll run out of free pencils and bumper stickers," I said.

"Last year the future Republicans' table gave me a lollipop, and it made me sick to my stomach," she said. "I told the future Democrats' club the other guys basically poisoned me, but they didn't do anything about it. Typical. I hate everybody."

I cracked up. "Well, I'm sure it had more to do with the fact the clubs use the leftover candy from the previous year. I think Tom's been getting to you with his conspiracy theories."

We got to the gym and saw the tables set up. There was a huge line at the student council's table because they were giving away cotton candy. I craned my neck, but Brendon wasn't there. Rory and I collected a bunch of pencils, some candy, and a flyswatter, but there was no sign of

Brendon, so we decided to sit on the bleachers and eat our cotton candy. I hadn't eaten cotton candy since I was five, and I didn't remember it being so thick and sticky.

"This is nasty. What flavor is this? Blueberry?" She passed her bag to me. I had gotten pink, but I tried some of hers.

"I think it might be raspberry. You can have mine. I think the food coloring stuff is probably cancer on a stick," I said, getting up to get a napkin. I was wiping my hands when someone tapped me on the shoulder.

"Having fun?" Brendon asked.

"I *was* until the future engineers club ran out of those cool notepads," I said.

"Well, I'll see what I can do," he said. He went over and came back with two notepads. "Will this make up for it?"

"It's a start. So...how are you?"

He shrugged. "Okay. It's been hectic trying to get this and the Halloween party organized," he said as his cell phone rang. "Great, Sam took off so now I have to go pick up a bunch of pumpkins and cider for the party tomorrow," he said, running his fingers through his hair. "Em, you want to go with me?"

"Yeah, sure. Let me go tell Rory," I said. I had to walk slowly so I wouldn't start skipping like a dork. I told Rory I was going with Brendon to pick up some Halloween stuff.

"The school's having a Halloween party?" she asked.

"It's for kids," I said. "You don't think he's going to ask me to sell tickets or pour punch while he goes out with some girl?"

"If he does then we'll key his car," she said. "You might want to wipe the blue crap off your lips before you go back over there though."

Brendon and I went to his car, and he cleared a bunch of papers and books off the front seat for me. He suggested we go to Muller's Orchard to pick up the stuff. I figured we could get everything at the grocery store, but he wanted to get real corn stalks. I hadn't been to an orchard since I was little, and it sounded like fun. We didn't talk much on the ride down. He pulled into the orchard parking lot and got a wheelbarrow, and we went to pick out a bunch of smaller pumpkins the kids could carve.

I picked up a pumpkin and then dropped it when I saw it had a slug on it.

"*Ugh*, I don't remember pumpkin picking being so slimy and gross when I was a kid," I said, wiping my hands on my jeans.

After we put the stuff in the car, he suggested we sit at one of the tables and have a doughnut and some cider. I wasn't a huge doughnut fan, and I've seen one too many TV reports on cider and diarrhea, but I ate half of a powdered sugar doughnut. I had to wipe my mouth constantly to get rid of my sugar mustache.

"Are you free tomorrow night?" he asked.

Was he asking me out? *Okay, play it cool. Don't get too excited. Remain calm.*

"Tomorrow...tomorrow...what's tomorrow? I think I'm free," I said.

"Do you want to help out at the party?" he asked.

Oh crap. He wanted me to keep an eye on the punch bowl and wipe runny noses so he could go out with his girlfriend—probably to some expensive restaurant or something. I'd have to weasel out of it gracefully.

"Because I was asked to write something on the party for the newspaper, and I thought I'd ask you if you wanted to do it so you could get a byline for your resume," he said.

Well, I did want to write for the newspaper because it would be cool to have an article to put with my resume when I tried for another internship at the local paper. I said I'd do it and asked if I'd have to wear a costume. He said he was borrowing a magician's cape from Jayson and going as a vampire. Okay, so it meant he was going, but was he bringing a date? I didn't have the guts to ask, and I wasn't sure I wanted to know anyway.

Brendon pulled up in front of my house at seven the next day. I had thrown together an elf costume from the *Cutie Pies* TV show. I had cut off the sleeves of an old baby doll dress of my mom's, made a little cap out of a washcloth, and found blue face paint at the drugstore. It had seemed like a good idea in my mind, but seeing myself completely blue was freaky. I wanted to look cute, but a blue face wasn't exactly hot. At least my hair ended up looking like the girl elf's. I walked up to his car, but there was somebody already sitting in the front seat. Somebody with red hair wearing a mermaid costume.

"Emme, this is Nicola," he said.

"Hey." She didn't even turn around to look at me. So the jerk had a date, and he just didn't feel like writing a stupid article for the newspaper. Now I had to sit through an evening with loud kids, and I'd probably break out from the blue makeup clogging my pores. Nicola got out of the car, and I got a better look at her costume. She had a shimmery skirt with a fishtail on it and a purple seashell top. The seashell bra was attached to a thin nylon shirt, but she might as well have been completely bare. Next to her it was like I was four years old and completely flat-chested because I didn't want to get blue face paint on my bra. She walked next to Brendon, and I trailed in behind them. There were mostly kids and parents inside, but also a few student council volunteers. Of the five girls who were helping out, there were two Marilyn Monroes and a Cleopatra, and there I was in my stupid blue elf costume. The worst part was most of the kids didn't know who the elf was, and they just thought I was a big blue weirdo.

Everybody had a job to do but me. I sat at one of the tables with a paper cup of orange punch. I forgot to bring any paper to write the story, so I got a pen and a bunch of napkins. Nicola didn't have anything to do either, unless you counted following Brendon around like a lost puppy. He was organizing the pumpkin-carving table, and he didn't need her hanging on him. I hoped one of the kids would slip and stab her with one of the safety carving knives. Brendon's friend, Sam, supervised the beanbag game. All you had to do was toss a beanbag through a giant cutout hole to get a prize, and I was bored so I went over and helped Sam run after the beanbags and hand out prizes. I saw Nicola sitting by herself, eating peanut butter kisses. I thought about going over to talk to her, but then she gave me the once over so I let her sit by herself.

"Emme, are you ready to go?" Brendon asked. I nodded, and the three of us walked to the car. She plopped herself in the front seat, but if she was his girlfriend, it was her place. Nicola had taken a trick-or-treat bag and offered Brendon a chocolate bar.

"Emme, want some candy?" he asked.

Nicola sighed and handed me a piece of taffy which had oozed out of its packaging. I thought about throwing it at the back of her head, but with my luck it'd boomerang and hit me in the eye. Brendon dropped her off first, but I did live closer to him. He walked her to the door, but they didn't kiss or even touch, although maybe it was because she was covered with glitter makeup.

"Are you going to move up to the front seat or am I your chauffeur?" he asked when he came back. I moved to the front. "Hey, did you eat anything at the party?" he asked. I shook my head. "Wanna stop and get something?"

We stopped at a diner where grease seemed to hang in the air. He ordered a burger and fries, and I ordered a side salad and French fries, which was the closest thing to a meatless option I could find. Brendon put some ketchup on his plate and then put a circle of ketchup around my plate like I always did.

"Oh, sorry. Force of habit," he said.

"It's okay. You got the better fries."

"Mine are all burnt."

"I love burned fries. So you won't mind if I steal a few?" I asked, sliding a fry off his plate.

"The menu says they make a great malted here," he said.

"What's the difference between a malted and a milkshake?"

He shrugged. "One tastes more like melted ice cream, and...I dunno. Good question. Should we get some?" I nodded. Grandma would have liked how he admitted he didn't know.

"Did I eat off the makeup around my lips?" I asked. He shook his head. "I forgot about my lovely elf complexion when you mentioned stopping somewhere. Everyone is staring at me because I'm blue."

"Not why they're staring," he said. I wasn't sure if he was flirting because he might be dating Nicola now, but I didn't want to get my hopes up and have him make a fool out of me.

"Well, I doubt they get many elves in here," I said as the waitress brought our malteds over.

He lifted up his straw and took a drink. I went to take a drink, got distracted, and the straw went up my nose. I left a little trace of blue on it, too. I don't think he noticed, but maybe he was just being polite.

"So, what do you think?" he asked. My heart jumped, but then I realized he was talking about the malt.

"It's good."

"I'll turn you into a junk food junkie yet," he said.

"I eat junk food. I love those peanut butter cups from the health food store," I said.

"They're *organic*," he said. I shrugged. He leaned over to get a napkin. "Your hair smells good."

"Essential oils," I said. He rolled his eyes. He always

thought my essential oil face and hair treatments were a waste of time. He didn't understand without them my hair would look like hay and my skin would freak out. Guys always expected you to look great, but they didn't understand it took some work. I wanted to ask him about Nicola, but I wasn't sure how to ask. Plus, I didn't want to look desperate or jealous.

"Did you get enough stuff for your story?"

"Yeah, I interviewed Sam and a couple of the kids' parents so I should be fine. I'll have it ready in time."

"Great, you can just drop it off to Lauren."

"Lauren?"

"Yeah, she's the one who asked me to do it, but I thought you'd do a better job. We should do this again. I've missed—I cannot believe this," he said, sitting up.

"What?"

"Brooke just walked in with her new boyfriend. Jayson's gonna lose it," he said. "Let's get out of here. She cheated on Jayson with him, and now they're going out. Just perfect."

Brendon seemed transfixed on Brooke and her new boyfriend, and it was like he forgot all about me. As we were leaving, I saw Brooke sitting there in a princess Halloween costume. With her hair up in the tiara, her dark roots were pretty noticeable.

Well, at least a mermaid hadn't ruined my night, even if a princess had.

Chapter 20

THE NEXT DAY, I went to the newspaper office to drop off my story. I hoped I wouldn't run into Lauren, but she was there with her feet up on her desk, talking on the phone. She put up her finger to signal me to wait. There was no place to sit so I stared at the posters on the wall. Lauren was wearing a blue zip-up sweatshirt and sweatpants. Her shiny hair was pulled back in a ponytail (a *bouncy* one of course), which showed off her diamond earrings. She had some pearly lavender lipstick on, the kind that makes most people look like a corpse, but on her it showed off her flawless complexion and rosy cheeks. Plus, she didn't need any other makeup with those gray eyes. I had spent forty-five minutes on my hair and makeup and wore a pair of designer jeans I got on sale and a cute fitted sweater I borrowed from Margaux, yet Lauren was hotter in her sweats and ponytail with hardly any makeup on.

"Sorry, talking to the assistant editor at the *Post*," she said.

Stupid namedropper—wait the *Post*? Where I had gotten the internship—the same one taken away from me?

"I'm interning there," she said.

"That's nice." Get me out of here. *She* got my position?

"This is my second time there. I started in the summer, but they wanted me to stay on for the fall. So what can I do for you?" she asked as I tried to keep myself from howling over the unfairness of the universe.

"Here's the Halloween party story. I e-mailed it to the submission address, but Brendon said you also needed a hard copy."

"Oh, I thought Brendon was going to write this," she said.

"He asked me to…is it okay?"

"I guess." She dropped it in a box and began typing furiously on her laptop.

"You're welcome." I hated her. I can't believe she got my internship at the *Post* and moved in on my ex-boyfriend. I could just imagine her and Brendon's life together—it would be like a glossy, preppy perfume ad. Their house would be in a magazine where they'd praise her for her good taste. Then their two perfect children Brendon Jr. and Lily (or whatever rich people name their daughters) would be dressed in perfect little outfits that matched the furniture. Meanwhile, I'd still be trying to work at the *Post* and wearing designer clothes from the final markdown sale rack at some bargain-basement store.

"Hey, what's wrong?" Rory asked when I sat down next to her.

"The universe hates me."

"Care to expand a bit?" she asked.

"Never mind. Did you get your essay done?"

"No, but I ran into Mr. Horowitz, and he says everybody's been stressing out over it so we're going to talk about it in class and it'll be due next week," she said.

Great, I stayed up all night trying to finish the essay and get the party article done. My intuition never helps me. Well, at least I could daydream during class.

"Feel like a movie this weekend?" Darren asked when he sat down.

I didn't have anything set for the weekend, but I didn't want to plan a date when I was still thinking about another guy. Of course, Brendon probably had plans with Lauren or the mermaid. I mean it was Friday so if Brendon did ask me to do anything it would probably be because somebody else had canceled on him.

"I don't know, Darren. Things are kind of up in the air," I said, pretending to search for something in my bag. I noticed my Riley Turner watch was right on top. I didn't want to have to give Darren a definite answer, so I grabbed my bag and rushed out when class ended. Brendon was standing outside waiting for me.

"How'd the article go?" he asked.

Great, he didn't come to see me, but to check up on me. "Fine, but I think Lauren wanted you to write it though," I said.

He shook his head. "Nah, I can't write. Anyway, I wanted to thank you for doing it. How about I buy you dinner?"

I could have pointed out we just had dinner last night, and I also could have said it was last minute and how dare he assume that I didn't have plans. Sure, I didn't, but I *could* have had a life. However, I was pathetic, so I said, "Okay."

Darren walked up behind me as Brendon left and squeezed my shoulder.

"So are we on for tonight or what?" he asked.

"Oh, I can't. I…" *I just made plans with my ex-boyfriend.* "I thought you meant Saturday when you said this weekend," I said, feeling awful.

His face fell. "I have to work tomorrow. Well, maybe some other time then. See ya."

I felt like a jerk for making plans with Brendon when Darren asked me first.

Rory, who had been eavesdropping, came over. "Are you guys back together?"

"We're...I don't know. I mean, I went to the Halloween party with him, but it was to write a story for the paper, and the girl with the red hair went with us. She went as a mermaid."

"Oh, too perfect. Was the mermaid his date?" she asked.

"I don't know. We dropped her off and got something to eat."

"It's a good sign if he dropped her off first. He obviously wanted to see you again if he asked you out today."

"But what if it is just to say thanks," I said.

"Emme, anybody could have written the article. Let's face it—it was an excuse to see you. And asking you to go pick out pumpkins? C'mon."

"They were heavy and somebody had to help him carry the doughnuts and stuff," I said as she made a face. "But he asked me out on a Friday. Doesn't it sound like somebody canceled, and he had a time slot available?"

"Then ask him what's going on between you guys," she said. "Let's get together tomorrow, and you can tell me everything."

I repeated the story to Margaux, who thought Brendon was interested in me, but the fact he was an Agretti, he probably liked the idea of dating more than one girl.

"He did move on pretty quick after Lauren," she said. I was relieved she didn't say how fast he had moved on after me. "I'd go, and if he acts like a jerk, then you'll know you made the right decision in the first place."

I wasn't sure what to wear. It was just dinner, but I had no idea where we were going to eat since there were a couple of nicer restaurants at the mall. I didn't want to get all dressed up like I thought it was a date, and then end up at the food court. I thought wearing a skirt would seem too "date-y" so I settled on a pair of brown fake-suede pants with a black sweater. It didn't look like I was expecting too much, but also didn't look like I was going to a place with a "kiddie land" either.

We ended up going to a nice restaurant where you wouldn't look out of place in jeans or in a dress. We ordered, and he started telling me about an embarrassing moment his dad had back when Senator Agretti accidentally fell over a chair and ended up with his hand in a cake when he tried to brace himself.

"It was the birthday cake for the oldest congressman—oh, hang on, it's my phone," he said, picking it up. "It's my mom. Better take this one."

"Sure, no problem," I said.

"Hey, Mom. What's up?" he asked, and then frowned. "Yeah, the pharmacy closes at eight, so if you call it in right now I can pick it up. Is Grandpa okay, though?"

He hung up the phone. "Em, I hate to do this, but my Grandpa was trying to open his own meds and knocked them all over. He tried to lean over to pick them up and fell out of his wheelchair."

"Is he okay?"

"Yeah, but I have to run and pick up a refill. I'm sorry about this—is it cool if we get takeout boxes?" he asked.

"Of course."

Brendon drove to the pharmacy and ran in to get his Grandpa's meds. "What's sad is I'm here so often picking up prescriptions they don't even blink an eye or ask questions anymore."

"Well, they probably know who you are," I said.

"Yeah, cause I'm here all the time."

"I meant, you know, the last name."

"Oh, right. I've gotta get this over to my grandparents', but I'll drop you off on the way," he said. "I'm going to stick around to make sure Grandpa didn't get hurt or anything. Sorry about tonight."

"It's fine," I said.

When he took me home, he walked me to the door and said he'd give me a call soon. I thanked him for dinner, and he drove off. It wasn't his fault our evening didn't turn out as planned, but it would have been nice to hear he missed hanging out with me.

Rory picked me up on Saturday and wanted to know how things went with Brendon. I told her we had barely taken a bite when he got a family emergency call.

"I overheard Lauren asking Brendon to go to a basketball game with her, and he blew her off," she said.

"When was the game?" I asked.

"I think it was today, but he said he had a ton of stuff to do this weekend."

"Maybe he thought she wanted him to write a story on it for the paper, and he was just trying to get out of it," I said.

"It was pretty obvious Lauren wasn't asking him to do an assignment. She was all over him," she said. "She made it clear she still likes him."

"Why wouldn't he want to go with her? Even *I'd* want to date her if I was a guy," I said.

"Have you ever noticed how rude she is?" Rory asked. "I wanted to write for the paper last year, and she talked down to me. She was so condescending, and she did it in this annoyingly sweet voice so you couldn't even call her on it."

I was pretty sure Lauren wouldn't let this thing with Brendon go. After all, I had seen her when she wanted something, and she had a lot more going for her than I did.

Brendon called me on Sunday afternoon and asked if I wanted to see a movie. I had no makeup on, my hair was up in a bun, *and* I was wearing sweats.

"Sam just dropped off free passes to see the sequel to *The Mummy's Revenge*. He said we should get there early to make sure they have enough seats," he said. "I'll pick you up in ten minutes."

"Um, I'm not ready at all."

"I'm sure you look beautiful. You hardly wear any makeup anyway. C'mon, please?"

Oh, Brendon, you naïve fool. I agreed and put on my favorite bright-pink sweater to give me a little color. I had just smeared on a little tinted moisturizer when I heard Brendon drive up. I whisked a mascara brush through my lashes and dabbed on some gloss. I had never gone out of the house wearing so little makeup before. He'd probably see me and turn around and drive to Nicola's house.

"Hey, you look great," he said.

Maybe he had lost a contact lens. When we got to the theater, he bought chocolate-covered peanuts, popcorn, and two bottles of water. He handed me the snacks while he put his wallet away. I poured the peanuts into his popcorn the way he usually did.

"Oh, I bought the popcorn for both of us. I thought greasy chocolate-y peanuts made you gag," he said.

"I don't mind," I said.

We had a few minutes until the movie started. He said Sam had already seen the movie, and it wasn't supposed to be too scary.

"Did you have a lot of homework this weekend?" I asked.

"Not much. Why, did you have a lot?"

"No, did you do anything interesting on Saturday?" I hoped I wasn't being too obvious.

"I slept in for once, got my car washed, and worked out. What about you?" he asked. I said I went to a movie with Rory.

The movie started and it was a *lot* scarier than I anticipated. When the Mummy's wrappings came off his decomposed face, Brendon put his hand up to shield my eyes.

"Sorry, I know you hate gross stuff," he said.

"Yeah, didn't expect it."

He put his arm around the back of my seat, and it was just like when we had been going out. I forgot how much I missed it.

After the movie, we stopped for coffee at the bookstore. We sat on the comfortable couch in the café, which was never available, and he brought a stack of magazines over for us to look at. I read a gossip magazine, while he read *Newsweek*. I always liked the way he and I could sit without having to talk all the time. We only had uncomfortable silences back when we first started dating, when I was a nervous wreck around him.

"Do you want to split a cookie?" he asked.

"Depends. Those huge ones no one can finish or a regular-sized one?" I asked, smiling.

"You know I'd *never* share a regular-sized one."

"Just checking."

When he took me home, I wondered if he was going to kiss me as he walked me to the front door. We hadn't specifically called this a date, and I still wasn't sure if Lauren or Nicola were in the picture. I wanted to get back together, but I didn't know what he wanted, and I was too spineless to ask. He ended up only kissing me on the cheek, but it definitely wasn't the kind of kiss you give to your grandmother.

Chapter 21

THE NEXT DAY, Brendon waited for me after class.

"Hey, you're not wearing all your bracelets," he said. After talking with Cheryl at the psychic fair, I had been wearing my crystals less and less.

"I'm not super into them right now."

"But you are wearing your watch," he said, smiling.

"Well, it goes with the outfit."

He laughed, and then reached over and took my hand. Okay, holding my hand in the hallway definitely meant something.

"Hey, are you going to math lab today? Because I can drive you home after class as long as you don't mind waiting for me during my seventh hour."

"I should go to work on my homework, so yeah, it'd be great."

I was in the math lab when he came to pick me up. Darren raised his eyebrows at me as he walked past us out of the room.

"What's his problem?" Brendon asked.

I just shrugged, and we left to go to get something to eat.

"Stargazer Deli, okay?" he asked.

"Sure." It was the one of the few fast-food restaurants we could agree on. He always got the bacon classic cheeseburger, and I ordered a peanut butter and banana sandwich and fries.

"So I applied to my dad's alma mater last month," he said.

"Have you heard anything yet?"

He shook his head, and I told him he'd probably get in.

"You think so? Sam told me I didn't have a prayer," he said, jamming a fry into his mouth.

"Why? You're an honor student, you're on a million committees, and you played soccer last year. What else are they looking for? Nomination for sainthood?" I asked.

"Well, you have to be in the top ten percent of your class," he said. "I am, but I'm having problems in my physics class. I even got myself a tutor."

"You'll be fine. My grandma always says worrying about something doesn't solve it, so just concentrate on doing your best," I said.

"Makes me wish I had told you before I told Sam."

"Will your dad be upset if you don't get in?"

"Well, all the men in my family have gone to one of two schools and only because two of them wanted to focus on constitutional law, so I pretty much have to get into one of them or else it's like I don't measure up, you know?"

No, I didn't, and I couldn't imagine the amount of pressure he was feeling.

"Did you apply to both?"

"Yeah, and to a safety school. Sad thing is my safety school *is* my own first choice," he said.

"What does your dad say about the safety school?"

"Huh? Oh, he has no clue it's where I want to go. I mean, I mentioned it had some great programs, but he basically blew me off."

"Does it have a better journalism program than the other two?" I asked.

He stared at me while chewing his French fry. "Yup, and it's where my favorite newscaster went to school. They help you get internships, bring in guys from the field—people who have gone in with the troops in Afghanistan and the reporter who was captured in Syria came last year. I watched a video of his talk online and it was *epic*."

"Your whole face lights up so much when you talk about this stuff. You need to try to talk to your dad again about it. Or maybe your mom."

"It won't go anywhere. My mom goes along with what my dad says, and there's no way he'd ever be okay with it," he said. "There is a scholarship to get in, and it's pretty prestigious. He might take it seriously if I won it, and maybe he'd entertain the idea of letting me go there for a semester, but then I know he'd make me transfer."

"Are you going to apply for it?"

"I don't know, but I'd have to write an essay on what story the news isn't telling today and why it isn't being covered."

"Do you have any ideas for it?"

"A couple. One on race relations, one on military suicides, and another on how families that decades ago would have fallen into the middle class are now living just above the poverty line."

"Wow, that's heavy stuff. Which one are you going to write on?"

"I've written something for all three, but I don't know which one to submit. If I do the military one, I risk my dad losing votes if my essay ever became public. And if I hand in the one about families...well, then people could go over my dad's voting record and point out anything he voted for which might have caused anything like what

I'm writing about. The race one is controversial, but probably the safest bet."

"Which one are you the most passionate about?"

"The military suicide one. My cousin had a hard time
when he came back from being overseas and...well, one
of my family members attempted suicide once, and I
know there's a stigma about it."

"Then why don't you go with what you're passionate
about? People should be able to separate what you do
from your dad," I said.

Brendon stared out the window for a minute. "I've
never told anyone this—not even a lot of people in my
family know this—but the person who attempted suicide
was my brother."

"Jayson?"

He nodded. "Yeah, it's part of the reason he's taking
time off from school. They say he's doing work with my
dad, but he's going to therapy, and nobody wants to rock
the boat."

"I had no idea. What happened?"

"Honestly, I don't know the whole story because it
happened while he was away at school. His roommate
was gone for the weekend, and luckily he called my mom,
and they went up there and got him before things got too
far. Jayson's never told me everything or how it went
down, but now you know why I got so upset when I saw
Brooke with her new boyfriend."

"Does she know what went on with Jayson?" I asked.

"I think she knows something went on, but I don't
think she knows how far it went. You know what drives
me nuts about this whole thing? Why do we have to keep
it so quiet? I get they don't want Jayson's personal business out there in the street, but even at home they *never*
talk about it. My dad tells him he can come to him with
anything, but you can tell Dad is uncomfortable about it,
and my mom keeps her books on suicide and depression

hidden in her bedroom where the maid won't see them. Mom won't order books online or download them because someone might trace them to her and wonder why she's buying them—I heard her say those words to my dad."

"Wow, is Jayson doing better?"

"I think so—hope so anyway. Family secrets suck. You know, they used to hide away Grandpa once he got sick so people could remember him the way he was. What's wrong with the way he is now? He had a stroke—nothing to be ashamed of. Yet when everything was going on with Jayson, they had Grandpa come to one of Dad's speeches, and I feel like it was to put the focus on Grandpa, so anyone who might be curious about why Jayson left school wouldn't pay attention to it."

"I'm sorry you've had to deal with all of this."

"Yeah, but I'm glad I told you. I feel a little better talking about it."

Reaching over, I squeezed his hand. I didn't need to ask him where we stood. Just knowing he could confide in me was all I needed.

"You can always talk to me."

"I know."

Chapter 22

THE NEXT DAY, Mr. Horowitz wanted us to go outdoors and write about nature in our journals. The memorial area seemed like the perfect spot, but I could hear a bunch of noisy kids playing soccer nearby. I had been there for five minutes when I noticed a spider web attached to my jeans. Between swatting at bugs and my hair blowing everywhere, I ended up writing about how next time I would remember to bring a hair clip. When Mr. Horowitz read my piece, he wrote I should let nature "overtake me" and not focus on the "outside world," but on the natural world. Whatever.

When I got home, Dad said Grandma had been throwing up again.

"Mom's been there all day. Do you want me to drop you off?" he asked.

Dad drove me to the hospice, and Grandma seemed so helpless lying there. I had never seen her so vulnerable. I was used to her hauling huge laundry baskets, cooking goulash, and yelling at game shows on TV, not lying there half-unconscious. There was this part of me that kept thinking if she wanted to, she could make herself well again. If she cared about us, she would fight and get out of this stupid bed and go home and make a pot of vegetable soup, and we could eat some carrot-cake muffins. Sometimes I felt like she was in there somewhere, and I almost wanted to scream loud enough for her to hear me.

I read to her for a while, and my mom said she had a migraine and wanted to go home. As we were driving, I checked my social media sites and saw a bunch of my friends posting about what they were doing after school. It was all stuff like practices, clubs, hanging out with friends, or their boyfriend or girlfriend. Then there was a post of Katia with her grandma, and they were going to yoga class together. Seeing everyone with their normal, uncomplicated lives was hard enough, but seeing Katia's grandma on a yoga mat while mine hadn't made eye contact with anyone in days? It was too much.

As soon as Mom pulled into the driveway, I grabbed my purse and told her I was going for a walk. I went all the way down to the elementary school in our neighborhood. There were a bunch of kids on the swings, and I wanted to be alone, so I went over and sat on the bleachers next to the baseball diamond. It was the first time I had been in complete silence in a long time. I tucked my hair into my jacket collar, put my phone ringer off, and stared into space. As long as I was outside I figured I might as well do my nature journal assignment, so I pulled a notebook out of my purse and found a pen. I started writing about the bugs and about how cold I was, but pretty soon it was all about the stuff I had been dealing with recently. I filled three and a half pages, but when I stopped to look it over, it shocked me what I had put down on the paper. I wrote how I didn't feel my writing was as good as everybody else's and how I didn't know if I would have been able to handle interning at the newspaper. Then I wrote about my feelings on how I wasn't sure if I was good enough for Brendon and if he actually liked me, and how there was a part of me which felt like if my grandmother truly loved me then she'd fight harder. I felt guilty even writing it, but I felt I needed to write it down because a little part of me had these nagging feelings.

I walked home, and Mom told me Brendon and Rory had called the home phone. Since I didn't feel like talking to anyone, I went upstairs to read. Kylie called later, and I had to pick up for her.

"Zach's driving me nuts. He went to Moby's with his friends the other night, and I thought he and I were doing something at night, so I was at home waiting for him to call while he was out with his stupid friends," she said.

"I hate men," I said.

"I thought you and Brendon worked things out," she said. "Hold on, other line."

She came back and said it was Zach calling to apologize.

"What was his excuse?" I asked.

She said he didn't realize she wanted to go out, and he said he'd make it up to her. He even made a special playlist for her. Gag me.

"And you're going to let him get away with it?" I said.

"It's not like he ran over my puppy," she said.

"Men are so self-centered. I feel like maybe I'm letting Brendon get away with too much stuff—like, yeah, we're getting along, but he did blow off a big moment for me, and the whole Lauren dance thing. Plus, I never—"

"You like him, right?"

"Yeah, but why should I always have to—"

"Give in?" she said.

"Right. I'm getting mad all over again," I said.

"Okay, you can tell me I've been reading too many of my mom's self-help books, but don't you think maybe you're getting mad at him to push him away?" she said.

"Hold on, let me get my copy of *Being You.*"

She came back on the line. "It says sometimes we put up roadblocks because we don't feel worthy of something, and we run from our fears instead of facing them."

"So you think I'm not good enough for him?" I asked. "You said it at the football game—"

"I didn't—the *book* said it. Maybe you feel unsure about some stuff, and instead of dealing with—"

This was getting way too close to what Cheryl had said. "Not in the mood for a therapy session right now. My grandma's still in a coma, I still have my stupid journal thing to type up, my grandpa's—I'm just not in a good mood right now," I said.

"You don't say. What's wrong with your grandpa?" she asked. "Is he sick, too?"

I didn't feel like going into the whole "my grandpa was wetting the couch, and he doesn't even realize my grandmother's gone half the time" thing.

"He's just upset over my grandmother," I said.

"Listen, I'm working at the coffee shop after school if you want to stop by. If my manager's not around, I'll slip you an apple cinnamon muffin," she said.

"Okay, I'm supposed to wait for Brendon after school. I'll tell him to meet me there."

I dropped by the bagel shop after class, and Kylie made me a white chocolate soy latte and gave me a chocolate chip muffin since they were out of the apple cinnamon ones.

"White chocolate is our new coffee flavor, but so far all of mine have been too sweet or not sweet enough," she said.

"It could do with a touch more chocolate," I said.

She put more flavoring in my latte and said she brought *Being You* for me to look at.

"Is this the book your mom reads while she's in the bathroom?" I asked. "Maybe I should wear rubber gloves or something."

She rolled her eyes, and I thumbed through it to make her happy. She had stuck a bookmark in the chapter on self-sabotaging, as if she was being subtle. Brendon came to pick me up, but said he had to drop me off without hanging out because he had a student council meeting at seven o'clock. I wanted to talk to him about my grandmother, but instead I was home in time to work on my math.

On Friday, Grandma's breathing had gotten worse. The nurses said she might not pull through, and Mom and I went to sit with her. I wasn't sure what to say because I didn't want to talk to her like this was our last conversation. Even though things were looking worse and worse, I still didn't want her to know I thought she might die. We stayed for three hours reading from her prayer books, but Grandma didn't even stir. Mom went straight to bed when we got home, but I stayed up listening to music and crying and didn't fall asleep until four in the morning.

Chapter 23

MY PARENTS WENT to the hospital early the next morning. Later Aunt Caroline and Uncle George came to the house, and I went with Caroline to the hospital while George stayed with Grandpa. The doctor told us to prepare ourselves, and I felt frozen inside. I wanted to scream, asking how you prepare yourself for something like this. Was it like bracing for a car accident? It seemed so crazy to say you could get ready for something like this.

We all took turns talking to Grandma. I sat outside her room wondering what to say to her for the final time. How did you sum up all those years in one moment? Aunt Caroline came out of the room and told me I could go in next. Standing up, my legs felt shaky. My anxiety spiked as I walked into her room. An unfamiliar, sickening sweet smell hit me. I had no clue what it was—it certainly wasn't the antiseptic cleaner I was used to smelling in this place. It almost made me gag. Grandma looked waxy and lifeless on the bed. I had seen her sleeping many times, and this wasn't anything like that peaceful dozing she did on the couch. This was a deep trance that made me look over at the monitors to see if she was still with us.

"Grandma," I said, reaching for her hand. "We're all praying for you, and I don't want you to be scared. Please know that we'll take care of Grandpa and do everything we can for him. I love you so much—" My voice broke, and the tears streamed down my face. Pretty soon I was crying so hard I began coughing and gagging. Aunt Caroline came into the room and put her arms around me.

"It's okay, Em. She knows. There's nothing more you need to say. She knows your heart."

Aunt Caroline and I left, and we were just pulling in the driveway when Uncle George came out of the house.

"The hospice just called. They said she passed away," he said.

I just stood there frozen in the driveway until Caroline pushed me back in the car.

I didn't say anything on the ride to the hospice. Grandpa sat next to me, but he didn't speak either. He just stared straight ahead, and I wondered if he was aware what was happening.

"Dad, are you okay?" my mom asked him.

"Mmm," he said with no emotion. I saw my parents exchange a look. Maybe Grandpa was in shock. I squeezed his hand, and he nodded at me.

When we got to the hospital, my mom went in the room first. Dad took me aside.

"Em, wait with Grandpa while I go talk to the doctor. We're worried what impact seeing your grandma will have on him right now," he said.

Uncle George and Aunt Caroline walked over and asked why we weren't in the room.

"Dad wants us to wait and get the all-clear from the doctor," I said, glancing in Grandpa's direction to let them know why without saying it out loud.

Uncle George rolled his eyes. "We are not going to coddle a grown adult," he said, taking Grandpa's arm.

"Wait, this could have serious—"

"*Enough*, Emme. He's going in."

I stood there shocked as my dad and the doctor walked up.

"Where's your grandpa?" Dad asked.

"George insisted we stop coddling him."

The doctor sighed. "Personally, I would not have subjected him to this because it could cause confusion."

"I would have had better luck stopping a moving tank," I said, feeling queasy.

"You don't have to go in if you don't want to," Dad said as the doctor went in to talk to the family.

"It's okay. Do you know what that weird smell in the room is?" I asked. "It was making me feel sick when I was here earlier."

"You mean like a decay smell?"

My eyes widened, and I felt dizzy. I put my hand out and grabbed the doorframe.

"Oh, kid, sorry. Did *not* think that one through. Okay, let's get you a chair."

I sat down and took a deep breath. My head felt like it was swimming, and my chest felt tight.

Uncle George came out into the hall. "You guys coming? Hurry up," he said, annoyed, and went back into the room without asking why I was sitting in a chair with my head almost in my lap.

"Em, you don't have to go in," Dad said.

"No, I need to make sure Grandpa's okay," I said, slowly getting up. "If I throw up though, three guesses on who I'm going to aim for."

Dad nodded. "I wouldn't blame you a bit. I'll crack a window to get some air going."

We walked in, and Grandma appeared like she was just sleeping, her mouth open. Caroline held her hand as a priest came in. Dad went to open a window and told my mom I wasn't feeling well.

"Here, why don't you sit down," Mom said.

The priest came over to me.

"I'm so sorry for your loss. It's hard to lose someone who is special to you," he said, squeezing my hand. "The memories will hurt at first, but later will bring you joy. And your grandmother would want you to remember them with joy."

My eyes filled up as I nodded. I wanted to say something back, but it was like words wouldn't come out.

He walked over to Grandma's bedside, and he must have said a prayer or something, but I didn't hear a word. I sat there feeling like I was watching the whole thing on TV. This didn't seem like real life. Aunt Caroline was staring at Grandma, and her eyes were filled with tears. My mom sat with her face scrunched in sadness and pain. Grandpa reached over to the nightstand and straightened the little prayer books, her rosary, and her comb. Then he picked up her tiny comb and held it to his heart, and I lost it. I shook and cried, and my mom squeezed my arm. I saw Dad walk Grandpa out of the room.

"We can go now," Mom said.

"Did you want to say a final good-bye?" Aunt Caroline asked.

"I just want out of this room," I said.

I took a deep breath as soon as I walked into the hallway, and the antiseptic smell filled my lungs. The priest gave me a hug.

"My grandpa hasn't been doing well since Grandma got sick. Please pray for him," I said.

"Of course, I will keep all of you in my prayers," he said.

We came home, and even the house felt different. It was like the energy had changed, and it was so quiet you could hear the refrigerator hum. I went to my room and cried.

"Em, dinner's ready. George made peanut butter sandwiches," my dad said. "You coming?"

I came down and ate two sandwiches because I had forgotten to eat after school today. Mom asked me if I wanted to call someone, but I said I was going to bed.

My family went to meet with a funeral director the next morning. They asked if I wanted to go with them, but I wanted to be by myself. I needed to be alone, and I didn't feel like I could cry in front of everybody. People kept calling the house to find out about the funeral. I didn't know anything, so I stopped answering the phone and only picked up when I saw Margaux's name on the home phone's caller ID. Margaux was probably the least sympathetic person I knew, but she ended up being the right person to talk to. She knew I hadn't been to a funeral before, and she wanted me to know what to expect at the funeral home and the church service.

"Do you want me to get your homework tomorrow?" she asked.

"Yeah, I guess. Thanks."

Mom came home and asked if I had talked to Kylie and Brendon yet.

"I don't feel like talking on the phone, but I told Margaux," I said.

"This morning Grandpa cried while eating his cereal, but when we got to the funeral home, he kept asking why we were there," she said.

"How was he when you told him?"

"First time, he said at least she wasn't in pain anymore. Second time, he seemed shocked, and the third time he nodded like he just had forgotten. I don't know, Em. Caroline wants her own doctor to evaluate him," she said.

"Has she mentioned nursing homes?"

"No, but your uncle did. You'll be happy to know she said Grandpa would stay with family unless there is a physical reason why we can't take care of him. We're going to work out the details in the days to come, but for now he'll spend six weeks with them, and then come stay with us to give them a break."

Grandpa came in the room then. "Emme, are you okay?" he asked.

"Yeah, Grandpa. I'm just sad."

"Me, too. I miss Mom," he said.

"Yeah, we all do," my mother said. "Why don't we go watch a movie for a little while."

Grandpa put his hand on my shoulder. "Want me to make you an ice cream cone like old times?" he asked.

My eyes watered as I nodded. "I'd love that."

Glancing over at my mom, I saw she had tears in her eyes, too. Even though I knew he might be asking me where Grandma was in an hour, I was going to hold onto this moment for a while.

Chapter 24

I DIDN'T FEEL like myself when I woke up the next morning. I felt numb—like a civil war could be going on outside my bedroom window and I'd just stare and blink as it went on around me. Even though I had slept for eight hours, I had no energy. All I wanted to do was to go back to bed, and I didn't feel like being put display or talking to people. I wanted to be alone, but I had to go to the prayer service for Grandma. Then a memory came flooding back, and I remembered I had gone to a funeral home once when I was eight years old. Maybe I repressed it, but I remembered being scared, and Grandma had taken me out into the hall and told me it was okay to cry and how sometimes she got scared at these things, too.

I hadn't left my house in two days. Margaux had been dropping my homework off, but I hadn't touched it. Brendon and Kylie had called, Rory had e-mailed, and Darren even stopped over, but I told my mom to tell everyone I was sleeping. I didn't want to see my friends, and I felt gross since I hadn't showered in two days. Mom made me wash my hair and told me to put on some makeup because I was a "little pale." What she meant was she didn't want people to be frightened by my appearance since I had dark circles and my eyes were like roadmaps because I had been crying so much.

"By the way, Brendon is going to be at the service," she said.

"Why? It's going to be super uncomfortable."

"He called the home phone since you weren't picking up your cell or answering your texts. He was concerned about you, and I thought you might want someone there with you," she said.

"Was it his idea or yours?" I asked, narrowing my eyes.

"He asked if you wanted him to be there, and I said it would be nice if he wanted to come," she said. "I thought you'd be happy."

We had just started hanging out together, and all I needed was for him to make some insensitive remark. Yeah, we could have deep conversations compared to most of the people I knew, but was he a shoulder to cry on? And let's face it—he had never seen me when I was this down. I didn't think he was shallow, but I wondered how he'd react if I fell apart or if Grandpa started acting confused. But then I figured if he got scared off by me being a complete mess then I didn't need him around. I had been just fine without him once, and I could do it again.

I was transferring my stuff into my nicer bag for the funeral when Cheryl's card fell out. Picking it up, I saw her e-mail address was on there. For some reason I felt the need to let her know my grandma had passed away, so I sent her a message. She probably wouldn't even remember who I was.

I put on Grandma's bracelet as I got ready. She hadn't met Brendon, but I knew she would have liked him. Even though I would never be able to ask her, I had a feeling somehow she'd let me know what she thought of him. As I rode with my parents to the funeral home, I started to get mad at myself for worrying about what Brendon would think about everything. I shouldn't have to worry about him. After all, this was supposed to be about Grandma and my family coming together. Not like I had seen much support. My mom spent all of her time with the caterers or the funeral director, and my cousin Ashleigh had decided not to come because she had a cheerleading competition coming up.

Aunt Caroline gave me a hug as soon as I walked into the funeral home. Most of the people walked right past me to get to my parents. Brendon wasn't there, so I went and sat on one of the couches and watched people come in. I didn't know what to do with myself, so I pulled out my phone and saw I had a message. It was from Cheryl.

Emme-

I am sorry to hear about your loss. Keep in mind we only feel great pain because we felt great love, and few people are privileged enough to experience truly selfless love. What you did by being there for your grandmother was an amazing thing, as is your being there for your grandfather now. While some see it as a burden, realize it's a privilege to be there and experience a purer form of love than most will ever know. I know it's tempting at this time to shut people out and fear losing someone else, but the saying is true about it better to have loved than lost then never to have loved at all. I hope things are going well for you with your boyfriend. Keep in mind we're all just trying our best, and people can say some stupid stuff when it comes to death, so try not to hold it against them—I only say this because I almost broke up with my boyfriend when my own grandfather passed.

You've got this, but if there's anything I can do please let me know.

Take care,
Cheryl

The funeral director put on a song about losing a loved one, and I swore the song could wring tears from concrete. I felt so alone, and I realized it was because I always sat with Grandma whenever we had to go to some family thing. She used to call me her pal and say we had to stick together. Now my pal had left me.

Father Jerzy arrived, and he greeted my parents and aunt and uncle.

"Is everyone here? Should we get started?" he asked.

"Wait, where's Grandma?" I asked, looking around. And then it hit me. Aunt Caroline stared at me with tears in her eyes.

"This will happen a lot as you get used to this," Father Jerzy said, squeezing my hand. "I did the exact same thing when my father passed away. You feel the loss more at family events where you're so used to seeing them."

My eyes were blurring from tears, and I tried to nod and pretend I was okay, but I was about to lose it.

"Be gentle with yourself," he said. "Grief doesn't heal overnight, but one day the good memories will ease things a bit."

Aunt Caroline and Grandpa sat on either side of me as Father Jerzy began to talk about Grandma. It was weird to hear him calling her "Franceska" because everyone called her "Frances." Someone put on a song, and I started crying because I had played the same song for her in the hospital. Caroline passed me the tissue box, and I rubbed my eyes without thinking about my mascara. My eyes started to burn, which only made me cry harder. When the service was over, I got up and went to the restroom. I hid out in the restroom until Caroline came looking for me.

"Emme, you have to come out and greet people. It's not polite," she said.

I was upset, but was I supposed to put on a happy face so no one will be offended? Taking a deep breath, I came out of the stall and splashed some cold water on my face. My face was red, and my lips were puffy. My appearance reflected how I felt, but maybe people would steer clear of me, and I could be alone. I walked out of the restroom and saw Brendon standing by the front door. Part of me wanted to run and hide among my family, but I went over to him wondering if he was going to be mad I had ignored his phone calls.

"Hey, how are you doing?" he asked. "Sorry I came in late. I got here on time, but when I got to the door—I dunno," he said, shrugging. "I guess I started thinking about my granddad, and it all kinda got to me."

I felt a pang of jealousy he still had grandparents, but I nodded.

"Grandparents are always the ones who spoil you and think you're perfect," he said. Way to comfort by reminding me of all the things I was going to miss. Why not just tell me there was no Santa Claus, too?

"I used to play basketball when I was in middle school," he said. "It was my first game, and I got confused and threw the ball into the wrong net. Everybody made fun of me, but my granddad said I had made a great three-pointer. Like he didn't even notice I had humiliated myself in front of the whole school."

"So sweet. You know, I used to take baton lessons, and we had this recital at the big auditorium downtown. I was super anxious and accidentally threw my baton into the balcony during a performance. So embarrassing, but Grandma said I was the best one on the stage because I didn't even need a baton."

"You were a baton twirler?" he said. "I'm trying to picture this."

"Yeah, and I took Hawaiian dance lessons, too," I said.

"Got any pictures of you in a grass skirt?" he asked.

"Gross, I was eight years old," I said, laughing.

We sat in silence for a few minutes, and then he

asked if I thought the grass skirt might still fit. We both started laughing, and my Uncle George glanced over and gave us a funny look.

"My uncle probably thinks I'm being inappropriate."

"If you don't have your sense of humor, then what do you have?" he asked.

"I'm glad you came," I said. "I would have understood if you didn't want to come, though, because I don't want to be here myself."

"I wasn't sure if you wanted me here because you didn't return any of my calls. I wanted to give you some space," he said. "But then I tried to read your mind, and I figured I should come."

I thought it was weird he said he "read my mind" because I had always found it strange when he'd know the exact moment to call, but I shrugged it off. After all, I was the one into all the New Age stuff, not him. I wanted to ask if he'd come to the funeral tomorrow since we had a half-day at school, but I didn't want to get rejected. He probably had a committee thing and wouldn't be able to make it.

"Hey, what time is the funeral?" he asked. "Do you mind if I come?"

"It's at noon."

"They're not going to play the stupid, sad song again, are they? They played that at my great-uncle's funeral. Actually, they play it at every funeral," he said. "It's like the new funeral anthem."

"I think it'll be strictly church music," I said.

"I'm holding you to it. I will bolt if I hear the song, but I'll take you with me. Deal?"

"Works for me."

"How's your grandpa holding up?" he asked.

I bit my lip. Aunt Caroline didn't want people to know Grandpa was dealing with dementia, so she had Uncle George sit with him at all times to field any questions Grandpa couldn't answer.

"It's kind of soon to tell," I said.

"Emme, we need you," Caroline said. "There are a lot of cousins you haven't talked to yet."

"Which is code for, 'stop talking to your boyfriend and do your civic duty,'" Brendon said, winking.

Boyfriend? "Yeah, you're probably right."

"I should head out, anyway. My mom is having dinner sent to your house tonight. She remembered you don't eat meat, though."

"How nice of her."

"She said people always drop off casseroles, and she couldn't bear the idea of you trying to find something meat-free to eat during this time," he said. "She painted a vivid picture of you sitting in front of a chicken noodle casserole and looking tragic. Jayson said he was about to go over and cook you a vegetable lasagna because of it."

"I don't know how you managed to make me smile twice on a day like this, but you did," I said.

"It's my job."

"Thanks for coming."

He leaned over and hugged me. "Anytime."

Chapter 25

I WOKE UP early on the day of the funeral, and I didn't know what to wear, but Mom let me borrow her red cashmere sweater.

"Can I wear red to a funeral? They always show everybody in black in the movies."

"You can wear anything you want, and Grandma always liked you in red. She always used to buy you red sweaters for school picture day. Every time I walked in her hallway, it would make me smile how all your school photos were in red," she said. "It's fitting you wear red."

I heard two Sweetie Gals songs on the way to the church.

"Hey Emme," Kylie said, coming over to hug me.

"I didn't know you were coming," I said. "Sorry I haven't called you back. I've been so out of it."

"I know, and it's a half-day anyway, so my mom let me cut out early so I could be here," she said. She told me everybody missed me at school, and she said Darren kept asking about me.

"Margaux is coming, and Rory said she'll call you tonight. Oh, Tyrell gave me a sympathy card to give you," she said, digging in her purse. "He said he'll help you with the math stuff when you get back, too."

"Tyrell is so thoughtful. You know, Brendon's supposed to come today," I said.

"Are you sure?" she asked. "The student council's supposed to have a mandatory meeting after school because it's a half-day. I guess he's going to miss it for you."

He probably forgot about the meeting when he said he'd come.

My mom and Caroline were worrying about whether there would be enough food for everyone at the luncheon after the service. We stood in the hall of the church and greeted everyone as they came inside. Margaux walked up, clutching Seth's arm. She was always hanging on him trying to show what a close couple they were. Meanwhile, he always seemed like he wanted to escape. I had to admit I was impressed he had agreed to come to a funeral with her. She must have told him about the luncheon afterward. I was still looking for Brendon when Caroline touched my arm and told me it was time to go inside.

My mom and Caroline walked in first with Grandpa, and then my dad, Uncle George, and I followed behind them. I sat next to my dad and Grandpa in the first bench. Grandpa got emotional, so I spent the service comforting him.

Father Jerzy ended the service, and the choir began singing "How Great Thou Art." The family was supposed to leave first, so I followed my dad out of the pew. Kylie waved to me as we walked down the aisle, and I noticed my cousins, Tara and Rodney, hadn't come to the funeral. I helped Grandpa down the steps to the church basement where the luncheon was being held. The tables were all set up, and Grandpa wanted to sit down. Kylie and Margaux stood in the doorway until I motioned them over. They didn't know what to say to Grandpa.

"Thank you girls for coming," he said. "Emme, you

should go and sit with your friends. I'll go sit with Alde-ans."

"This might be super inappropriate and all, but who is the hot guy with the highlighted hair?" Margaux asked as Grandpa went over to sit with his nephews.

"Don't you have a boyfriend?" I asked.

"Yeah, but Seth's in the bathroom," she said. "I'm free to look as long as I don't do it in front of him."

"The one in the navy suit? I know he's my cousin, but I don't see this side of the family very often. I'm guessing either Fredrick or Austin," I said.

"How old is he?" she asked.

"I don't know. I think they're both still in high school. Um, Seth is on his way over here," I said.

"Margaux, only you would try to pick someone up at a funeral," Kylie said. "Next time, don't bring a date."

I could tell Margaux was wishing she hadn't brought Seth. Mom walked by and told us to wait until everyone else had gone in the food line.

"We weren't expecting this many people to come, but Theresa's whole family came, and she has twenty grand-kids," Mom said. She handed me some money. "If they run out of food you can run to the fast food place next door."

Father Jerzy came over and gave me a hug. "Why aren't you guys in line for lunch?" he asked. "Aren't you hungry? We've got lots of good food."

I explained my mother's worries about there not be-ing enough food for everyone. He shook his head.

"The women who cook for these events always make extra so everybody can have seconds or even thirds. Go help yourselves," Father said. "Just save me a cupcake—chocolate, not vanilla."

We got in line and piled our paper plates high with potatoes, pasta salads, and rolls. I hadn't eaten much the night before, and I was starving. I even went back for seconds. Seth and Margaux hit the dessert table, and they brought us each a piece of spice cake and a cupcake.

"Margaux, we've gotta take off," Seth said. "I have to be at work by three."

Margaux started to get up, but Kylie said her mother was going to pick her up after the luncheon, and she could give her a ride home. Seth left and Margaux forced me to get information on my cousin.

Aunt Caroline brought Austin over to the table, and Margaux moved right in on him. She even ended up getting a ride home with him. Father Jerzy came over to say we were going to the cemetery next, so Kylie gave me a hug and promised to call me later.

"I'm sorry he didn't show today," she said. "I'm sure he wanted to be here."

"Whatever, it's fine. I'm so grateful you were here, Ky. Thank you."

I got in my Uncle George's car to ride over to the cemetery.

"You okay, Em?" Caroline asked.

"Yeah, my boyfriend was supposed to be here, but I guess he couldn't make it."

"Well, it was nice of him to come yesterday and for his family to send over dinner."

"I would have felt out of place coming if I were him," George said. "He came yesterday, and it was nice your friends came today to support you."

"Way more than Tara and Rod did," Caroline said. "I asked their mother where they were today, and she lied straight to my face and said they had school today, when I know full well St. Lucy's had the day off."

"You know, Margaux left with Austin," I said.

"You're kidding me? Austin's supposed to be at the cemetery because he's a pallbearer," she said.

We arrived at the cemetery, and Mom told me to pick a rose from the flower arrangement next to the door as we walked into the chapel. It didn't matter that Austin left because the funeral director wheeled the casket in. Father Jerzy said a few words and had my grandma's sister, Theresa, and Grandpa both sprinkle holy water over the casket. That's when it hit me—this was final. My grandmother was actually in the box in front of us, and we were going to leave her. I could feel my anxiety rising as I realized this was the last time I'd ever be in the same room with my grandma. Adrenaline pumped through my body as the people started filing out, but I just sat there. Once I left this room, I wouldn't have a grandma anymore. How could everyone just walk out and go about their lives? Caroline put her hand on my shoulder.

"Honey, it's time," she said.

I wanted to be the last one out, so I waited until everyone had passed by, and then put my hand on the casket. I didn't know what to say, so I said "good-bye" to Grandma in my head and placed the rose on top. I sat in the backseat and cried quietly the whole way home. It started to rain when we got out of the car, and I wanted to go back and tell them they couldn't leave my grandma out in the rain. I couldn't stand the thought of her being outside in the rain and getting cold. Crying, I went up to my room and tried to write in my journal, but I had too much going on in my head to put into words. Brendon and Kylie both called, but I wasn't in the mood to talk to anyone.

I came downstairs at five o'clock, and there were still a few family members at the house. My grandpa was sitting with his cousin, Eddie, who was speaking Polish to him. Grandpa couldn't remember where he had slept the night before, but he could suddenly speak in Polish without any hesitation. My older cousin Carla came over to sit with us when Eddie left. She had lost her grandmother last summer, and I hadn't gone to the funeral because I had plans to go to the beach with Kylie the same day. Yet here Carla was, and she had taken off a day of work for my grandmother.

Grandpa started to cry, which made me cry, and Carla didn't know what to do. She and I were never close, seeing as she graduated from high school when I was in the first grade, but she sat there with us and tried to be supportive. If I had been her, I would have backed away slowly and left the room. I asked her for her e-mail address before she left. She seemed surprised, but wrote it down for me.

After everyone left, I went upstairs and took off my makeup. Putting on my favorite fuzzy pajamas, I got into bed. I put a cartoon on my laptop and just wanted to forget about my life for a little while.

Chapter 26

EVERYONE SWEARS THEY'RE going to be there for you when someone dies, but three days later there's nobody around. Before the funeral, people brought crappy casseroles and gelatin salads over for days. After the last one was gone, my dad realized there was no food in the house. I had noticed, seeing as I don't eat gelatin or casseroles, but did anybody care I was practically starving? Nope. Mom asked me to go to the store with her. Grandma and I used to go grocery shopping together every Thursday night. She liked this grocery store that was a half-hour away because it was cuter than the usual warehouse-like ones and was part of a strip mall. First we'd go look at the candles and decorations at the stationary store next door. Grandma always bought cards for people. She had sent me one for every holiday, always with a twenty-dollar bill inside. Halloween was the first time I hadn't gotten a card from her.

Next, we'd go to this little clothing store where I'd usually find a sweater or something and she'd buy it for me. I never asked her to buy me anything—in fact, sometimes I even tried to talk her out of spending money on me—but she had to get me something. There was one time when I tried on a bunch of stuff and I liked it all, but I told her I didn't need any more clothes. I didn't want to be like my cousin Tara who only spent time with her so she could get stuff. But while I was changing, Grandma took everything I tried on up to the counter and bought it for me.

After we went to the clothing store, we'd stop and have hot chocolate at the bookstore café while reading tabloids. We'd always read who was dating whom and then try to figure out if it was a real relationship or if they were just together to promote a movie. Then we'd *finally* get to the grocery store and load up. Grandma was into organic food. She might have eaten a lot of red meat, but at least it was organic. She always said preservatives were bad for you, and she got me buying all organic fruit and things. However, when it came to junk food and ice cream, as long as it was in the health food aisle, she didn't care. She'd buy gluten-free cookies, all natural cream cola, rice chips, and we'd always go through the ice cream drive-through on the way home. Then we'd go back to their house, and I'd watch TV with Grandpa and finish my ice cream while Grandma did the crossword puzzle. Now it felt like I couldn't even drive past a grocery store without wanting to cry.

When Mom and I walked into the store, my chest felt tight. Then I saw a box of the organic cookies Grandma liked and started crying right in the aisle.

"Emme, I know, it's hard, but Grandma wouldn't want you to be sad," Mom said as she dug through her purse for a tissue. "All I have is an old receipt from the drugstore. Try not to get the ink on your face when you blow your nose."

"Can I get the cookies?" I asked. "And a bottle of the natural soda?"

"I don't care, but I don't want you to be miserable. You know you're going to just sit there crying and eating," she said. "Oh man, they have those rice chips she always ate. Get two bags. I want to drown my sorrows, too."

As much as I missed Grandma, it also felt like I was starting to miss Grandpa, even though he was still here. He would constantly ask, "Where's Mom?" and sometimes he'd even ask, "Is Pop home from work?" about his own father who had died years before I was born. But at least Grandpa didn't seem scared like Grandma had been. He might not have known whose house he was in, but he seemed happy if I put on a ball game and gave him some Cheezy Kurls and a glass of fruit punch.

In the past, we always spent Thanksgiving at my grandma's house. She used to make the turkey, dressing, cranberry sauce, mashed potatoes, and a big pumpkin pie for dessert. Now Caroline and my uncle were coming over to eat a meal my dad had picked up premade from the supermarket. How depressing. Mom had the Thanksgiving Day parade on for Grandpa. I didn't think it was necessary to get dressed up since it was just my aunt and uncle, but Mom told me to change out of my jeans. I put on my beige pants and my favorite black turtleneck sweater. I didn't feel like doing my hair so I pulled it back into a ponytail.

Caroline brought over some flowers for the table, and everyone was trying to be upbeat, but it wasn't working. The only sounds we made during dinner were eating noises, and I realized how disgusting it was to listen to someone chew. I only ate the mashed potatoes and corn because the stuffing had bits of turkey in it and the green bean casserole had bacon in it. There was also a sweet potato dish, but it had marshmallow in it and the thought of mixing candy and potatoes grossed me out. I cut a big piece of pumpkin pie since I was still hungry.

"Emme, you should eat your dinner and not just the dessert," George said.

"I did eat my dinner, but there's meat in the stuffing

and in the beans," I said.

"So pick the meat out," he said.

"You can still taste the—"

"George, leave her alone," Caroline said. "Let's just have a nice family dinner."

He sighed. "I just think—"

"Emme's old enough to decide for herself," she said.

I made sure to put extra soy whipped cream on my pie just to annoy him. He told me about the importance of animal protein, and how I'd basically shrivel up and die without it.

"Interesting, well, I need to catch up on my homework, so I should head upstairs," I said.

I overheard George say it was rude of me to leave when I had company over, but Mom said I needed to make up the assignments from the days I missed for the funeral.

I sat on my bed and flipped through my phone. I knew Kylie was at her grandmother's house, Brendon was with his grandparents', and Margaux had gone to Kentucky to visit her family. However, Rory had said that her family wasn't super traditional so I took a chance and called her.

"What's up?" I asked.

"My whole family is crazy right now. My uncle overcooked the turkey, and my aunt called him stupid, and now everybody's mad at each other. What's going on with you?" she asked.

"I dunno. Everything's weird. I needed an escape from everybody," I said.

"How's your grandpa taking it?" she asked.

I didn't want to tell her Grandpa's dementia had now gotten to the point where he didn't always remember my grandmother had passed away. Rory would feel uncomfortable and probably say how bad she felt for me, and I didn't want her pity. In fact, I was sick of everybody looking at me with those sad oh-you-poor-thing eyes. I had enough of that at the funeral. Instead, I said it was difficult for him.

"It's hard because we always spent the holidays with her," I said.

"Yeah. I'm supposed to go to Frankenmuth with my family for the holiday walk tomorrow," she said.

"Do you have to go?" I asked. "Maybe we could do something."

"Much better! Do you want to get together at your house?" she asked.

My aunt made a big deal about not telling people about Grandpa's dementia, and I didn't want Rory to come over and have it come out she already knew. Plus, the family room still smelled a little bit like urine from yesterday's accident.

"I kinda want to get out of my house because my uncle's driving me crazy," I said, which wasn't a lie.

"Well, maybe you could come with us to Frankenmuth. They have all the holiday stuff up there, and I'll go nuts if I'm left alone with my family for another minute." She went to ask her mom if I could come.

"Yup, it's fine. We'll pick you up at seven tomorrow," she said.

I went downstairs to tell my mom, and my aunt said we were supposed to go shopping tomorrow.

"I already told Rory I would go with her," I said.

"Maybe you should have asked first," my uncle said as he scrubbed the carving knife. I wondered if he wanted to use it on me.

Caroline sighed. "We don't come to town that often, but if you'd rather go out with your friend…"

"We won't be out long. Rory's been a good friend to me, and she's going through some family stuff right now," I said. No need to elaborate on the fact her family's problem was an overcooked turkey.

Mom said I could go, and I offered to help with the dishes. Unfortunately, I had forgotten we used the good plates, which meant they had to be dried by hand. At least I didn't have to wash the gravy boat or the plate the turkey was on because grease made my stomach roll. When I was in the fifth grade I threw up after my mom left a pan of pot roast grease out on the counter.

We went into the family room to watch football after the dishes were done. Normally after the game, we watched *It's a Wonderful Life*, but the disc was at my grandparents' house. Instead, we watched some old Christmas film set in an orphanage with a couple of priests who needed to raise money or else the little orphans would end up homeless. The whole thing was so depressing, watching the tiny children complaining about being hungry. The movie was supposed to inspire people to focus on giving rather than receiving during the holidays, but I honestly didn't know why everybody raved about this movie, which was basically just close-ups of small children crying over being cold and hungry. I bet this movie was why so many people killed themselves over the holidays. Well, this movie and having to spend so much time with their families. I was starting to feel a little suicidal myself when the telephone rang.

"Hey, you picked up. How was your Thanksgiving?" Brendon asked.

Seriously? You blow off my grandma's funeral after saying you'll be there and that's your opener? "Depressing. How was yours?"

"Okay. My grandparents asked about you," he said. "Then my cousin ate too much and puked at the table."

"Charming."

"Every year he and his brother try to outdo each other, and this year he spewed all over," he said. "So anyway, how are you holding up?"

"Still trying to get used to everything."

"Yeah, I'll bet. Oh, I gotta go. My dad's serving dinner to the homeless downtown, and he wants Jayson and
me to go. Talk to you later."

I wondered if I should have said something to him
about feeling hurt he didn't text me to say he wasn't coming at the very least. But I didn't have it in me to get into
an argument. Things weren't perfect, but at least he had
come to the funeral home and was there for me when I
was losing it.

Chapter 27

RORY'S FAMILY CAME to pick me up the next day, and we sat in the back of the van with her cousin, Heidi, who was seven. Rory and I couldn't talk since Heidi kept interrupting, but at least her family wasn't fighting anymore. Rory and I decided to get tickets for the carriage ride, and while we were waiting in line, I saw one of the carriages go by carrying Brendon and Lauren.

"Emme, where are you going?" Rory asked. She ran after me and grabbed my arm. "What's the matter?"

"Brendon's with Lauren," I said.

"You saw them here?"

"In the carriage. They were sitting together," I said as my stomach tensed.

"But I thought you guys were back together," she said.

"So did I."

"C'mon, don't let him ruin this," she said. "I've got the tickets and we're next. We're going to go on the carriage ride and have fun. Maybe they'll put us in with some cute guys, and you can forget all about him."

The last thing I wanted to do was to get into one of

those carriages, but I knew Rory had been looking forward to it so I followed her. Why should everybody's holidays suck just because fate had decided to dump on me? The driver helped us in, and we had to share the coach with a family who smelled like garlic. Not exactly the happy ride we hoped for. Why couldn't Lauren have to sit next to the garlic family? I'm sure the other people in her coach all smelled like expensive cologne and had brought hot chocolate for her drinking pleasure. The ride was okay with the exception of the garlic and horse poop smell. The driver let us off near the nativity scene, and we walked around, looking at the lights.

"Em, they have roasted chestnuts. We've gotta get some," Rory said, pulling my arm.

I had never had roasted chestnuts before, and they were mushier than I expected. I liked the smell and the way they warmed my hands more than I liked the taste. I was about to suggest we get some hot chocolate when I saw Brendon standing on the other side of the chestnut cart. I grabbed Rory's arm and hid behind the giant snowman display.

"Brendon's right over there," I said. "Okay, who is he with?"

"Um, some blonde-haired chick, but I don't see Lauren," she said

I peered around the snowman. "That's his mom. I wonder where Lauren went."

"Can we go inside and get something to drink?" she asked. "My nose is about to fall off from frostbite."

I followed her inside a candy store, and she bought me a licorice rope and some taffy to cheer me up. We sat drinking hot chocolate and watching two guys make fudge.

"Why does every tourist place in Michigan sell fudge?" I asked. "You could go to the gas station and it's like, 'Did you get any fudge?'"

"I dunno, but I like to watch the taffy pull. See the blue kind? I'd love to dye my hair the same color, but I'd have to bleach it first, and it might dry my hair out too much," she said. "Look, Brendon just walked in with his parents."

"Is Lauren with him?" I asked, and Rory stood up to see him better.

"Yeah, I think she's with her parents, and I'm guessing her brother. Her brother's kind of hot," she said, and I glared at her. "What? He's hot in a preppy lawyer way. Not my type anyway."

"I'm going to the bathroom," I said. I stayed in there until Rory came in and said Brendon and Lauren had left.

"I can't believe he took her on some family thing. I wonder if she had dinner with them yesterday. She was probably sitting next to him when he called me," I said.

We finished our drinks and went to meet Rory's family. The kids had gotten candy canes from Santa Claus, and they were all sticky. We were walking back to the van when my foot slipped.

"Ew-wie kablooey," Heidi said, pointing at me, and I realized I had stepped in horse poop. I hated Thanksgiving.

When I got home, I asked Caroline where Grandpa was, and she said he had already gone to bed.

"Okay, I'll just go say good-night."

"Don't bother him. He might be asleep by now."

"Right," I said, but I went to check on him in case whoever put him to bed forgot his nightlight and glass of water or put his glasses on the wrong side of the bed where he wouldn't find them.

I walked into his room, and his face lit up with a smile.

"Hey, Grandpa," I said, plugging in his nightlight and moving his glass of water closer. "You okay in here?"

"Yes, sweetie. Oh, I forgot to tell you, Dennis told me at the funeral he's going to call you because he had to leave early. It was nice to see him again."

My heart hurt as I told him thanks for the message. I closed the door behind me, and my dad was in the hallway.

"Grandpa doing okay?" he asked.

"Yeah," I said, but my eyes welled up with tears. Dad hugged me and I sobbed on his shoulder.

"It's going to be okay. We'll figure something, kid. I promise."

Chapter 28

CAROLINE AND GEORGE left early the next morning. I was exhausted, but I dragged myself out of bed to eat breakfast with them. Grandpa was going back with them for a few weeks, and I started to get emotional when I hugged him as they were leaving.

"I'm going to miss you, sweetie," he said. "You be a good little girl."

My eyes started watering. "Did you take those crystals with you, Grandpa?"

I figured he wouldn't know what they were or even remember I had given them to him, but he pulled them out of his pocket to show me. "I didn't forget, Emme," he said, smiling. He hadn't called me by my name in weeks.

I started crying as I waved from the window. It had been hard with him here, having to constantly show him where the bathroom was, telling him where Grandma was when he asked, but now with him actually leaving I felt sick. Would George and Caroline know how he liked his snack? Would they be patient with him when he got confused? George had zero patience, and I prayed he would understand Grandpa couldn't help it.

I tried going back to bed for a nap, but I couldn't fall asleep. I got up and went for a jog to clear my mind, but it was freezing out, so I came back home and got in the shower. It felt good to be in a steamy room and just to be alone for a while. My skin was glowing when I got out of the bathroom. I slipped on my terrycloth robe and went downstairs to eat lunch. My dad made veggie patties and hash browns. I was on my third helping of hash browns when the phone rang.

"Hey Em. What's up?" Brendon asked.

I hadn't expected him to call. Maybe I either completely misread him the last few weeks, and we had never been back together in the first place, or else he was making a fool of me. I thought I'd have more time to decide how I was going to react. Part of me considered hanging up on him, but decided to act like I didn't care if he was with Lauren.

"Did you have fun on the carriage ride?" I asked.

"Huh?"

"I was there yesterday. I saw you and Lauren in the carriage together," I said.

"Em, I don't want you to get the wrong idea about Lauren and me. It was just a coincidence she was in Frankenmuth with her family," he said, explaining how Lauren's parents played golf with his, and they ran into each other.

"I'm in the middle of eating lunch right now," I said.

"Oh, okay. Well, call me later. Maybe we can go see a movie or something," he said.

I didn't answer. I just hung up the phone, and Mom said I sounded rude.

"Who were you talking to?" she asked.

I shrugged. I didn't want to get into it since she had been out of it since Grandma died. Plus, I didn't want my parents to know Brendon might have been seeing someone behind my back, so I said it was Darren and stuffed another veggie patty in my mouth. After lunch, I called Rory to see if she wanted to get together. Her family was still in town, and she had to babysit for the kids. I was hoping she'd ask me to come over and babysit with her, but she didn't mention it. Instead I went downstairs, and my parents were getting ready to go out.

"Where are you going?" I asked.

"I forgot we had these stupid opera tickets," my mom said. "My manager gave them to me weeks ago, and she'll be upset if I don't show up. Are you going to be all right here by yourself?"

I didn't want to be alone, but I didn't want to say I needed my mommy and daddy to stay home with me. Besides, my mom needed a distraction right now, and I didn't want to ruin her night out. Dad said I could invite a friend over to watch a movie.

"Everybody's out of town, and Rory has to babysit," I said.

"How about Brendon?" Mom asked.

I didn't want to make a big deal out of it, and I pretended I might call him. I'd much rather be alone than have him think it was okay to hang out with his ex all the time. However, fifteen minutes after they left, I was starting to get anxious. I hadn't been home alone in a long time since Grandpa had been staying with us. Now I was all by myself and hearing creaks and groans I had never heard before. The home phone rang, and I checked the Caller ID, but it said "cellular call," and it was a number I didn't recognize.

"Hi, Em."

Crap. It was Brendon. He had used someone else's cell phone because he knew I wouldn't pick up for him.

"Do you want to see a movie tonight?" he asked.

"I don't feel like going out," I said.

He didn't give up. "We could hang out at your house, or I could come get you and we could — "

Something fell upstairs and made a huge banging sound. My whole body went cold.

"I just heard a noise upstairs, and there's no one up there," I said. My eyes darted around the room.

"Do you want me to come over and check it out?" he asked.

I was furious with him, but I was more scared than I was mad.

"Okay, come over," I said.

"On my way. Do not go upstairs."

Like I was going to run up there to investigate whatever made the sound. Just because he thought I was stupid enough to take him back and believe his lame excuses did not mean I was a complete fool.

He was at my house in five minutes, and he went upstairs to check on what had made the noise. I tried to remember if my room was halfway decent. He came back downstairs and said one of the shelves in the guestroom had fallen, and all the stuff was on the floor. I followed him into the room and piled up the books.

"Sorry, guess I was just a little nervous. I haven't been home alone in a while," I said.

"It's no big deal," he said. "Do you want to rent a movie or something?"

I nodded and went to get my purse. He followed me into my bedroom.

I saw a pair of baby-blue underpants hanging on the arm of my chaise lounge. He sat in the chair, but didn't seem to notice my undies until he leaned back and knocked them onto the floor. He glanced down to see what he had dropped.

"I believe these are yours," he said, handing them to me with a smile.

I snatched them from him and tossed them in my hamper. This was just great. First, he thought I was dumb enough to believe he and Lauren "just bumped into each other." Then, I acted like a baby over a noise. Now he got to embarrass me by finding my panties. Maybe I could accidentally set off the alarm at the video store to add to the evening. Why couldn't I just be normal?

We headed to Movie Mania, and he told me to pick out the film. Brendon didn't like romantic comedies, but he didn't say anything when I picked one out. He also hated it when girls drool over hot actors, so I purposely picked a movie with Rex Davidson in it. I'm not into Rex at all, but a lot of girls at school have pictures of him in their lockers.

"I want this one," I said, and he went up to pay for it. Normally, I'd ask his opinion, and I always offer to pay or at least split the cost with him, but not today. We got in the car, and I put on the radio.

"I didn't know you liked Rex Davidson," he said, holding up the movie.

"He's hot," I said, staring straight ahead.

"Well, Audrey Macintosh is pretty hot, too, so I guess it won't be too hard to watch."

I hadn't even noticed she was in the film. Brendon never said stuff about any actress he thought was cute, and I figured he knew what I was doing. After all, he always said he hated it when Margaux would talk about how she was in love with the lead singer from Lone Shark right in front of Seth. He said it was rude, even if the guy was a rock star and it was just a fantasy thing.

"Do you want to get some snacks?" he asked.

"Don't care."

He pulled into the Stop-N-Go, and grabbed a bag of potato chips. They had a bunch of organic chips, but I pretended I couldn't find anything. He got a bottle of soda and asked me what I wanted. I stood in front of the cooler and said they didn't have the juice I wanted. He grabbed a bottle of water for me and went up to pay. He gave me the water, and I held it but I didn't open it. I was upset he thought he could make a decision for me, like I was being too difficult. We got back to my house, and I went into the kitchen. I poured myself a bowl of chips and got my own bottle of water from the fridge. Even though it was the same brand, I left the water he had bought for me sitting on the counter.

"Should we start the movie?" he asked.

I shoved the disk into the DVD player, and the previews started. The movie was bad from the beginning, and the acting was horrible. Brendon made a joke during the film, and I picked up the remote and rewound the part he talked through, even though I didn't care what I missed. I got up to get something else to eat and noticed we had the same brand of chips he had bought at the store, so I brought my bag into the family room and poured them into my own bowl.

"My chips too dirty for you?" he asked, and I shrugged. "Okay, someone's mad at me. Mind telling me what I did?"

"Shh, I want to see this part," I said, picking up the remote to turn up the volume.

"Em, what did I do?" he asked.

"Are you going to talk through the whole movie?"

"I told you I just ran into Lauren at the festival. Obviously you don't believe me."

"Whatever," I said.

"I should go. I thought things were going to be different this time, but if you can't trust me then I don't know what to do," he said, but he didn't get up.

"Fine, go."

He got up and walked out of the room. I heard him close the door behind him, and I went into the kitchen. He had left the water bottle on the counter. I went to lock the front door behind him, but saw he was sitting outside on the porch, so I opened the door.

"Forget your keys?" I asked.

"Can we please talk?"

"Fine," I walked back into the house, and he followed me. It had started snowing, and there were snowflakes melting on his collar.

"I'm not interested in Lauren," he said. "I had no idea she was going to be in Frankenmuth. My dad just ran into Mr. Hartnet—"

"I'm not a jealous person, but I don't like being replaced every time I'm not around. You know, I wasn't the one who started dating as soon as we got into a fight," I said.

"Yes, you did," he said. "You started hanging around that one guy."

"Darren? He's just my friend from class."

"Well, Sam overheard Darren telling some guys you had been all over him at some party."

"What? I never even—I hate when guys imply stuff. *Ugh*, I want to kill him."

"Yeah, my reaction, too," he said.

"But you were the one throwing your girlfriends in my face," I said. "I mean, you and Lauren kissed *right* in front of me."

"She kissed me, and honestly it caught me off guard."

I rolled my eyes. "What about the mermaid?" I asked.

"Who?"

"The girl who dressed up as the mermaid for Halloween," I said.

"Nicola was my co-chair on the planning committee...and I might have offered to drive her because I wanted to make you jealous," he said with a smile.

"How mature," I said.

"You have no idea how upset I was when I heard about you and Darren," he said. "At first, I didn't believe it, but you were *always* with him. It made me sick to think you were already over me."

We stood there staring at each other in the hallway. The phone rang, and I left him standing there. It was Kylie calling from her grandmother's house. I pulled the phone into the pantry and whispered that Brendon was here and told her what had happened.

"Oh wow. Do you have your copy of *Being You* around?" she asked. "There's a whole section on this."

"It's upstairs in my bedroom. What do I say to him?" I asked.

"Do you still like him?" she asked.

"Yes."

"Do you trust him?"

"Yeah," I said.

"And are you finally over the I'm-not-good-enough crap?" she asked.

"Thank you, Kylie. You've been a tremendous help."

"Just tell him you want to…um…you know Margaux would know exactly what to say," she said.

"And Margaux would have him buying her a present at the end of the argument, too," I said. Biting my lip, I realized I didn't have it in me to handle another loss in my life. I felt so empty now with Grandma gone and Grandpa going through so much and not being at our house anymore—I physically couldn't handle any more drama or pain. "Okay, I'm going to go in there and pretend to be Margaux."

"Good luck," she said. "Call me later."

I went back into the hall, and Brendon was sitting on the stairs. I sat next to him and said I believed he and Lauren had just run into each other. Pretending to be someone else gave me courage. I felt like I could say anything I wanted because it wasn't coming from me.

"It threw me the way you just shut me out," he said. "And it hurt to see you had moved on. Before, I felt like we had this connection—like I could almost read your mind."

I wanted to tell him how miserable I had been without him, but I didn't. I had always been honest about my feelings, and it hadn't gotten me anywhere. Kylie was right—I didn't feel like I was good enough for him, and I had never felt comfortable around his friends either. Maybe Margaux was smart to hold back and have some control over the relationship. From now on I was going to follow her lead.

"I just want things to be okay between us. I know you were jealous over Nicola, but—"

"I wasn't jealous of her, just upset you picked *her* of all people. It made me look bad," I said. It was like I was quoting Margaux. "But I didn't honestly think you were interested in her."

He stared at me. "Oh, okay. So...do you want to watch the rest of the movie?" he asked.

"Let's go out. I didn't have dinner, and I'm starving," I said as I grabbed my coat. "How about Finnigan's? I'm craving something fried and greasy."

We got into his car, and I put on some music. He pulled into the parking lot, and I asked him to drop me off at the door because Margaux always insisted her dates do it. We sat down to order and decided to split some potato wedges and fried zucchini. The waiter put crayons on the table in case we wanted to draw on the paper tablecloth. I picked up a red crayon and started to draw a house. Brendon grabbed the blue crayon and drew a swimming pool.

"Maybe I don't want a pool at my house," I said. "Make it a tennis court."

"Oh, so it's *your* house. Fine, I'll make my own," he said and he drew a fence between the house and the pool.

After we ate, we walked downtown and went into one of the gift shops. The store was crowded, and a guy pushing a stroller bumped into Brendon's leg.

"I hate crowds," Brendon said after the guy with the stroller had apologized. "Can we get some air?"

We walked back outside, and I pulled my hands inside of my sleeves and crossed my arms to keep warm. Brendon saw me freezing and gave me his navy scarf. I suggested we stop for hot chocolate, and we went to Beanie Weanies. We waited in a long line, and the little boy behind me had a hacking cough. Grandma always told me to say a prayer and imagine a white light around you whenever you were around sick people. We got our drinks, but there was no place to sit. We stood by the garbage cans and waited for somebody to leave. Two young guys started to get up, and Brendon shot over there and nabbed the table.

"Great save," I said.

"You know, I'm not a people person," he said. "Maybe politics isn't for me."

"You could always try modeling if law school doesn't work out," I said, smirking.

He rolled his eyes. "Yeah. I'm not even sure I'm going to go to law school."

"I thought your family had your ten-year plan mapped out forever. Law school, then politics. Something change?" I asked.

He shrugged. "It's hard to get into law schools, and isn't there some study which says someday there will be two lawyers for every person or something?"

"I don't know, but you have a lot of time before you have to make a decision," I said. "Have you heard from the colleges you applied to yet?"

He shook his head. "Nope, but I'm going to South Bend next weekend with my parents to check out the campus."

I hadn't even thought about the fact he'd be moving out of state if he got accepted. He'd be miles away and meeting tons of new people, and he wouldn't want to be stuck with me anymore. He seemed deep in thought, and I wondered if he was thinking the same thing. Brendon was bound to meet girls who had a lot more in common with him than I did. It was probably a school full of Lauren Hartnets. He'd probably wait until after prom to dump me. Unless he decided Nicola would look better than Lauren in the prom pictures. Then he'd dump me and take her to prom. With my luck, she would get a full scholarship to the same college, and they could spend every moment together.

"Em, do you want to split an espresso brownie?" he asked.

I snapped back to attention. "Sure."

"Kind of dozed off there, huh?"

"I was just daydreaming about my other boyfriend," I said, and I tried to look underneath my eyelashes the way Margaux did when she would flirt with somebody. Margaux had a way of flirting with a guy, while letting him know she had other offers. She knew how to work the whole lashes thing, too. Unfortunately, I think Margaux's mascara worked better than mine because it made me look like I had a nervous tick or something. Brendon stared at me funny as he got up to get a brownie. When he came back, I broke my half of the brownie into little pieces the way Margaux did, and I tried the eyelash thing again.

"Do you have something in your eye?" he asked, leaning over.

"Uh, yeah." It was either lie or admit my attempt to be cute sucked. Margaux should teach a course on this stuff.

After we ate, we got in his car and drove around to look at the Christmas lights. I relaxed and forgot all about trying to be Margaux. We had fun picking out which houses we wanted to live in when we got older.

"I love the red brick house," I said. "Look at that sun porch."

"Okay, that's where we'll live when I'm a journalist and you're a best-selling author," he said.

I was about to say I wanted a garden when I realized

he had talked about us being together in the future. Did he mean it, or had it slipped out and now he regretted it? Would he get my hopes up if he were going to dump me after prom? He dropped me off at home, and I called Kylie as soon as I took my coat off.

"So are you guys okay or what?" she asked.

"Yup, we made up, but—"

"But? Now what?" she asked.

"He's going to be going to be out of state next fall," I said. "And I'm sure he's going to want to see other people."

"Girl, will you just stop thinking so much and relax? He might want to keep seeing you. Besides, fall is a long time away. You could break up way before. He could die before fall ever comes around," she said. "*You* could die before then."

"You're so comforting," I said. "I almost made a fool of myself doing the flirty eye thing Margaux does. He thought I had something in my eye."

"I tried to smack my lips like she does when she wants a guy to notice her mouth, but I ended up smearing my lip gloss all over, and nobody told me," she said. "I didn't even notice I had a peach smear under my lips until I got home from school."

"Wait, did you do it last week? I thought you had impetigo," I said. "I even threw my pen out after you borrowed it."

"Zach thought I had it, too, and he was freaked out I might be contagious. Luckily, we're no longer in the impress-me stage, and I just told him it was lipstick," she said.

"I'll have you know I threw out my favorite pen, too. You know, Margaux needs to write a how-to book," I said.

"Yeah, but her advice would only be good for relationships you want to last less than a month or on guys whose minds you want to mess with," she said. "Geez, poor Seth."

"Actually, she broke up with him before she left for Kentucky. It's poor Austin now," I said.

It was a good thing I never saw Austin at any of the family reunions because it would be uncomfortable, since Margaux would end up dumping him, too. It always took guys a long time to date after she was through with them.

"You know, Margaux isn't the best role model for a decent relationship," Kylie said. "Zach and I only got together *after* I stopped playing games with him, and now he's my best friend, too."

Kylie might have been right, but Margaux had two things I had been craving: self-confidence and control when it came to relationships.

"Still, you might want to call Austin's parents and tell them to cancel any life insurance policies they might have on him. I hear they don't cover suicides, and it would be a shame for his parents to waste all that money."

"How do you know it won't be different with—" I broke off laughing. "Sorry, couldn't say it with a straight face. But who knows? Maybe it will be different with Austin. People can change."

Chapter 29

BRENDON HAD BEEN quiet since his trip to his dad's old school. It didn't take my intuition to tell it hadn't gone well. I wanted to ask him, but I figured he didn't want to talk about it. Sam asked about the trip as we were walking out of school together.

"Nothing much happened. Just took the tour," Brendon said. "We've gotta go. I need to stop at the bookstore before I take Emme home."

He didn't say anything on the way to the bookstore. He didn't even wait for me when he got out of the car. In fact, he headed straight for the resources section and started pulling books off the shelf.

"What are you looking for?" I asked.

"Um...nothing," he said as he flipped through a thick college guidebook.

"I'm going to go walk around," I said.

"M'kay," he said without looking up.

For all he knew I was going to walk out the front door. I didn't want him to think I was just going to sit around waiting for him, so I grabbed a copy of a novel I wanted to get and hid out in the travel section. Let him wonder where I was. However, he found me and asked if I wanted to get something to drink in the café.

"Two soy lattes," he said when we got up to the counter.

"Wait, I want one of those mango-infused waters," I said, putting my hand on his arm.

We sat down, and he put his books on the floor beside him. I put my paperback on the table and struggled to open my bottle. He reached for the bottle, but I managed to open it myself.

"What are you looking at?" I asked.

"Just some college prep books," he said, taking a drink.

"For what? Do you have to take some more tests or something?" I asked.

"Kinda. It's not super interesting." He put the top back on his coffee and stood up. "Are you ready?"

I followed him in line, and he handed me his keys and said I could wait for him in his car.

"But I was going to buy this book," I said, showing him the paperback.

He grabbed it from me. "I'll get it for you," he said.

I glanced over to see if there was some cute girl working the register, but there was a guy behind the counter. It was weird he wanted me to meet him in the car, but I had no reason to stay. I went out to the parking lot and started the car so I could listen to the radio. Brendon opened the door and handed me my book. I offered to pay him back for it, but he shook his head.

"Are you okay?" I asked.

"Just tired. I had a big test today, and I'm worn out," he said. He didn't say another word until he pulled in front of my house.

"Hey, call me later, okay?" he said without even looking at me.

I went inside and called Margaux. I thought maybe

she'd know why Brendon was acting so weird, but she had just gone out with my cousin, and she wanted to tell me all about it.

"We went to Augustine's for dinner, and he paid, of course—"

"You know, it is polite to at least offer to split the check," I said.

"Whatever, and then we went to see the new Anthony Matthews movie," she said, telling me how Austin had brought her peach roses.

"See, red's predictable, but peach is unique and more expensive, especially at this time of year," she said.

"I like getting red roses. Well, I only got them once, but I—"

"They're nice, but they show zero imagination," she said.

I told Margaux how weird Brendon had been acting after school.

"He's probably getting too comfortable with you," she said.

"What do you mean?"

"You know, like he feels like he doesn't need to impress you anymore."

"What do I do?"

"Ignore him a little bit," she said.

Margaux said I should pretend that I was too busy to call him tonight. She thought Brendon took me for granted. I took her advice and didn't call him. He e-mailed me around nine o'clock, but I didn't write back.

Chapter 30

I WAS WALKING down the hallway with Kylie in the morning when I saw Brendon standing with his friends. He said "hi" to me, but I just gave him a smile. Margaux said to be mysterious and unavailable. I went to my locker and put my books away.

"Did you get my e-mail?" he asked.

"I didn't read it until late last night. I was super busy," I said.

"Did you have lots of homework?" he asked.

Actually, I had watched a *Cutie Pies* marathon and spent the rest of the night doing an astrological chart I had promised Rory a while back, but he didn't need to know my plans. I shrugged.

"Everything okay?" he asked.

"Yeah, why?" I asked.

"I dunno. You're acting weird," he said. "Are you sick or something?"

Great, I tried to act mysterious, and he thought I was coming down with something. I said I was fine, and he asked if I wanted to go to the movies after school.

"I thought today was the college prep meeting," I said.

"It'll probably be boring, and it's not like I don't know about it all already," he said. "Meet me at my car, okay?"

I thought it was weird he was going to miss the meeting where the counselors go over all the things you needed to do to get ready for college, but I guess he did have a zillion books on it. I told Kylie and Margaux about it, and Kylie thought he just needed a break from college prep stuff.

"Uh-oh," Margaux said. "He's missing the meeting so you guys can go somewhere private and *talk*."

"But they're going to a movie so they can't talk much," Kylie said.

"Yeah, *or* make a scene," Margaux said. "He wants to break up."

"What? Are you sure?" I asked.

Margaux said she had broken up with three different guys at the movies.

"I always waited until they show the last preview, so the guy can't throw a fit because the theater's quiet. Sometimes the guy leaves, which is great because then I don't have to worry about what to say when the movie's over," she said. "Oh, but make sure he pays for your ticket."

"You let the guy pay for you, and *then* you dump him?" Kylie asked with her eyes wide.

"Sometimes, but Emme will be in the opposite position, so she should definitely get him to pay. It would suck to buy your own ticket and then get dumped," she said.

"Yeah, I'll bet," Kylie said. "I can't believe you."

Margaux pointed out I'd be stuck at the theater afterward since Brendon was the one driving. She said I should go into the mall afterwards and call my parents for a ride home because it would be too humiliating to get a ride home from him.

"Brendon is not going to dump her," Kylie said. "Besides, if he wanted to break up with her, he could just go to the meeting and then dump her afterward. He doesn't need to miss the meeting, too."

"You guys, should I break up with him first?" I asked.

Kylie said we didn't even know if he wanted to break up with me.

"You should find out what was going on with him," she said.

But Margaux wasn't as optimistic.

"Dump him first," she said.

My heart was in my stomach as I walked to his car. He was listening to his favorite *Fat Losers* album when I got in the car. He didn't say much as we drove to the theater. I hadn't actually thought he was going to break up with me, but now he seemed like he had something on his mind.

"Is everything okay?" I asked.

"Do you mind if we skip the movie and just go somewhere and talk?" he asked.

The cheap jerk wasn't even going to pay for my ticket! He was just going to dump me in the lobby and save himself the ticket price. He took my arm and led me into the mall entrance. We sat outside a department store, and I leaned back and folded my arms across my chest. I wasn't going to make this easy for him.

"I'm not going to my dad's school," he said.

"Huh?"

"I met with a counselor while I was there, and it's not going to work out. It's not just my physics grade either. There are so many people applying and I—I dunno. I don't want anybody to know yet because…well, no one thought I had a chance to get in anyway," he said.

"I did, but are you sure there's no chance?" I asked.

"I'm on the wait-list."

"That's good, isn't it?"

He shook his head and said he had met with our school counselor when he got back, and Mrs. Bergin said that it would be next to impossible to move up on that list. She told him he'd need to apply to other schools right away.

"I should have applied to more backup schools, but I was so determined to get in, so I only applied to two others, and I don't want to go to either one."

"You've still got a while to decide what to do, right?"

He shrugged. I had two more years before I had to start worrying about colleges, and I didn't have an idea of where I wanted to go to school. I wasn't sure what to say to him, so I thought about what Margaux would do and asked if he still wanted to see the movie. Maybe he needed a distraction, and after all, Margaux wasn't good at deep conversations, so I figured she'd want to get away from the weirdness and see a movie. I even ordered her favorite combo at the concession stand: bottled water and fat-free gummy bears. Brendon didn't say anything during the previews, but he did offer me some of his popcorn and chocolate-covered peanuts. After the movie, we went to a department store. I was feeling Margaux-like, so I dragged him over to the makeup counter while I tried on a lipstick.

"What do you think?" I asked, trying Margaux's famous lip smack.

He shrugged and said it was nice. I bought it, and then made him wait while I tried on some jeans. He sat in a chair next to the dressing rooms, looking bored. I started to feel bad, so I suggested we stop for lattes at Beanie Weanies. There were a lot of people there, so I told him to get a table, and I'd order for us. I asked the guy behind the counter for extra soy whipped cream and tried doing Margaux's lip smack. I apparently nailed it because I got my extra whipped topping, and he didn't even charge me for the white chocolate flavoring I had in my latte. I brought the drinks over to the chairs Brendon had saved for us.

"What were you doing?" Brendon asked, glaring at me.

"What?"

"The way you were acting with the guy behind the counter."

I acted like I didn't know what he meant.

"I couldn't hear what you were saying, but it sure seemed like you were flirting with him," he said.

"I wasn't, but I guess he was kinda flirting with me," I said. Margaux always acted like she couldn't help she was irresistible.

Brendon stood up and said he wanted to go, but I tugged on his arm and said I wanted to finish my coffee first. He sat back down, but he barely said two words to me. I tried asking him questions, but he kept giving me one-word answers. Finally, I gave up and we left. The whole playing-hard-to-get thing was supposed to make him like me more and give me control over the relationship since I had always felt like *he* was in control before. At least it was how it worked when Margaux did it. The guys would always call her right after they dropped her off. Of course, she was too busy to take the call, but they still called all the same. Only Brendon didn't call me at night, and he barely spoke to me in the hall the next day. I asked Margaux what I did wrong, and she blew it off.

"It's a typical guy thing. You take a little control away, and they've gotta go all out and show you they've still got the power. It's classic," she said, rolling her eyes.

Later, I told Kylie I had followed Margaux's advice, and now Brendon was acting weird. She asked if anything happened at the movies. I didn't tell her about Brendon not getting into his dad's old school since he didn't want anyone to know.

"I would just ask him what's up," she said. "But I wouldn't take Margaux's advice. I mean, has she ever had a relationship which has lasted longer than her attention span?"

Kylie's advice made more sense, and at least she and

Zach had been going out for a while. I was going to write him a note, but Margaux told me not to put stuff in writing. I decided I would leave the math lab a little early to make sure I caught up with him after his last class. However, Tyrell had other ideas.

"The math teacher suggested I work with you to help you get caught up," he said. "I don't know if it's something you wanna do, but I could stay after the lab's over, and we could go over your homework."

I did need the extra help in math, so I stayed. I saw Brendon standing outside the lab, and I went to tell him that I needed to work with Tyrell a little longer.

"I can call my mom for a ride if you have to go," I said.

"Fine, whatever," he said, walking away.

I had to fight to concentrate on what Tyrell was showing me. We worked for a half-hour, and he asked if I had a ride home.

"I'll call my mom," I said.

"I can give you a ride home if you want."

We were walking out to his car when we saw Brendon and Sam sitting on a bench. I knew they were talking about me because Sam nudged Brendon when he saw me.

"Do you want me to wait for you?" Tyrell asked, and I shook my head.

"No, but thanks for helping me today."

"No problem. I needed the extra tutoring points for student council anyway," he said.

I sat down, and Sam got up and made some excuse to leave. I asked Brendon if everything was okay, and he shrugged. I tried to put myself in my Margaux persona, but I figured her solution would be to go after Sam and flirt with him to make Brendon jealous, which was not the right thing to do at the moment. Maybe I needed to drop the whole Margaux thing. It was obvious Brendon was upset about something, so I asked him if he wanted to talk.

"Let's go sit in your car. It's freezing out here," I said.

He switched on the heat in the car, and I rubbed my hands together as the windows started to fog up.

"What's going on with you?" he asked. "You've been acting weird lately."

"Me? You're the one who blew me off in the hall this morning."

He started to say something else when somebody knocked on his window. He rolled it down. "What?"

"Can I get a ride home, man?" Sam said. "My car wouldn't start.

"Fine, get in," Brendon said.

Sam lived further out than me, so Brendon dropped me off first. I was hoping we'd get to talk, but at least he asked if I wanted to hang out after school tomorrow, so he couldn't have been too mad at me.

Margaux, Kylie, and I did a three-way call later to talk about the whole Brendon thing.

"You know what? We should do the new *Healthy Self* thirty-day challenge," Kylie said. "We'll get fitter, healthier, and—"

"You think I need to lose weight?" I asked.

"*No*, it's just part of the program. My mom ordered it, and I just thought you might want to do it," she said. "By the way, did you hear Lauren got into Senator Agretti's old school?"

"Seriously? I wonder if she applied there because Brendon did," I said.

Margaux snorted. "Duh, of course. Seriously, she might as well just pee on him to mark her territory."

"Margaux, shut up," Kylie said.

"Whatever. Anyway, the important thing is if Brendon *knew* she was applying there," Margaux said. "Em, do you think he knew?"

I hoped Lauren was just trying to follow Brendon, but what if they had planned this whole thing while they were dating? What if he convinced her to apply there so they could go to college together, wear matching American flag sweaters with big scarves while drinking hot chocolate, and jump into leaf piles just like a preppy clothing catalog. At least now I didn't have to worry about them reciting poetry to one another in South Bend, but still, what if they *had* made plans to go to school together?

"Don't worry about it," Kylie said. "She was probably trying to follow him—like she always does. She's so pathetic."

Kylie was trying to make me feel better, but Lauren was far from pathetic. After all, she was pretty much the "Most Likely to Succeed" poster girl. While she was out overachieving and saving the world without messing up her perfect, bouncy hair, I was trying to get through each day. I tried to push away the image of Lauren and Brendon holding hands and drinking hot chocolate under a stadium blanket, but of course, I had to go and ask him about it the next day. We were sitting in the bookstore café when I asked him if he knew she had applied to the same school as him.

"Huh? Yeah, I think she mentioned it," he said as he flipped through a news magazine.

"Did you know she got in?"

He glanced up for a second, and then shook his head. I couldn't read his expression. Was he thinking, "Crap, I dumped the wrong one," or "Well, it sucks Lauren got in, and I didn't," or maybe "Will she shut up so I can read this article?"

He just stared at me. "I'm getting a muffin. You want anything?"

I wanted a chai latte, but he got up before I could answer. I followed him in line as he picked up a blueberry fat-free muffin.

"You know, they should call those things frosting-less cupcakes because they're not any healthier—"

"Can I have one day without a food lecture? Please?" he said.

"Fine." I shoved a five-dollar bill at him. "I want a chai latte."

He handed me the money when he brought my drink over to the table. I thought he'd apologize for ripping my head off, but he didn't say anything. He just stared at his magazine. Brendon had been different ever since he found out he wasn't going to his dad's alma mater. I thought about asking if he wanted to do something this weekend, but I didn't want to get shot down. What happened to the guy who used to e-mail me the weather report every night?

"Your horoscope says you shouldn't overspend this weekend," he said.

"You read my horoscope?" I asked.

"Every day," he said.

"Even when we weren't together?"

He nodded,

"I read yours, too."

"Did you read Derrick's as well?" he asked.

"Who? Oh, *Darren*? No. Why?" I asked, trying to hide a smile. He *had* been jealous of Darren.

He shrugged. "I just thought since you started hanging out with him two minutes after we had a fight, maybe you thought *he* was your soul mate. You were supposed to find your soul mate in your number five year, weren't you?" he asked. "So did you?"

I wasn't sure what to say, and I was afraid to set him off, so I said I thought he didn't believe in that kind of stuff. He started to answer when Margaux came over with my cousin. I was surprised she was still with Austin.

"Can we sit with you guys?" she asked. "Austin, bring over two chairs and get me a gingerbread latte and a lemon bar, but not the kind that has the crumbly junk on top of it. I only like the ones with powdered sugar on top."

"So what's up? Ooh, horoscopes," she said, pulling the paper out of Brendon's hands. "Mine says to utilize this opportunity to streamline your position. What's Austin's sign, Em?"

I remembered going to a birthday party for either him or his brother a million years ago, and I thought I had been wearing a sundress at the time, so I guessed it was some time in the summer.

"So like a Cancer or Leo?" she asked. "I hope he's a Leo, I'd hate to have some moody guy dragging me down."

Brendon stood up. "I need to make a call."

"Margaux, Brendon's a Cancer," I said when he left.

"I know, and from the look on your face when I walked in, the moody guy *was* bringing you down. So what's his problem? Did he get sparkling water on his sweater label?" she asked, rolling her eyes.

"No, he's just—"

"Is this the kind of lemon bar you wanted?" Austin asked, coming over. She nodded and asked him what his sign was. "Leo."

"Are Leos and Aries compatible?" she asked. I nodded. Maybe it explained why he was still in the picture. On the other hand, Cancers and Leos, Brendon and my signs, weren't exactly destined to be together...even if sometimes I felt like we were.

"I am so dreading winter break," she said. "We have to go to my Aunt Patti and Uncle Randolph's for Christmas Eve, and Patti wears the same Santa Claus sweater every stinking year. It's like she thinks it won't be Christmas for the rest of us if she doesn't have it on."

"Didn't she give you the design-your-own-sweatshirt kit one year?" I asked.

"Mm-hmm. You see what I'm dealing with. Plus, my uncle makes the same stupid joke each year about asking Santa for a sports car. Seriously, I could record my whole conversation before I go in because they ask the same crap about school, and then Randolph goes on about the 'importance of education.' What he should do is tell me to stay in school so I don't end up like him. Kidding."

My mouth dropped open, and I glanced over at my cousin to see his reaction, but he was smiling at her. "You crack me up," he said.

She blushed and fed him a bite of her lemon bar. What was this?

Brendon came back to the table looking madder than before. "Everything okay?" I asked. He nodded. "Well, we better get going so you don't miss your meeting. See you guys later."

I heard the song they played at the funeral home as we walked out of the bookstore. I hoped it was a sign from Grandma things were going to be okay. Brendon opened the car door for me.

"Why did you lie and say I had a meeting?" he asked.

"Well, Margaux can be a lot to handle, and I was getting strong let's-get-out-of-here vibes from your direction," I said. "Did I read that right?"

"You always do."

"What do you mean?"

"I don't know, but in the past it's felt like you could read my mind. You just seem to understand me when no one's ever been able to get what I'm dealing with being in my family. And what's even weirder is…well, I'm sorta able to do it with you," he said. "I knew something was wrong with your grandma before you told me about the stroke. It's why I was at your locker that day. I had a feeling and—"

"Wait, back up. What do you mean?"

"Even before we started going out I'd get these feelings about you. I saw you during the school year last year, and I had this feeling we were supposed to, I dunno, be together. So when I walked into our summer class, I knew it was meant to be, and I wasn't surprised at all when Mrs. Rae had us working together. Then I'd have these dreams about you—I'm weirding you out, aren't I?"

I shook my head. "No, I mean, maybe a little, but keep going. I want to hear this."

"I'd know when I was supposed to call you, and I'd always seem to get this feeling when you needed me. At first, I thought it was a coincidence, but there was *too* much going on. It threw me the day the numerology book said that thing about the soul mates," he said. "I never told you this, but the day I came to your house to look at your computer, my mom asked me where I was going and when I told her she said, 'She must be your soul mate if you're leaving the house for her during the basketball playoffs.'"

"You missed a playoff game to help me?"

"Yup, but once we got to know each other better—I got a little scared by how well you seemed to get me. Most people try to imagine what my life must be like or act like they get it, but you seemed to see past all the stuff people assume and actually got what I was dealing with. For the first time I felt like someone understood me and what I was going through—from my family's expectations, to my grandpa being sick, and the whole pressure to be someone or something I'm not."

"You haven't had other people you could talk to?"

"Nope. If I complain in the slightest they act like I'm ungrateful. I don't get to be myself fully because, well, like you said, there's a five-year plan already set up for me," he said.

"Your dad is a nice guy though—he wouldn't do all that stuff to help other people if he wasn't. I think he'd listen to you if you showed him how important journalism is to you."

Brendon ran his fingers through his hair. "I think I am going to talk to him about it. But, Em, something else has been bothering me—other than the college admissions people telling me I'm a big, fat, stinking loser."

"You're not a loser."

"Yeah, well, I've felt like one with the hot and cold thing you've been running on me. It's like we're back to-gether—oh no, we're not. Every time I felt like we were getting close again, you'd pull back."

I glanced down at my hands and then saw my brace-lets. It hit me. Cheryl was right about the way I hide be-hind New Age stuff instead of dealing with things head on, and I realized I had been holding back with Brendon because of all the other things going on in my life. And maybe Kylie was right—I didn't feel good enough for Brendon, so I didn't share my real feelings.

"You know, I don't think we talked about how I felt when you blew me off the night of the reading and then the whole Lauren thing—it hurt me you went to the dance with her."

"But I thought it was pretty obvious homecoming night who I wanted to be with when I kissed you at the after party," he said.

I shifted. "Honestly, I didn't know what the kiss was about. I think the whole thing with you and Lauren was always on my mind. Your relationship with her was a lot…well, it was much more serious than I ever got with a guy, and I didn't know if she had some sort of hold over you because of it."

"Yeah, we did date for a while," he said. "But that was history."

"And that's what my ex said, and then he cheated on me with the last girl he dated."

"But that was *him*, not me."

"Same situation."

"How?"

I swallowed. "Well, John's ex was…well, they had slept together, and when I told him I wasn't ready for anything like that, he said it was fine, but he went back to her because...well, he knew she'd be okay with it."

Brendon stared at me, but didn't say anything.

"I pretty much figured you and Lauren had the same kind of relationship," I said.

"I'm not going to lie to you—we did. But it also complicated everything. She got weird afterwards. I'm not saying I wasn't taking it seriously, but she got super codependent, like it was assumed we'd go to the same college and law school and get married. That part of the relationship put all this pressure on us. I felt guilty when I realized I couldn't be with her anymore—like I had to stay with her, and I think it's why we stayed together for so long. And there was this one time last year when I told her we needed to take a step back. It was because she started talking about if we should get married while we were in law school or wait until we graduated. It was the same day she yelled at me for forgetting our six-month anniversary, which I didn't even know was a thing. And when I say yelled, I mean she let me have it."

"Wow."

"Yeah, and I said we were moving too fast for me, and she said, 'What did you think it meant when we slept together?' I spent the whole night apologizing and feeling like I didn't have the right to break it off with her."

"What happened to make you change your mind?"

"Only Sam knows about this, but...well, she was over at our place, and she made a comment about Jayson having no direction for his life and how she hoped I didn't turn out like him. It hit me wrong because he was going through some stuff, and she knew he was struggling—not about the suicide attempt, but she knew he was having serious issues. I thought she was being pretty cold, and I told her I wanted to break up. Honestly, I couldn't see myself staying with someone who could be so heartless. She waited a day and then told me she thought she was pregnant."

"What?" It felt like my heart went into my throat.

"Yeah, well, a few days later it came out she lied, and I was like, there is no way we can keep going on."

"Then why are you still letting her in your life so much? She e-mails you, texts you—the dance thing—"

"I felt guilty. Seriously, the whole relationship got so complicated after it. And it was a huge mistake."

I sat back in the seat. "Life was so much easier when dating meant passing notes in the hallway, drinking out of the same juice box at lunch, and sharing crayons."

He laughed. "Those were the days. I'm sorry if I did anything to make you feel like you did when you were with John. Instead of trying to reassure you I wasn't like him, I guess I got offended that you thought I was."

"Well, it wasn't just him. I think my whole experience getting over the betrayal and everything that went on with my grandparents threw me off. Maybe I pushed you away a bit."

"You think?" he said.

"In my defense, it's a little hard to go out with some-one half the school wants to be with."

"Only half the school?" he asked with a smirk. "I'd like to think I'm good-looking enough to make a few guys question some stuff."

I cracked up. "Wow, so modest."

"Em, I miss being with you. I've never had anything like this before, and I don't want to lose you."

"Me neither. You know, I went to a psychic fair, and I was trying to figure out how the stars aligned for us, look-ing to tarot cards and stuff to see if we were meant to be. This lady there was like, stop getting caught up in the New Age stuff. She told me to listen to my common sense and see the situation as it is. I think I was hiding behind the New Age stuff instead of dealing with real life."

"Like when we went out, and you were oh-so-subtly

trying to figure out how we connected with numerology to see if we had a future together?"

My face got warm. "You picked up on what I was doing?"

"Yup."

"How embarrassing."

"Eh, it was cute, but I don't need number connections to tell me how I feel about you," he said. "I mean, even my mom likes you, and she doesn't like anybody."

"Well, I am adorable."

"Too true."

"But there's something else I think we need to talk about. I held back a lot of stuff—you know how I felt resentful about Lauren and all, and how I was being kind of standoffish to you around Thanksgiving."

"Oh, you mean when you were being a little Margaux and acting super cold?"

I squirmed. "You picked up on the Margaux stuff, too?"

"Uh-huh, but I figured you were just trying to sort out if I was telling the truth about running into Lauren in Frankenmuth."

"Well, part of it, but I was..." I paused, feeling anxious. "Um..."

"Emme, you can tell me anything," he said, putting his hand over mine.

"I know you had a student council meeting the day of my grandma's funeral, but I was hurt you didn't come when you said you would."

"I did come."

"What?"

"I was there, but I got super overwhelmed because I started thinking about how my granddad's health hasn't been good, and I went into the hallway before I had an anxiety attack in the church. The whole thing threw me a lot more than I expected it to, and I was kind of a mess, so I left before the luncheon started. I went up to your grandpa and asked him to tell you I had to leave and said I'd call you later."

My mouth dropped open. "Oh my goodness, that's what Grandpa meant—he got you confused with his cousin the first time he met you, and when he told me Dennis gave him a message—oh wow, I thought he was confused."

"What do you mean?"

"Grandpa started showing signs of dementia right after my grandma's stroke. My aunt doesn't want to talk about it, but he can't be alone anymore."

"Oh wow, so you've been dealing with losing your grandma and him being sick, as well?"

"Yeah, it's been a lot to handle. Probably why I thought life made more sense and felt in control with all the New Age crap. I was counting on my bracelets to keep me safe and grounded."

"So numerology and horoscopes might be off, but I have been getting some signs about you," he said. He said he had been hearing Sweetie Gals songs on the radio all the time, too, like I had. "It's either some sort of sign we're supposed to be together, or the group is getting back together."

"If only they would reunite," I said. "But getting back to us—why didn't you ever tell me you had a feeling about us being meant to be before?"

He shrugged. "Didn't want to creep you out. I just had this gut feeling you and I were meant to be, and then there's the fact every single day my intuition was basically saying, 'Stupid, go get her.'"

"You always managed to call or be around at the right moment, too, but I didn't realize you had been feeling anything as well."

"Do you remember the day I was on a plane, and we had all that turbulence? When it dropped, all I could think about was you. I've never been so scared in all my life, and yet all I could think about was you. I told my dad about it the other day, and he said he had a similar reaction before. He said near-death situations take away all the fake stuff and make you realize what matters. Then he said it was why he backed off on micromanaging Jayson. He said Jayson's attempt made him realize all that matters was Jayson being happy and well. It didn't matter where he ended up."

"So maybe he'd be open to hearing about your dream," I said.

Brendon shook his head, smiling. "I just told you my near-death experience made me think of you, and you come back with wanting me to talk to my dad about pursuing my dream?"

"Trust me, the first part was *not* lost on me, but I want what's best for you, too."

"Maybe the first part was a little overwhelming?"

I laughed. "A bit, but I liked it."

"Well, it's something."

"And I wouldn't mind if you started looking at schools a little closer. No pressure. I'm not mapping out our future, but I wouldn't mind spending time with you next fall."

"You're more likely to map out our destinies in the stars anyway," he said, laughing. "But I got to admit, I like where you're going with this."

"Well, I'll leave the horoscopes alone for a while, but I do think I'll check my intuition from time to time."

"Is that what it's called? You'll have to tell me more," he said, leaning in to kiss me. "Does this mean we're not reading each other's minds? Because I was starting to wonder."

"You know, maybe you could stop reading my mind between eight and ten at night so I can watch my favorite TV shows," I said, and he shook his head and kissed me again. "Well, at least you could telepathically help me with my math tests."

"I'm not advanced with telepathy yet, but I'll work on it. After all, my horoscope said I'm supposed to involve myself in a new project," he said. "But you never answered me about your number five year—did you find your soul mate?"

"You know, I think I just might have."

"Well, I know I did."

I kissed him. "Good to know."

"Oh, and I downloaded an application to another school...it's forty minutes away."

"*That* far?"

He cracked up. "Willing to try a long-distance relationship?"

"I think we can make it work."

"You don't need to check the stars first or get a sign?" he asked.

"Nope, all signs point to yes."

"That's what I like to hear."

About the Author

KRYSTEN LINDSAY HAGER writes about friendship, self-esteem, fitting in, frenemies, crushes, fame, first loves, and values. She is the author of *True Colors, Best Friends... Forever?, Next Door to a Star, Landry in Like,* and *Competing with the Star (The Star Series: Book 2)*. Her work has been featured in *USA Today, The Flint Journal, The Grand Haven Tribune, The Bellbrook Times* and on Living Dayton.

Acknowledgments

MY PARENTS, AMY, Laura Turner (the Louise to my Thelma), Riley Turner, the Dubicki family, Stephanie Taylor (thank you, thank you, thank you!), Opal Campbell (Bluebell forever), Cindy Madison, Lisa Frederick, Leslie McKee., the Yott family, the Palczewski and Ignatowski families, Lorraine Carey, James Gordon, the Sova Family, the Plachecki family, the Nielsen family, Dale Weller, the Slaters, and the Ambrus family.

My readers whose time and support mean so much.

My A-team: Pia P., Vivian G., Anna O., Emily V., Suzanne V., Pat F., Jen H. (Mrs. Screech), Kim M., Tina C., Jennifer F., Big smoochies!!